PENGUIN 🐧

EARLY IRISH MYTHS AND SAGAS

ADVISORY EDITOR: BETTY RADICE

These early Irish stories, probably first written down around the eighth century, represent the foremost written repository of the oral tradition of the Iron Age Celts who flourished in Europe during the seven centuries before Christ. As well as creating economic, social and artistic foundations throughout the continent, their myths and tales have been said to be the earliest voices from the dawn of western civilization. But later, with the growth of Viking and Roman empires, the Celtic influence declined until it was only in Ireland, on the fringes of Europe and less exposed to the new traditions, that their original culture was preserved in a beautiful and elusive language with themes foreshadowing those still current in the inspiration of Yeats, Synge and Joyce.

JEFFREY GANTZ received a doctorial degree in Celtic Languages and Literatures from Harvard University in 1972. He lives in Cambridge, Massachusetts, where he works as a newspaper editor and journalist. He has also translated *The Mabinogion* for Penguin Classics.

EARLY IRISH MYTHS AND SAGAS

Translated with an introduction and notes by

Jeffrey Gantz

Penguin Books

PENGUIN BOOKS

Published by the Penguin Group
Penguin Books Ltd, 80 Strand, London WC2R 0RL, England
Penguin Putnam Inc., 375 Hudson Street, New York, New York 10014, USA
Penguin Books Australia Ltd, 250 Camberwell Road, Camberwell, Victoria 3124, Australia
Penguin Books Canada Ltd, 10 Alcorn Avenue, Toronto, Ontario, Canada M4V 3B2
Penguin Books India (P) Ltd, 11 Community Centre, Panchsheel Park, New Delhi – 110 017, India
Penguin Books (NZ) Ltd, Cnr Rosedale and Airborne Roads, Albany, Auckland, New Zealand
Penguin Books (South Africa) (Pty) Ltd, 24 Sturdee Avenue, Rosebank 2196, South Africa

Penguin Books Ltd, Registered Offices: 80 Strand, London WC2R 0RL, England

www.penguin.com

First published 1981

056

Printed in Great Britain by Clays Ltd, Elcograf S.p.A.
Set in Intertype Lectura

ISBN-13: 978–0–140–44397–4

www.greenpenguin.co.uk

MIX
Paper from
responsible sources
FSC
www.fsc.org   FSC® C018179

Penguin Books is committed to a sustainable
future for our business, our readers and our planet.
This book is made from Forest Stewardship
Council™ certified paper.

Contents

Contents

Introduction

Early Irish Myths and Sagas

One day, in winter, Derdriu's foster-father was outside, in the snow, flaying a weaned calf for her. Derdriu saw a raven drinking the blood on the snow, and she said to Lebarcham 'I could love a man with those three colours: hair like a raven, cheeks like blood and body like snow.'

'The Exile of the Sons of Uisliu' (p. 260)

This passage, from one of the finest stories ever written in Ireland, evinces much of what Irish literature is: romantic, idealistic, stylized and yet vividly, even appallingly, concrete. Most of all, it exemplifies the tension between reality and fantasy that characterizes all Celtic art. In Ireland, this art has taken many forms: illumination (the books of Durrow and Kells), metal work (the Ardagh Chalice and the Tara Brooch), sculpture (the stone crosses at Moone and Clonmacnois), architecture (the Rock of Cashel and the various round towers), music (Turlough O'Carolan). But this tension manifests itself particularly in the literature of Ireland, and most particularly in the myths/sagas – no more precise description is possible, at least for the moment – that survive in Irish manuscripts dating back to the twelfth century.

There are many reasons why this should be so. To begin with, these stories originated in the mists of Irish prehistory (some elements must predate the arrival of the Celts in

Ireland), and they developed through the course of centuries until reaching their present manuscript state; consequently, they manage to be both archaic and contemporary. Their setting is both historical Ireland (itself an elusive entity) and the mythic otherworld of the Síde (Ireland's 'faery people', who live in burial mounds called 'síde' and exhibit magical powers), and it is not always easy to tell one from the other. Many of the characters are partially euhemerized gods – that is, they are gods in the process of becoming ordinary mortals – so that, again, it is not easy to tell divine from human.

At bottom, this tension between reality and fantasy is not accidental to the circumstances of literary transmission and formation but rather an innate characteristic, a gift of the Celts. The world of the Irish story is graphic: blood spurts not only from the calf flayed for Derdriu but also from the lips of Anlúan as his head is thrown across a table (in 'The Tale of Macc Da Thó's Pig'); the 'hero' of 'Bricriu's Feast' is tossed from the balcony of his house on to a garbage heap; the warriors of Ulaid (the Irish name for Ulster) are all but roasted in an iron house (in 'The Intoxication of the Ulaid'). Yet this story-world is also magically bright and achingly beautiful. Two pairs of lovers – Mider and Étaín (in 'The Wooing of Étaín), and Óengus and Cáer Ibormeith (in 'The Dream of Óengus') – turn into swans. The hero of 'The Destruction of Da Derga's Hostel' can dispatch several hundred foes without even reaching for his weapons; Macc Da Thó's pig is so large that forty oxen can be laid across it. Myth obtrudes upon reality at every turn. In 'The Destruction of Da Derga's Hostel', a bird descends through a skylight, sheds his bird outfit and sleeps with the woman Mess Búachalla, thus fathering the story's hero, Conare Már; in 'The Wooing of Étaín', Mider's wife, Fúamnach, turns her rival Étaín into a scarlet fly; in 'The Wasting Sickness of Cú Chulaind', Cú Chulaind is horsewhipped and then healed by two women from the otherworld (shades of the German women in Fellini's *Casanova*). In these Irish stories, then, the pride and energy of reality are allied with the magic and beauty of fantasy – and the result is infused with a rare degree of idealism. In the otherworld of 'The Wooing of Étaín', not only are bodies white as snow and cheeks red as foxglove, but there is no 'mine' or 'yours'.

The Celts

The traditions of these early Irish stories originated with the Celts, an Indo-European group who are the ancestors of the Irish, the Scots, the Welsh, the Cornish, the Bretons and the people of the Isle of Man. When and where this group first appeared is, rather fittingly, an elusive, even controversial, question. The conservative view, and perhaps the most prevalent, is that the Celts surfaced with the beginning of the Iron Age in Europe, roughly 1000 B.C.; and this is certainly the earliest period in which the archaeological testimony affords positive proof. Myles Dillon and Nora Chadwick, however, propose to date the first Celtic settlements of the British Isles to the early Bronze Age (*circa* 1800 B.C.) and to identify the Beaker Folk as Celts.[1] Leon E. Stover and Bruce Kraig go further still: comparing the Classical descriptions of the Iron Age Celts with what they infer from burials at Stonehenge and Únětice (a cemetery near Prague), they propose to classify 'the Wessex and Únětician warriors as formative Celts' and conclude by claiming that the Celts 'emerged as a dominant people in Europe by the beginning of the third millennium B.C.'[2] The controversy is largely semantic. Wessex as presented by Stover and Kraig does look like an early form of what is described by Posidonius and Caesar, but then so does the heroic society of Homer's *Iliad*, and of course there is no linguistic evidence at all.

Presumably, from the beginning of the third millennium on there developed, in Europe and subsequently in Britain and Ireland, heroic societies that gradually became, both culturally and linguistically, Celtic.

In any event, by the beginning or the early part of the first millennium B.C., the Celts clearly had emerged, not as a subset of their Slavic or Germanic or Italic neighbours but as a discrete Indo-European ethnic and cultural group; moreover, during the course of that millennium, they became the dominant people in non-Mediterranean Europe. From their homeland (probably in Bohemia), they expanded westward into France and Spain and, eventually, Britain and Ireland; southward into Italy; and eastward into Turkey, where they became the Galatians of St Paul. These early Celts took with them not only their chariots and their iron swords but also a distinctive geometric/linear art, called Hallstatt (after an important cemetery in Austria). By 500 B.C., a new art form had sprung up, this called La Tène (after a site in Switzerland); much less restrained than its predecessor, La Tène is a kind of baroque development, all curves and spirals and luxuriant plant and animal outgrowths. At this time, too, the Celts began to come under notice of the Classical authors: Herodotos, writing in the mid-fifth century, described the *Keltoi* as tall (by Mediterranean standards) and with light skin and hair and eyes, boastful and vainglorious but demonic in battle, childlike and ostentatious but hospitable, fond of hunting and feasting and music and poetry and glittering jewellery and bright colours; and his impressions were confirmed by subsequent accounts, particularly those attributed to Posidonius in the first century B.C.[3]

With their energy and warlike temperament, the Celts were able to expand quickly; by 390 B.C., they had sacked Rome, and by 279 B.C., Delphi. Many tribes settled in France, where the Romans called them Gauls, but their numbers also included the Boii (Bologna, Bohemia), the Belgae (Belgium) and the Helvetii (Switzerland); moreover, their settlements included Lutetia Parisiorum (Paris), Lugudunum (Lyon), Vindobona (Vienna) and Mediolanum (Milan), and they also named the Sequana (Seine) and the Danuvia (Danube). Unfortunately, Celtic tribal free-spiritedness was no match for Roman civic organization. Caesar's defeat of Vercingetorix, at Alesia in 52 B.C., signalled the decline of the Celts' hegemony in Europe; thereafter, they were overrun and assimilated. As a distinct entity, Celtic language and culture disappeared in Europe (though of course their influence persisted); in Great Britain, the Celtic tribes were driven back into Scotland, Wales and Cornwall (from where they eventually reclaimed Brittany) by the numerous incursions of Romans, Angles/Saxons and Normans.

Ireland was a different story. By virtue of its westerly and isolated geographic position, this island remained free of Roman colonization; thus, Irish society did not change appreciably until the advent of Christianity (in the fifth century) and the arrival of Viking raiders (some time thereafter). Consequently, the culture of the Iron Age Celts survived in Ireland long after it had been extinguished elsewhere. It is this conservatism that makes the early Irish tales, quite apart from their literary value, such a valuable repository of information about the Celtic people.

The Irish

As elusive as the date of the Celts' emergence in Europe is the date of their arrival in Ireland. Such megalithic tombs as Knowth, Dowth and New Grange, which now appear to date from the middle of the fourth millennium, testify to the presence of an indigenous, pre-Celtic culture; but how soon afterwards Celts – even formative Celts – appeared is open to controversy. If the Bell-Beaker people are viewed as proto-Celts, then one might say that they – assuming they reached Ireland as well as Britain – represent the beginnings of Celtic culture in Ireland; against this, archaeological evidence of large-scale immigration to Ireland between 2000 and 600 B.C. is wanting. If the indigenous population evolved into a Celtic one at the behest of a small number of aristocratic invaders, however, no such large-scale immigration would have been necessary. In any event, we know that Celts of the Hallstatt type reached Ireland by the middle of the sixth century-and that Celts continued to migrate to Ireland and Britain until the time of the Belgic invasion in the first century B.C.

How and in what form they arrived is even more uncertain. According to Lebor Gabála (The Book of Invasions), our earliest copy of which dates from the twelfth century, Ireland was subjected to six invasions, those of Cessair, Partholón, Nemed, the Fir Bolg, the Túatha Dé Danand and the sons of Mil Espáne. Irish history being what it is, the particulars of the Lebor Gabála account are open to question; what matters is that Ireland was, or was felt to have been, settled by a succession of different tribes. That these people actually arrived in separate waves – as opposed to filtering in more or less continuously – is moot; but the early tales do reflect the existence of different ethnic groups.

The Ireland of these tales is apportioned into four provinces, called, perversely, cóiceda, or 'fifths': Ulaid (Ulster), Connachta (Connaught), Lagin (Leinster) and Mumu (Munster). The fifth province was probably Mide (Meath), though there is also a tradition, probably artificial, that Mumu was once two provinces. Either this fifth province was original and disappeared (while the word cóiced persisted), or else the original four provinces became five after the emergence of a new power centre. Mide, which encompassed both Bruig na Bóinde (New Grange) and Temuir (Tara), is the setting for the early mythological tales, and this argues for its status as an original province. On the other hand, Mide was also the territory of the Uí Néill, who by the fourth century had supplanted the Ulaid as the dominant power in Ireland; this argues for its being a later addition. Moreover, the name Mide, which means 'middle', looks palpably artificial – of course, the entire province set-up may be artificial.

In any case, there are, in the stories of this volume, four centres of action. Mide, with its numerous burial mounds, is the setting for the early mythological tales. It is peopled by the Túatha Dé Danand (the People of the Goddess Danu), who, though presented by Lebor Gabála as a wave of invaders, appear in these tales as the denizens of the otherworld, the Síde. They interact freely with the ordinary people of the mythological stories, and they also appear in some of the more historical tales. Ulaid, with its capital of Emuin Machae (near present-day Armagh), is the primary setting for the historical (insofar as any of the Irish tales are historical) sagas of the Ulster Cycle; its king is Conchubur son of Ness, but its champion is the mythic hero Cú Chulaind. The arch-enemies of the Ulaid (province names apply to the people as well) are the Connachta, who have their capital at Crúachu, in the west of Ireland. These people may well have originally occupied Mide, for their queen, Medb, is often identified as the daughter of the king of Temuir, and she may once have been a fertility goddess. It also seems more logical that Ulaid's foe should have been centred in adjacent Mide rather than in the distant west; and this in fact would have been true if the Ulster Cycle tales reflect the historical conflict between the Ulaid and the emerging Uí Néill of Mide. The tradition that the Connachta were the enemies of the Ulaid coupled with the fact that Connachta was now the name of Ireland's western province would have given the storytellers sufficient reason to move Medb and her husband, Ailill, from Temuir to Crúachu. Finally, there are the people of Mumu; they play a more peripheral role in the Ulster Cycle, but the king Cú Ruí son of Dáre does figure prominently in several tales.

When the events related in these stories might have taken place is yet another mystery. The Alexandrian geographer Ptolemy, who wrote in the second century A.D. but is believed to have drawn upon sources at least two hundred years older, provides evidence that Ireland was then Celtic-speaking; however, few of his names – and they are restricted both in number and in location – suggest those of our stories, so that one might suppose the people of these stories (insofar as they were real) had not yet appeared. At the other end, the milieu of the tales predates the advent of Christianity, while the circumstances of the Ulster Cycle must predate the Uí Néill appropriation of Emuin Machae. Kenneth Jackson has placed the formation of the Ulster tradition somewhere between the second century B.C. and the fourth century A.D., which seems entirely reasonable.

What Irish life was like during this period is, fortunately, *not* such a difficult question. On the one hand, we have the evidence of the Classical authors, Posidonius (via Diodorus Siculus and Strabo) and Caesar – evidence that was taken from Gaul and Britain but must surely have been valid for the Irish Celts as well. On the other, we have not only the evidence of the stories but also that of the Irish annals and genealogies and law tracts.

What emerges from the collation of this evidence is a culture of extraordinary vitality and beauty. Irish society exhibited the same tripartism that Georges Dumézil perceived elsewhere in the Indo-European world: a warrior class headed by a king; a priestly class (the druids); and a class of farmers and free men. The king of a *túath*, or tribe, was often subject to an over-king, to whom he gave assurances of allegiance and from whom he received some kind of support; the over-king, in turn, might have been subject to his provincial king. (The idea of a high king or king of Ireland is probably a fiction, fabricated by later peoples – notably the Uí Néill – to provide a historical justification for their claim to rule Ireland and perpetuated by the romanticism of subsequent tradition.) Kingship seems originally to have been sacral – indeed, the 'kings' in the mythological tales are barely euhemerized gods. In some traditions, the tribal king was ritually married to the tribal goddess (Medb, for example); in others, he had a sympathetic relationship with the land: if he were healthy and virile, the land would be fertile, while if he were blemished or impotent, the land would become barren. (This Wasteland idea is not, of course, exclusively Celtic.)

In 'The Destruction of Da Derga's Hostel', a druid partakes of the flesh and broth of a slaughtered bull and then lapses into a deep sleep, wherein he is expected to see the form of the new king. In later Irish history, however, the king was chosen from an extended family unit; and his position, continually contested by other family members (just as in fifteenth-century England), was far from secure. Curiously, the kings of the Irish stories are not battle leaders: either they betray vestiges of divinity (Cú Ruí, for example) or they have a young champion as heir and rival. Examples of this second pattern – which reflects the relationship of Agamemnon to Achilles and anticipates those of Arthur to Lancelot and Mark to Tristan – are legion: Mider temporarily loses Étaín to his foster-son Óengus; Conchubur loses Derdriu to the young warrior Noísiu and relinquishes supremacy in battle to Cú Chulaind; Cet rather than King Ailill is the champion of the Connachta.

The second class of Irish society, the priests, is more controversial. Popular notions of white-robed druids overseeing human sacrifices, cutting mistletoe with golden sickles and chanting spells over magic cauldrons persist – and not without reason. But Strabo points out that the druids

concern themselves with questions of ethics in addition to their study of natural phenomena. And because they are considered the most just of all, they possess the power to decide judicial matters, both those dealing with individuals and those involving the common good. Thus they have been known to control the course of wars, and to check armies about to join battle, and especially to judge cases of homicide. When there is a large number of these last, they suppose there will be a large return from the land as well. And both they and others maintain that the soul and the cosmos are immortal, though at some time in the future fire and water will prevail over them.[4]

Diodorus, moreover, makes mention of

certain *philosophoi* and religious interpreters, men highly honoured, whom they call Druids ... It is their custom not to make any sacrifice without one of these *philosophoi*, since they believe that offerings should be rendered to the gods through the agency of those well acquainted with the divine nature (on speaking terms, one might say), and that requests for favours should likewise be made by these same men. In matters of war too the *philosophoi* are readily obeyed, they and the singing bards, and this by enemies as well as their own people. Often, in fact, when battle lines are drawn and armies close ground with swords and spears poised, they will step out into the middle and halt both sides, as if enchanting wild beasts. Thus even among the most savage barbarians, the spirit yields to the arts, and Ares reveres the Muses.[5]

Valuable as they are, these Classical accounts, at second hand and biased, should not be accepted at face value: the druids were, most probably, neither human-sacrificing savages nor great moral philosophers. Certainly, there is no evidence of either role in the Irish tales. In the mythological stories, druids are magicians: in 'The Wooing of Étaín', Fúamnach, who has been reared by the druid Bresal, is able to turn her rival, Étaín, into first a pool of water and then a scarlet fly; in 'The Destruction of Da Derga's Hostel', Ingcél's druids bring about Conare's death by making him thirsty. The druids of the Ulster Cycle, however, are little more than wise old men (reminiscent of Nestor), though they claim some power of prophecy. Cathub and Senchae are greatly revered for their sagacity and for their peace-making ('Bricriu's Feast' and 'The Intoxication of the Ulaid' fully confirm Diodorus's account of druidic intervention between combatants), but they display neither magical powers nor moral philosophy. It seems that the process of becoming a druid was a protracted one – according to Caesar, it could take twenty years – and involved the study of myth/history, law, science, religion and philosophy. Since the Celts in general and the druids in particular were averse to writing their knowledge down (out of fear that it might be corrupted if outsiders found it, but doubtless also because of the druids' desire to preserve their privileged status), all this material had to be memorized. In short, the druids appear to have been the caretakers of whatever knowledge – from magic to science – their people possessed. •

The third class of people were free men who farmed and herded. As the clients of a chieftain or other landowner, they received rent of the land, perhaps some stock, and some protection from enemies; in return, they surrendered a portion of what the land yielded and did some kind of service for their landlord. The upper class of these tenant farmers took possession of the rented stock after seven years; the lower classes did not and were in effect serfs. At the bottom of the social scale were the slaves; these were often people captured from neighbouring tribes, but they do not appear to have been numerous.

Irish society, especially that of the historical tales, was an aristocratic one. The strongholds of the Ulster Cycle – Crúachu and Emuin Machae – are not cities but rather compounds where the king lives with his household and where he regales his chieftains with feasts and entertainments: poets, singers, musicians, jugglers. These strongholds may also have been centres for rounding up stock in autumn and for the holding of annual fairs, such as the one described at the beginning of 'The Wasting Sickness of Cú Chulaind': 'Each year the Ulaid held an assembly: the three days before Samuin and the three days after Samuin and Samuin itself. They would gather at Mag Muirthemni, and during these seven days there would be nothing but meetings and games and amusements and entertainments and eating and feasting.' And drinking. Such a lifestyle dictated an expansionist policy towards one's neighbours, since, in order to distribute wealth to their clients, kings and chieftains first had to accumulate it. Even in the mythological stories, the importance of land and possessions is patent: in 'The Wooing of Étaín', Óengus asserts his right to land from his father, the Dagdae, and it is the wealth of Bruig na Bóinde that enables him to compensate his foster-father, Mider, when the latter is injured.

The Irish year was divided into two parts: winter and summer. The first day of November, called Samuin, was both the first day of winter and the first day of the new year; the feast has since given rise to Hallowe'en/All Saints' Day and contributed the bonfire to Guy Fawkes celebrations. Samuin was a day of changes, of births and deaths; it was an open door between the real world and the otherworld. Óengus (in 'The Wooing of Étaín') dispossesses Elcmar of Bruig na Bóinde at Samuin, and he finds his beloved (in 'The Dream of Óengus') at Samuin. It is at Samuin that Da Derga's hostel is destroyed and Conare Már is slain (the death of a king at

Samuin is so common as to suggest regeneration myths and ritual slaying); it is at Samuin that, in 'The Wasting Sickness of Cú Chulaind', beautiful birds appear at Mag Muirthemni and Cú Chulaind is entranced by Fand; it is at Samuin that, in 'The Intoxication of the Ulaid', the Ulaid charge off to the south-west of Ireland and are nearly burnt inside an iron house. Proinsias Mac Cana has called Samuin 'a partial return to primordial chaos ... the appropriate setting for myths which symbolise the dissolution of established order as a prelude to its recreation in a new period of time';[6] and there can be no doubt that Samuin was the most important day of re-creation and rebirth in Ireland.

The first day of May, called Beltene, marked the beginning of summer; this feast has since given rise to May Eve/ Walpurgisnacht and May Day. Beltene was a less important day, and, consequently, less information about it has survived; the name seems to mean 'fire of Bel' (Bel presumably being the Irish descendant of the continental god Belenos) or 'bright fire', and there is a tradition that cattle were driven between two fires on this day so that the smoke would purify them. In any case, the rites of Beltene were probably directed towards ensuring the fertility of land and stock. The Welsh hero Pryderi is born on the first of May, and this fact coupled with the unusual circumstances of his birth (the concurrent birth of colts, the otherworld visitor) suggests that Beltene was also a day when the real and the fantastic merged.

The beginnings of spring and autumn were also celebrated, but even less is known about these holidays. Imbolg, which fell on the first of February, seems to have been the beginning of the lambing season; it is also associated with the goddess Brigit (Briganti in Britain), whose successor, Saint Brighid, has her feast day, significantly, on the first of February. Lugnasad, which fell on the first of August, was named after the god Lug and seems to have been a harvest festival; if so, it was probably a late addition, since harvest time (that is, the end of the grazing season) in a pastoral (as opposed to an agrarian) community would have fallen closer to Samuin. In any case, the opening sentences of 'The Wasting Sickness of Cú Chulaind' show that the annual autumn round-up and assembly of the Ulaid took place at Samuin.

For Celtic and Irish religion, there is a wealth of evidence: the testimony of the Classical writers, especially Caesar; that of Gaulish sculpture and inscriptions; and that of the surviving Welsh and Irish myths. The resultant picture, however, is far from clear. Caesar identifies a Gaulish pantheon headed by Mercury and including Apollo, Mars, Jupiter and Minerva; corroborating evidence is so absent, however, that one has to suspect he is simply pinning Roman tails on a Celtic donkey.[7] It is the Gaulish sculptures and inscriptions (we have no stories, unfortunately) that attest to the true nature of Celtic religion: no pantheon, but rather localized deities with localized functions; and this accords with what we know of the Celts politically, for they had little tolerance for centralized authority, even their own. The more widespread and possibly more important deities include Lugos (Mercury in Caesar, Lug in Ireland, Lleu in Wales; he gave his name to Lyon, Leiden and Liegnitz (Legnica), as well as to the Irish autumn festival of Lugnasad); Belenos, whose name means 'bright' and who might have been a rough counterpart to Apollo; Maponos (Mabon in Wales, the Macc Óc in Ireland; his name means 'great son'); Ogmios, whom Lucian describes as the Gaulish Herakles and as a god of eloquence;[8] Cernunnos, whose name means 'horned' and who presumably is the horned figure on the Gundestrup cauldron; and Epona, a goddess whose name means 'great horse'. Much attention has been given to the trio of Esus, Taranis and Teutates in Lucan[9] and to the sacrifices with which they allegedly were appeased (hanging, burning and drowning, respectively), but their true importance is uncertain. Evidence as to how these and other Celtic gods (who are literally too numerous to mention) related to each other – the kind of testimony we find in Greek mythology – is totally lacking.

The evidence of the Irish tales, our third and final source, is abundant, but it has suffered from faulty transmission, political distortion, historical overlays and church censorship; the result is no clearer than that from the continent. The Ireland of the tales comprises two worlds, 'real' and 'other'; but the line between them is not well demarcated. Even the location of the otherworld – which should not be confused with the Classical underworld – is uncertain: sometimes it is to the west, over the sea; sometimes it is in the south-west of Ireland (where it may be called the 'House of Dond', Dond being a chthonic deity); but usually it is found in the great pre-Celtic burial mounds of the Síde, of which the most important in the tales is Bruig na Bóinde, today's New Grange. The Irish otherworld is, not surprisingly, a stylized, idealized version of the real one: everyone is beautiful, and there is an abundance of beautiful things, and the joys of life are endless – hunting, feasting, carousing, perhaps even love. Paradoxically (of course), though this otherworld makes the real one seem a shadow by comparison, it is the Síde who are the shadows, for they have no physical strength for fighting; just as Pwyll, in 'Pwyll Lord of Dyved', is asked to fight on behalf of the otherworld ruler Arawn, so Cú Chulaind, in 'The Wasting Sickness of Cú Chulaind', is asked to fight on behalf of the otherworld ruler Labraid Lúathlám. The Síde are distinguished primarily by their power of transformation: they move invisibly, or they turn themselves (and others) into birds and animals. But they exert no moral authority, and, while they can injure and heal, they do not have that power over life and death characteristic of the Greek Olympians. Often they seem just like ordinary humans.

Relatively few of the names from Gaulish inscriptions reappear in Ireland – given the decentralized nature of Gaulish religion, this is not surprising. Lug is the major figure in 'The Second Battle of Mag Tured', but in the stories included in this volume he appears prominently only as the father of Cú Chulaind. The Macc Óc is a central character in both 'The Wooing of Étaín' and 'The Dream of Óengus', but he has been so thoroughly euhemerized that there is no trace of the Gaulish Maponos; and such names as the Dagdae, Mider, Bóand, Étaín, Cáer Ibormeith, Medb and Cú Ruí have no apparent continental counterparts. Many of the quasi-divine figures in these tales are associated with animals or with natural features. The name Bóand, for example, means 'white cow'; but Bóand is also the Irish name of the river Boyne. At the outset of 'The Wooing of Étaín', Bóand sleeps with the Dagdae, whose other name, Echu, means 'horse'; Frank O'Connor saw this 'love affair' between a horse god and a cow goddess as a reconciliation between Bronze Age invaders and the indigenous Neolithic civilization, which gives some idea of how old these stories might be.[10] Like Rhiannon in 'Pwyll Lord of Dyved', Macha of 'The Labour Pains of the Ulaid' is a euhemerized horse goddess; and the same may be conjectured of Étaín, whose epithet Echrade means 'horse troop'. A number of the Síde appear as birds: Mider and Étaín leave Temuir as swans, and Óengus (Mider's foster-son) and Cáer Ibormeith return to Bruig na Bóinde as swans; Conare Már's unnamed father discloses himself to Mess Búachalla in the form of a bird; and Fand and Lí Ban first present themselves to Cú Chulaind as birds.

Strabo's testimony, the evidence of lavish grave goods

buried with the wealthy, and the identification of the Boyne burial mounds as the dwelling place of the Síde all suggest that the Irish did believe in a life after death. But the Irish otherworld was not simply an anticipated joyful afterlife; it was also – even primarily – an alternative to reality, a world that the hero might enter upon the invitation of a king or a beautiful woman. Inasmuch as this otherworld, no matter how beautiful, is not quite human (there is, for example, no winter), the hero never stays; but the alternative – and thus the tension – is always present.

Finally, there is the language, as beautiful and elusive as any aspect of Irish culture. Just as the Celts were a distinct Indo-European entity, so their languages formed an independent branch of the Indo-European language tree; nonetheless, Celtic is more like Italic (that is, the Romance languages) than it is like any of the other Indo-European language groups, and many place and personal names in Gaulish are very similar to those in Latin. For example, the Gaulish suffix -rix (as in Vercingetorix) is the counterpart of the Latin word rex, both meaning 'king'.

In the British Isles, the Celtic languages divided into two groups, one spoken primarily in Britain (and comprising Welsh and, eventually, Cornish and Breton), the other spoken primarily in Ireland (and comprising Irish Gaelic and, eventually, Scottish Gaelic and Manx Gaelic). The most obvious (though not necessarily the most important or fundamental) difference between the two groups is that Indo-European q^u became p in the British languages (the word for 'four' was petwar) and c in the Irish group ('four' was cethair).

At the time our stories are purported to have taken place – which is to say any time before the fourth century – the Irish language probably looked a good deal like Gaulish and not so very different from Latin. By the time these stories were being written down, however – and this could have begun as early as the seventh century – drastic changes had taken place: many final syllables had dropped away, many medial vowels had disappeared and many medial consonants had been simplified or lightened. Thus, the word for 'horse', *equus* in Latin, had become *ech* in Ireland at this time. The language of the tales, then, is quite different from that of the time they describe; and this makes the correlation of the stories' proper names with those in earlier sources (such as Ptolemy's geography) even more difficult. Although the syntax of the new language was straightforward, the morphology was not: regular verb conjugations often looked wildly irregular, and word roots occasionally disappeared altogether. The principles of phonetic change were aesthetic rather than semantic; the resultant language was soft and subtle, verb poor but noun-and-adjective rich, static and yet vital.

Irish Storytelling

Irish literature – meaning whatever was written down in Irish – of this time encompassed a broad area, including history, genealogy and law tracts; but it is poetry and narrative prose that are relevant to the early Irish myths and sagas. The earliest poetry was alliterative and syllabic, with end-rhyme appearing later. In Welsh literature, there are epics told entirely through the medium of verse – the *Gododdin*, for example; in Ireland, however, the storytelling medium is invariably prose. Some of the very archaic poetry is essential to the tales in which it appears; thus, the rhetorics in the early part of 'The Cattle Raid of Cúailnge' help to clarify the relationship among Ailill, Medb and Fergus.[11] The poetry in 'The Exile of the Sons of Uisliu', on the other hand, reinforces the narrative, adds detail – mostly descriptive – and provides weight; but it could be omitted without loss of sense. Conceivably these myths/ sagas were at one time recited entirely in verse; what remains, however, is largely decorative.

The earliest form of transmission must have been oral. Storytelling was a favourite entertainment among the Celts, and one version of 'The Voyage of Bran' states that Mongan (an Ulaid king who died about A.D. 625) was told a story by his *fili* (a kind of poet) every winter night from Samuin to Beltene. Presumably, the storytellers did not memorize entire tales – rather, they memorized the outlines and filled in the details extemporaneously. Eventually, perhaps as early as the seventh century, the tales began to be transcribed; and thereby two processes, rather opposite in effect, were initiated. In many cases, tales are reworked and acquire a literary veneer; this is certainly true of the Book of Leinster opening to 'The Cattle Raid of Cúailnge', and it would seem to apply to 'The Cattle Raid of Fróech' and to the concluding section of 'The Wasting Sickness of Cú Chulaind'. But these same tales have also deteriorated considerably by the time they reach our earliest (twelfth-century) surviving manuscripts. This deterioration is not likely to have originated with the storytellers themselves, for a long tale would naturally be prolonged over several evenings (which would be in the storyteller's interest, since during that time he would be enjoying his host's hospitality); and in any case, as James Delargy has pointed out, no audience would 'have listened very long to the story-teller if he were to recite tales in the form in which they have come down to us'.[12] The people who wrote these stories down, however, were – for the most part – not literary artists; and of course, they lacked the incentive of an appreciative (and remunerative) audience. Banquet-hall transcription cannot have been easy, and the scribe doubtless grew weary before the storyteller did; consequently, it is not surprising that spelling is erratic, that inconsistencies abound (this could also result from a story-teller's attempting to conflate multiple traditions) and that many tales deteriorate after a promising beginning. Some formulaic passages, such as in 'The Destruction of Da Derga's Hostel', are represented simply by 'et reliqua'. As manuscripts were recopied, moreover, additional errors inevitably appeared. Some areas are manifestly corrupt, and in the case of the archaic poetic sections it seems doubtful whether the scribes understood what they were writing. All this is hardly surprising – just consider the problems attendant upon the texts of Shakespeare's plays, only four hundred years old – but it should be remembered that what survives in the manuscripts, however beautiful, is far from representative of these stories at their best.

The Irish Manuscripts

The language of these tales varies considerably as to date; but at its oldest, and allowing for some degree of deliberate archaism, it appears to go back to the eighth century; one may assume the tales were being written down at least then, if not earlier. Unfortunately, Scandinavian raiders were legion in Ireland at this time, and they tended to destroy whatever was not worth taking away; consequently, very few manuscripts predating A.D. 1000 have survived. Among the missing is the Book of Druimm Snechtai, which belonged to the first part of the eighth century and included 'The Wooing of Étaín', 'The Destruction of Da Derga's Hostel' and 'The Birth of Cú Chulaind'.

Of the manuscripts that have survived, the two earliest and most important for these tales belong to the twelfth century. Lebor na huidre (The Book of the Dun Cow) is so called after a famous cow belonging to St Cíaran of Clonmacnois; the chief scribe, a monk named Máel Muire, was slain by raiders in the Clonmacnois cathedral in 1106. Unfortunately, the manuscript is only a fragment: though sixty-seven leaves of eight-by-eleven vellum remain, at least as much has been lost. Lebor na huidre comprises thirty-seven stories, most of them myths/sagas, and includes substantially complete versions of 'The Destruction of Da Derga's Hostel', 'The Birth of Cú Chulaind', 'The Wasting Sickness of Cú Chulaind' and 'Bricriu's Feast' as well as an incomplete 'Wooing of Étaín' and acephalous accounts of 'The Intoxication of the Ulaid' and 'The Cattle Raid of Cúailnge'.

The second manuscript, which is generally known as the Book of Leinster, is much larger, having 187 nine-by-thirteen leaves; it dates to about 1160 and includes in its varied contents complete versions of 'The Cattle Raid of Fróech', 'The Labour Pains of the Ulaid', 'The Tale of Macc Da Thó's Pig' and 'The Exile of the Sons of Uisliu' as well as an unfinished and rather different 'Intoxication of the Ulaid' and a complete, more polished 'Cattle Raid of Cúailnge'. Two later manuscripts also contribute to this volume: the Yellow Book of Lecan, which offers complete accounts of 'The Wooing of Étaín' and 'The Death of Aífe's Only Son' and dates to the fourteenth century; and Egerton 1782, which includes 'The Dream of Óengus' and has the date 1419 written on it.

These manuscripts do not, of course, date the stories they contain. Our earliest complete version of 'The Wooing of Étaín' appears in the fourteenth-century Yellow Book of Lecan, yet we have a partial account in the twelfth-century Lebor na huidre, and we know from the contents list of the Book of Druimm Snechtai that the tale was in written form by the early eighth century. What we do not know — and probably never will — is whether the Druimm Snechtai version was very different from the one in the Yellow Book of Lecan, whether the tale assumed written form earlier than in the eighth century, and what the tale was like before it was first written down. Even the surviving manuscripts, which we are fortunate to have, are far from ideal: obscure words abound, some passages seem obviously corrupt, and there are lacunae and entire missing leaves.

The Irish Material

Convention and tradition have classified the early Irish tales into four groups, called cycles: (1) the Mythological Cycle, whose protagonists are the Síde and whose tales are set primarily among the burial mounds of the Boyne Valley; (2) the Ulster Cycle, which details the (purportedly historical) exploits of the Ulaid, a few centuries before or after the birth of Christ; (3) the Kings Cycle, which focuses on the activities of the 'historical' kings; (4) the Find Cycle, which describes the adventures of Find mac Cumaill and his fíana and which did not achieve widespread popularity until the twelfth century. Although these categories are useful, it should be remembered that they are also modern (no particular arrangement is apparent in the manuscripts, while it seems that the storytellers grouped tales by type – births, deaths, cattle raids, destructions, visions, wooings, etc. – for ease in remembering) and artificial. Characters from one cycle often turn up in another: the Síde-woman Bóand is introduced as Fróech's aunt in the Ulster Cycle's 'Cattle Raid of Fróech'; the otherworld-figure Manandán appears in the Ulster Cycle's 'Wasting Sickness of Cú Chulaind' and in the Kings Cycle's 'Adventures of Cormac'; Ulaid warriors join the invaders in the Mythological Cycle's 'Destruction of Da Derga's Hostel'; Ailill and Medb, king and queen of Connachta, take part in the Mythological Cycle's 'Dream of Óengus'. Also, one should not suppose that the Mythological

Cycle is populated exclusively by deities or that the other cycles are inhabited exclusively by mortals: many of the 'humans' are barely euhemerized gods, many of the 'gods' behave much like humans, and the two groups are often difficult to distinguish.

The material of these tales encompasses both impacted myth and corrupted history. Although Irish mythology does evince the tripartism detected by Georges Dumézil in other Indo-European cultures ('The Second Battle of Mag Tured' is on one level an explanation of how the priests and warriors – Dumézil's first two functions – wrested the secrets of agriculture from the third function, the farmers), its fundamental orientation seems more seasonal than societal, for the mythic subtexts of the tales focus on themes of dying kings and alternating lovers. (This strong pre-Indo-European element in Irish mythology probably derives both from the Celts' innate conservatism and from the fringe position of Ireland in the geography of the Indo-European world.) These themes are stated most clearly in 'The Wooing of Étaín' and 'The Exile of the Sons of Uisliu'. In the former story, Bóand passes from her husband, Elcmar, to the Dagdae (also called Echu) and then returns to Elcmar; Étaín goes from Mider to Óengus and back to Mider, from Echu Airem to Ailill Angubae and back to Echu, and from Echu Airem to Mider and back (in some versions) to Echu. In the latter tale, Derdriu passes from an old king, Conchubur, to a young hero, Noísiu, and back to Conchubur after Noísiu's death; when Conchubur threatens to send her to Noísiu's murderer, she kills herself. Sometimes, the woman's father substitutes for the dying king (this variant appears in the Greek tales of Jason and Medea and Theseus and Ariadne): Óengus has to win Étaín away from her father in 'The Wooing of Étaín' and Cáer Ibormeith away from hers in 'The Dream of Óengus'; Fróech has to win Findabair from Ailill and Medb – but primarily, and significantly, from Ailill – in 'The Cattle Raid of Fróech', while Cú Chulaind has to win Emer from Forgall in 'The Wooing of Emer'. Sometimes, the dying king is absent, and the regeneration theme is embodied in the wooing of a mortal hero by a beautiful otherworld woman (whom he often loses or leaves): Cáer Ibormeith seeks out Óengus in 'The Dream of Óengus', Macha comes to Crunniuc in 'The Labour Pains of the Ulaid', Fand appears to Cú Chulaind in 'The Wasting Sickness of Cú Chulaind'. (This variant persists even into the Find Cycle, where Níam's wooing of Oisín becomes the basis of Yeats's 'The Wanderings of Oisín'.) And sometimes the theme treats only of the dying king: in 'The Destruction of Da Derga's Hostel', Conare Már is slain, at Samuin, in the hostel of a chthonic red god; in 'The Intoxication of the Ulaid', Cú Chulaind is nearly burnt, also at Samuin, in an iron house in the southwest of Ireland (where the House of Dond, an Irish underworld deity, was located). Centuries of historical appropriation and Christian censorship notwithstanding, these regeneration themes are never far from the narrative surface; and in their ubiquitousness is apparent their power.

As history, the early Irish tales verge upon wishful thinking, if not outright propaganda. The Ulster Cycle, however, does appear to preserve genuine traditions of a continuing conflict between the Ulaid (who appear to have concentrated in the area round present-day Armagh) and the Uí Néill (who were probably centred at Temuir, though for reasons suggested earlier – see page 7 – they have been moved to present-day Connaught by the storytellers); in any case, it is a valuable repository of information about the Ireland of prehistory – what Kenneth Jackson has called 'a window on the Iron Age'[18] – with its extensive descriptions of fighting (chariots are still the norm) and feasting (an abundance of strong words and strong drink) and dress (opulent, at least for the aristocracy) and its detailing of such institutions as fosterhood, clientship and the taking of sureties. The important but not very surprising conclusion generated by this information is that the Irish society represented by the Ulster Cycle is still very similar to the Gaulish civilization described by Caesar; and there are good reasons to think it not very different from the Celtic world of an even earlier period.

What is surprising, though, is that these tales – which betray a natural and unmistakable bias towards the Ulaid and against the Connachta – do not more consistently depict Ulster society at its zenith. Cú Chulaind is the only true hero in the Ulster Cycle, and his deeds are more often superhuman than heroic; Conchubur, as early as 'The Boyhood Deeds of Cú Chulaind', serves notice that he will be largely a *roi fainéant*; and among the Ulaid warriors there is, 'The Cattle Raid of Cúailnge' excepted, more talk than action. Odder still, in many of the best-known and most important tales, there are clear instances of parody. In 'The Death of Aífe's Only Son', the Ulaid are awestruck by the feats of a seven-year-old boy; in 'The Tale of Macc Da Thó's Pig', Ulaid and Connachta are reduced to fighting over a dog (at least, in 'The Cattle Raid of Cúailnge', the bone of contention is a bull), and the Ulaid are ridiculed and put to shame by the Connachta champion; in 'The Intoxication of the Ulaid', Cú Chulaind loses his way and leads the Ulaid on a drunken spree across Ireland, while the two druids guarding Cú Ruí's stronghold bicker and quarrel; and in 'Bricriu's Feast', the wives of the Ulaid warriors squabble over precedence in entering the drinking hall, while Bricriu is accidentally flung out of his house and on to a garbage dump. Conchubur's treachery (equivalent to Arthur's murdering Lancelot) in 'The Exile of the Sons of Uisliu' eliminates any doubt: the society of the Ulster Cycle, for all the splendour that attaches to it, is a society in decline.

This Translation

The purpose of this translation is to offer accurate, idiomatic renderings of a representative sample of early Irish stories. For reasons of space I have had, unfortunately, to limit my selection to tales from the Mythological and Ulster cycles, which often seem earlier in feeling and more characteristically Celtic. Two prominent stories from the represented cycles have also had to be omitted. 'The Second Battle of Mag Tured' is a valuable enumeration of the Túatha Dé Danand, but as a tale it is of less interest, and it stands somewhat apart from the mythological tales presented here. The centrepiece of the Ulster Cycle, 'The Cattle Raid of Cúailnge', could fill a small volume by itself; and though the Book of Leinster version opens very promisingly, the narrative quickly deteriorates. Moreover, modern translations are available elsewhere.

As in my translation of the Welsh Mabinogion, I have not attempted to be absolutely literal. Where a scribe has written 'et reliqua', I have expanded; where repetitions and duplications and irrelevant interpolations appear, I have removed them. Where the manuscripts are obscure or corrupt, I have had to guess. Most tales are translated entire; but where an archaic rhetorical section is hopelessly obscure, or where a long poetic passage seemed expendable, I have omitted it. Some flaws, unfortunately, are irreparable: there is a puzzling non sequitur near the beginning of 'The Destruction of Da Derga's Hostel', and the Book of Leinster and Lebor na huidre fragments of 'The Intoxication of the Ulaid' do not quite meet. The stories are arranged chronologically (so far as one can tell).

All Celtic proper names are spelt in their Old Irish forms, which seemed preferable to anglicizations and modernizations; this should not cause undue concern, but the reader may want to glance at the note on geographic names. The pronunciation guide is an approximation; Old Irish is more phonetic (and thus easier) than English, but a few inconsistencies persist. The map indicates the location of the major strongholds and natural features (to show every place name would have been impractical); the bibliography, while not exhaustive, will afford a useful starting point.

I would like to thank Will Sulkin and Betty Radice for their help and encouragement, and my brother Timothy for his numerous valuable suggestions.

Bibliography

DIPLOMATIC EDITIONS

Lebor na huidre: Book of the Dun Cow, edited by R. I. Best and Osborn Bergin (Dublin: Royal Irish Academy), 1929.

The Book of Leinster, five volumes, edited by R. I. Best, Osborn Bergin and M. A. O'Brien (Dublin: Dublin Institute for Advanced Studies), 1954–67.

TEXTS

'Tochmarc Étaíne' (The Wooing of Étaín), Y B L 985–98; edited by Osborn Bergin and R. I. Best in *Ériu* 12 (1937): 137–96.

'Togail bruidne Da Derga' (The Destruction of Da Derga's Hostel), L U 83a1–99a47 and Y B L 91a1–104.10; edited by Eleanor Knott in *Togail bruidne Da Derga* (Dublin: Dublin Institute for Advanced Studies), 1936.

'Aislinge Óengusso' (The Dream of Óengus), Egerton 1782; edited by Eduard Müller in *Revue Celtique* 3 (1882): 344–7.

'Táin bó Froích' (The Cattle Raid of Fróech), L L 248a12–252b6; edited by Wolfgang Meid in *Táin bó Fraích* (Dublin: Dublin Institute for Advanced Studies), 1967.

'Noínden Ulad & Emuin Machae' (The Labour Pains of the Ulaid & The Twins of Macha), LL 125b42–126a30.

'Compert Con Culaind' (The Birth of Cú Chulaind), LU 128a–128b47; edited by A. G. van Hamel in *Compert Con Culainn* (Dublin: Dublin Institute for Advanced Studies), 1933.

'Maccgnimrada Con Culaind' (The Boyhood Deeds of Cú Chulaind), L U 4855–901, 4924–54, 4973–5033, 5035–210; edited

28

by John Strachan in *Stories from the Táin* (Dublin: Royal Irish Academy), 1944.

'Aided óenfir Aífe' (The Death of Aífe's Only Son), Y B L 214a–215a; edited by A. G. van Hamel in *Compert Con Culainn* (Dublin: Dublin Institute for Advanced Studies), 1933.

'Serglige Con Culaind & Óenét Emire' (The Wasting Sickness of Cú Chulaind & The Only Jealousy of Emer) LU 43a1–50b14; edited by Myles Dillon in *Serglige Con Culainn* (Dublin: Dublin Institute for Advanced Studies), 1953.

'Scéla mucce Maicc Da Thó' (The Tale of Macc Da Thó's Pig), L L 112a1–114a54; edited by Rudolf Thurneysen in *Scéla mucce Meic Dathó* (Dublin: Dublin Institute for Advanced Studies), 1935.

'Mesca Ulad' (The Intoxication of the Ulaid), LL 261b25–268b49 and L U 19a1–20b31; edited by J. C. Watson in *Mesca Ulad* (Dublin: Dublin Institute for Advanced Studies), 1941.

'Fled Bricrend' (Bricriu's Feast), LU 99b1–112b48; edited by George Henderson in *Fled Bricrend* (Dublin: Irish Texts Society), 1899.

'Longes macc nUislend' (The Exile of the Sons of Uisliu), L L 192b11–193b24 and Y B L 749–53; edited by Vernam Hull in *Longes mac n-Uislenn* (New York: Modern Language Association), 1949.

TRANSLATIONS

Ancient Irish Tales, edited by T. P. Cross and C. H. Slover, various translators (New York: Henry Holt), 1936; reprinted, with a revised bibliography by C. W. Dunn (New York: Barnes and Noble), 1969.

Lebor Gabála Érenn (The Book of the Invasions of Ireland), five volumes, edited and translated by R. A. S. Macalister (Dublin: Irish Texts Society), 1938–54.

Táin Bó Cúalnge from the Book of Leinster (The Cattle Raid of Cúailnge), edited and translated by Cecille O'Rahilly (Dublin: Dublin Institute for Advanced Studies), 1967.

The Táin (The Cattle Raid of Cúailnge and other Ulaid stories), translated by Thomas Kinsella (Dublin: Dolmen Press, 1969, and London: Oxford University Press, 1970).

Táin Bó Cúalnge from the Book of the Dun Cow, edited and translated by Cecille O'Rahilly (Dublin: Dublin Institute for Advanced Studies), 1978.

BIBLIOGRAPHY

Bibliography of Irish Philology and of Printed Irish Literature, edited by R. I. Best (Dublin: National Library of Ireland), 1913.

Bibliography of Irish Philology and Manuscript Literature 1913–41, edited by R. I. Best (Dublin: Dublin Institute for Advanced Studies), 1942.

BOOKS RELATING TO IRELAND

Rudolf Thurneysen, *Handbuch des Altirischen*, 1909; translated by D. A. Binchy and Osborn Bergin as *A Grammar of Old Irish* (Dublin: Dublin Institute for Advanced Studies), 1946; revised edition, 1961.

Rudolf Thurneysen, *Die irische Helden- und Königsage* (Halle: Max Niemeyer), 1921.

T. F. O'Rahilly, *Early Irish History and Mythology* (Dublin: Dublin Institute for Advanced Studies), 1946.

Gerard Murphy, *Saga and Myth in Ancient Ireland* (Dublin: Cultural Relations Committee of Ireland), 1961.

K. H. Jackson, *The Oldest Irish Tradition: A Window on the Iron Age* (Cambridge: Cambridge University Press), 1964.

S. P. Ó Ríordáin, *Tara: The Monuments on the Hill* (Dundalk: Dundalgan Press), 1954.

S. P. Ó Ríordáin and Glyn Daniel, *New Grange* (London: Thames & Hudson), 1964.

Bibliography

BOOKS RELATING TO THE CELTS

T. G. E. Powell, *The Celts* (London: Thames & Hudson), 1958.

Myles Dillon and Nora Chadwick, *The Celtic Realms* (New York: New American Library), 1967.

Nora Chadwick, *The Celts* (Harmondsworth: Penguin), 1970.

Anne Ross, *Everyday Life of the Pagan Celts* (London: Routledge & Kegan Paul), 1970.

Duncan Norton-Taylor, *The Celts* (Alexandria, Va: Time-Life), 1974.

Barry Cunliffe, *The Celtic World* (New York: McGraw-Hill), 1979.

Alwyn Rees and Brinley Rees, *Celtic Heritage* (London: Thames & Hudson), 1961.

Proinsias Mac Cana, *Celtic Mythology* (London: Hamlyn), 1970.

Stuart Piggott, *The Druids* (London: Thames & Hudson), 1968; reprinted (Harmondsworth: Penguin), 1974.

K. H. Jackson, *A Celtic Miscellany* (London: Routledge & Kegan Paul), 1951; reprinted (Harmondsworth: Penguin), 1971.

The Mabinogion, translated by Jeffrey Gantz (Harmondsworth: Penguin), 1976.

CONTEMPORARY RETELLINGS

James Stephens, *Deirdre* (1913).

J. M. Synge, *Deirdre of the Sorrows* (1909).

W. B. Yeats, *On Baile's Strand* (1904); *Deirdre* (1907); *The Green Helmet* (1910); *At the Hawk's Well* (1915); *The Only Jealousy of Emer* (1916); *The Death of Cuchulain* (1937).

A Note on the Pronunciation of
Irish Words and Names

Although the spelling system of Old Irish may seem confusing at first, it is still more consistent than that of English. Moreover, the actual pronunciation is not at all difficult.

Consonants. These are mostly as in English; the major difference is that some are softened when they stand alone in medial or final position. Consonant clusters tend to be pronounced as they would be in English.

b (initial): *b*oy; *b* (medial or final): ne*v*er or *w*in.
c (initial), *cc*: *c*ane, never *c*inder; *c* (medial or final): eg*g*.
ch: Scottish lo*ch* or German Ba*ch*, never *ch*urch.
d (initial): *d*og; *d* (medial or final): ra*th*er.
f: *f*ort.
g (initial): *g*irl, never *g*in; *g* (medial or final): German Ma*g*en.
h: *h*ill.
l, *ll*: *l*ow.
m (initial), *mb*, *mm*: *m*ow; *m* (medial or final): ne*v*er or *w*in.
n, *nd*, *nn*: *n*ew.
p (initial): *p*ort; *p* (medial or final): ca*b*in.
r, *rr*: Italian se*r*a.
s, *ss* (before *a*, *o* or *u*, or after when final): *s*in, never ro*s*e; *s*, *ss* (before *e* or *i*, or after when final): *sh*ow.
t (initial), *tt*: *t*ow; *t* (medial or final): a*dd*.
th: *th*in.

A Note on the Pronunciation of Irish Words and Names

Vowels. These are largely as in continental languages.

a, ai: father.
á, ái: law.
áe, aí: aisle.
e, ei, éo, éoi: bet.
i: pin.
í, íu, íui: keen.
ía, íai: Ian.
o, oi: pot.
ó, ói: lone.
óe, oí: oil.
u, ui: put.
ú, úi: moon.
úa, úai: moor.

Stress. This usually falls on the first syllable. Unstressed vowels, when not long, are usually reduced to the sound of *a* in *sofa*.

A Note on Irish Geography

In this translation, all Celtic place names are given in their original Old Irish forms rather than in anglicizations. This should cause neither undue concern nor any great confusion; but, for the reader's convenience, the most important names are listed here together with their English equivalents.

Ériu: the island of Ireland.

Albu: originally, the island of Britain; later, northern Britain; still later, just Scotland.

Bretain: the southern part of the British isle; the people of that area.

Ulaid: Ulster, especially the area between Armagh and Dundalk; the people of that area.

Connachta: Connaught, especially the area round Crúachu (see the map); the people of that area.

Lagin: Leinster; the people of that area.

Mumu: Munster.

Mide: Meath, but really modern Meath and Westmeath; the eastern part may be called Brega.

Bruig na Bóinde: New Grange.

Temuir: Tara.

Dún Delga: Dundalk.

Áth Clíath: Dublin.

Bend Étair: Howth.

Áth Lúain: Athlone.

Bóand: the river Boyne.

Life, Ruirthech: the river Liffey.

Sinand: the river Shannon.

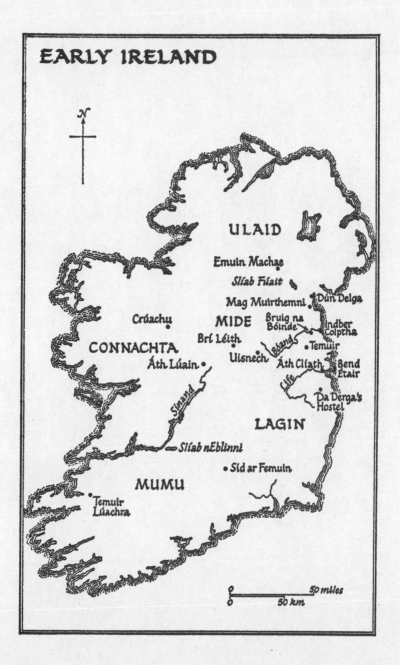

EARLY IRELAND

N

ULAID

Emuin Machae

Slíab Fúait

Mag Muirthemni   Dún Delga

Crúachu   MIDE   Bruig na   Indber
                        Bóinde   Colptha
        Brí Léith
CONNACHTA   Uisnech   Temuir
        Áth Lúain
                Áth Clíath   Bend
                            Etair
    Stnand
                    Da Derga's
                    Hostel
            LAGIN

        Slíab nEblinni

            Síd ar Femuin

MUMU

    Temuir
    Lúachra

0   50 miles
0   50 km

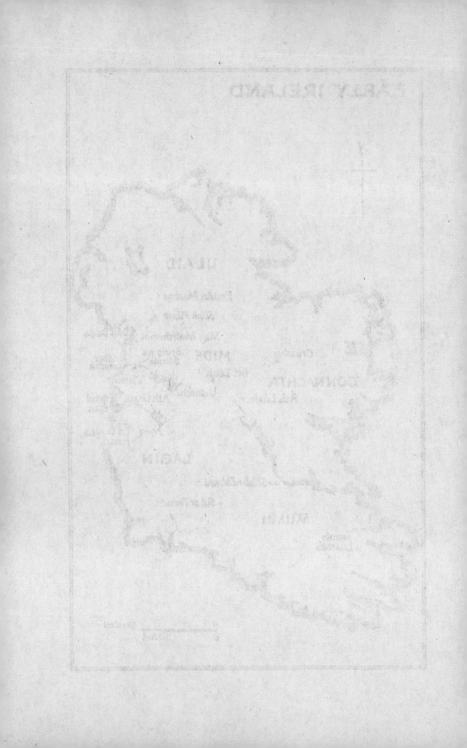

The Wooing of Étaín

Introduction

Apart from being a remarkable tale, 'The Wooing of Étaín' has a remarkable history. Although it is preserved in Lebor na huidre, the beginning of the first section and the ending of the third are missing, and only the short second section is complete. This situation persisted until this century, when a complete version of the story was discovered lying innocently among a part of the Yellow Book of Lecan housed in Cheltenham; and in 1937 the complete text of 'The Wooing of Étaín' finally appeared in print.

The three sections are virtually independent tales. The first comprises a set of variations upon the regeneration theme of the rival lovers; thus, in the opening episode, Bóand goes from her husband Elcmar to the Dagdae and then back to Elcmar. Óengus's efforts to win Étaín away from her father represent a variant of the type found in the Welsh 'How Culhwch Won Olwen', while his concealing her from Mider suggests that the two gods were originally rivals. In the second section, Echu and Ailill are the rival claimants, Ailill's love-sickness recalling that of Gilvaethwy in 'Math Son of Mathonwy'; Étaín goes from Echu to Ailill and back to Echu. In the final section, it is Mider and Echu who contest Étaín, and the tasks assigned Mider recall those imposed upon the Dagdae in the first section and those imposed upon Culhwch; Étaín goes from Echu to Mider, back to Echu (in the person of her daughter), back to Mider and, in some traditions, back to Echu – the uncertain conclusion underlines the seasonal motif.

'The Wooing of Étaín' is also a kind of legal primer. The first section, wherein Óengus gains possession of Bruig na Bóinde (at Samuin, naturally), demonstrates that the Irish had a poetic sense of law. Frank O'Connor says that 'The trick – borrowing the use of New Grange for a day and a night and then claiming successfully that this means for all time – has some esoteric meaning which I cannot grasp';[1] but there is nothing esoteric here. Óengus's argument that 'it is in days and nights that the world passes' explains everything. Mider uses the same trick in the third section, for, in claiming that Echu has 'sold' Étaín, he is clearly arguing that 'My arms round Étaín and a kiss from her' entitle him to permanent possession of her, that it is in embraces and kisses that love is spent. (Actually, since the last fidchell game is played for an open stake, Mider could simply have asked for Étaín outright; but perhaps then Echu would not have kept the bargain.) Since Echu does not accept this argument – he claims that he has not sold Étaín – Mider is forced to trick him a second time; thinking that he has picked out Étaín from among the fifty women, Echu pledges himself content, but actually he has chosen his own (and Étaín's) daughter. Mider's name, appropriately, seems to derive from a Celtic root meaning 'to judge'.

The Wooing of Étaín

There was over Ériu a famous king from the Túatha Dé
Danand, and Echu Ollathir was his name. Another name for
him was the Dagdae, for it was he who performed miracles
and saw to the weather and the harvest, and that is why
he was called the Good God. Elcmar of Bruig na Bóinde
had a wife whose name was Eithne, though she was also
called Bóand.[2] The Dagdae wanted to sleep with Bóand,
and she would have allowed him, but she feared Elcmar and
the extent of his power. The Dagdae sent Elcmar away,
then, on a journey to Bress son of Elatha at Mag nInis; and
as Elcmar was leaving, the Dagdae cast great spells upon
him, so that he would not return quickly, so that he would
not perceive the darkness of night, so that he would feel
neither hunger nor thirst. The Dagdae charged Elcmar with
great commissions, so that nine months passed like a single
day, for Elcmar had said that he would return before night-
fall. The Dagdae slept with Elcmar's wife, then, and she
bore him a son, who was named Óengus; and by the time
of Elcmar's return, she had so recovered that he had no
inkling of her having slept with the Dagdae.

The Dagdae took his son to be fostered in the house of
Mider at Brí Léith in Tethbae, and Óengus was reared there
for nine years. Mider had a playing field at Brí Léith, and
three fifties of the young boys of Ériu were there together
with three fifties of the young girls. And Óengus was their
leader, because of Mider's love for him and because of his

handsomeness and the nobility of his people. He was also called the Macc Óc, for his mother had said 'Young the son who is conceived at dawn and born before dusk.'[3]

Now Óengus fell out with Tríath son of Febal (or Gobor) of the Fir Bolg – Tríath was also a fosterling of Mider and was the other leader at play. Óengus had no mind to speak with Tríath, and he said 'It angers me that the son of a slave should talk to me', for he believed that Mider was his father and that he was heir to the kingship of Brí Léith, and he did not know of his relationship to the Dagdae. But Tríath answered 'It angers me no less that a foundling who knows neither his mother nor his father should talk to me.' Óengus went off to Mider, distressed and in tears at having been shamed by Tríath. 'What is this?' asked Mider. 'Tríath has mocked me and thrown it in my face that I have neither father nor mother.' 'False,' replied Mider. 'Who are they, then, my father and my mother?' 'Echu Ollathir is your father, and Eithne, the wife of Elcmar of Bruig na Bóinde, is your mother. I have reared you without Elcmar's knowledge so it would not pain him that you were conceived behind his back.' 'Come with me, then,' said Óengus, 'that my father may acknowledge me and that I may no longer be hidden away and reviled by the Fir Bolg.'

Mider set out with his fosterling to speak with Echu, thus, and they came to Uisnech Mide at the centre of Ériu, for that is where Echu dwelt, with Ériu extending equally far in every direction, north and south, east and west. They found Echu in the assembly, and Mider called him aside to speak with the boy. 'What would he like, this youth who has never been here before?' asked Echu. 'He would like his father to acknowledge him and give him land,' answered Mider, 'for it is not right that your son be without land when you are king of Ériu.' 'A welcome to him,' said Echu, 'for he is my son. But the land I have chosen for him is still occupied.' 'What land is that?' asked Mider. 'Bruig na Bóinde, to the north,' said Echu. 'Who is there?' asked Mider. 'Elcmar is the man who is there,' said Echu, 'and I have no wish to disturb him further.'

'What advice, then, can you give the boy?' asked Mider. Echu answered 'This: he is to go into the Bruig at Samuin, and he is to go armed, for that is a day of peace and friendship among the men of Ériu, and no one will be at odds with his fellow. Elcmar will be at Cnocc Síde in the Bruig with no weapon but a fork of white hazel in his hand; he will be wearing a cloak with a gold brooch in it, and he will be watching three fifties of youths at play on the playing field. Óengus is to go to Elcmar and threaten to kill him, but he should not do so provided he obtains his request. That request is that Óengus be king in the Bruig for a day and a night, but Óengus must not return the land to Elcmar until the latter agrees to abide by my judgement. Óengus is to argue that the land is his by right in return for his having spared Elcmar – that he requested the kingship of day and night and that it is in days and nights that the world passes.'

Mider set out for his land, then, and his fosterling with him, and on the following Samuin, Óengus armed himself and went into the Bruig and threatened Elcmar; and the latter promised him a kingship of day and night in his land. Óengus remained there as king of the land during that day and that night, and Elcmar's people did his will. The next day, Elcmar came to reclaim his land from the Macc Óc, and at that, a great argument arose, for the Macc Óc said that he would not yield the land until Elcmar had put the question to the Dagdae before the men of Ériu. They appealed to the Dagdae, then, and he adjudged the rights of each man according to their agreement. 'By right, the land now belongs to this youth,' Elcmar concluded. 'Indeed, it does,' said the Dagdae. 'He hewed at you menacingly on a day of peace and friendship, and since your life was dearer to you than your land, you surrendered the land in return for being spared. Even so, I will give you land that is no worse than the Bruig.' 'What land is that?' asked Elcmar. 'Cletech, and the three lands about it, and the boys from the Bruig playing before you every day, and the fruit of the Bóand for your enjoyment.' 'Fair enough – let it be thus,' said Elcmar, and he set out for Cletech and built a fort there, and the Macc Óc remained in the Bruig.

One year after that, Mider went to the Bruig to visit his foster-son, and he found the Macc Óc on the mound of the Bruig, it being Samuin, with two groups of boys playing before him and Elcmar watching from the mound of Cletech to the south. A quarrel broke out among the boys in the Bruig, and Mider said 'Do not trouble yourself – otherwise Elcmar may come to the plain. I will go and make peace among them.' Mider went, then, but it was not easy for him to part them; moreover, a sprig of holly was hurled at him, and it put out one of his eyes. Mider returned to the Macc Óc, his eye in his hand, and said 'Would that I had never come to seek news of you, for I have been shamed: with this blemish, I can neither see the land I have come to nor return to the land I have left.' 'Not at all,' answered the Macc Óc, 'for I will go to Dían Cécht, and he will come and heal you. Your own land will be yours again, and this land will be yours also, and your eye will be healed, without shame or blemish.'

The Macc Óc went to Dían Cécht and asked him to come and save his foster-father, who had been injured in the Bruig on Samuin; and Dían Cécht came and tended to Mider until the latter was well. Mider said, then, 'Since I have been healed, it would please me to leave now.' 'Well that,' said the Macc Óc. 'But stay for a year and see my warriors and my people and my household and my land.' 'I will not stay,' answered Mider, 'unless I have a reward.' 'What sort of reward?' asked the Macc Óc. 'Not difficult that,' answered Mider. 'A chariot worth seven cumals and clothing appropriate to my rank and the fairest woman in Ériu.'⁴ 'I have the chariot and the clothing,' said the Macc Óc, whereupon Mider said 'I know of the woman whose beauty surpasses that of every other woman in Ériu.' 'Where is she?' asked the Macc Óc. 'She is of the Ulaid,' answered Mider, 'daughter of Ailill, king of the north-eastern part of Ériu; Étaín Echrade is her name, and she is the fairest and gentlest and most beautiful woman in Ériu.'

The Macc Óc went to seek Étaín, then, at the house of Ailill in Mag nInis, where he was welcomed and where he spent three nights. He announced himself and told of his race and his people and said that he had come to ask for Étaín. 'I will not give her to you,' said Ailill, 'for there is no profit in it. The nobility of your family and the extent of your power and your father's is so great that, if you were to shame my daughter, I would have no recourse.' 'Not at all,' replied the Macc Óc, 'for I will buy her from you here and now.' 'You will have that,' answered Ailill. 'Tell me what you want,' said the Macc Óc. 'Not difficult that,' replied Ailill. 'Twelve lands of mine that are nothing but desert and forest are to be cleared so that cattle may graze on them and men dwell there at all times, so that they may be suitable for games and assemblies and meetings and fortifications.' 'That will be done for you,' said the Macc Óc. He went home, then, and complained of his predicament to the Dagdae; the latter, however, cleared twelve plains in Ailill's land in a single night: Mag Machae, Mag Lemna, Mag nÍtha, Mag Tochair, Mag nDula, Mag Techt, Mag Lí, Mag Line, Mag Muirthemni.

The task having been accomplished, the Macc Óc returned

to Ailill and demanded Étaín. 'You will not have her,' said Ailill, 'until you divert from the land towards the sea twelve great rivers that are in springs and bogs and moors: the fruits of the sea will be brought to all peoples and families, thus, and the land will be drained.' The Macc Óc went to the Dagdae and again bewailed his predicament, and the Dagdae in a single night caused the twelve great rivers to run towards the sea, where they had never before been seen. These were the rivers: Findi, Modornn, Slenae, Nass, Amnas, Oichén, Or, Bandai, Samuir, Lóchae.

This task also having been accomplished, the Macc Óc again went to Ailill and demanded Étaín. 'You will not have her until you buy her,' said Ailill, 'for after you take her away I will have no further good of her, only what you give me now.' 'What do you want, then?' asked the Macc Óc. 'I want her weight in gold and silver, for that is my share of her price. Everything that you have done so far has profited only her family and her people.' 'You will have that,' said the Macc Óc. The woman was brought to the centre of Ailill's house, and her weight in gold and silver was handed over. That wealth was left with Ailill, and the Macc Óc took Étaín home with him.

Mider welcomed the two of them. He slept with Étaín that night, and the following day his clothing and his chariot were given him, and he thanked his foster-son. He stayed a year in the Bruig with Óengus, and then he returned to Brí Léith and his own land, and he took Étaín with him. As he was leaving, the Macc Óc said 'Look after the woman you are taking with you, for there awaits you a woman of dreadful sorcery, a woman with all the knowledge and skill and power of her people. She has, moreover, my guarantee of safety against the Túatha Dé Danand.' This woman was Fúamnach wife of Mider, from the family of Béothach son of Íardanél; she was wise and clever, and she was versed in the knowledge and power of the Túatha Dé Danand, for the druid Bresal had reared her before her engagement to Mider.

Fúamnach welcomed her husband, and she spoke much of friendship to them. 'Come, Mider,' she said, 'that you may see your house and your lands, that the king's daughter may see your wealth.' Mider went round all his lands with Fúamnach, and she showed his holdings to him and to Étaín. He took Étaín back to Fúamnach, then. Fúamnach preceded Étaín into the house where she slept, and she said to her 'The seat of a good woman have you occupied.' With that, Étaín sat in the chair in the centre of the house, whereupon Fúamnach struck her with a wand of scarlet rowan and turned her into a pool of water. Fúamnach went to her foster-father Bresal, then, and Mider left the house to the water that had been made of Étaín. After that, Mider was without a woman.

The heat of the fire and the air and the seething of the ground combined to turn the pool of water that was in the centre of the house into a worm, and they then turned the worm into a scarlet fly. This fly was the size of the head of the handsomest man in the land, and the sound of its voice and the beating of its wings were sweeter than pipes and harps and horns. Its eyes shone like precious stones in the dark, and its colour and fragrance could sate hunger and quench thirst in any man; moreover, a sprinkling of the drops it shed from its wings could cure every sickness and affliction and disease. This fly accompanied Mider as he travelled through his land, and listening to it and gazing upon it nourished hosts in their meetings and assemblies. Mider knew that the fly was Étaín, and while it was with him he did not take another wife, for the sight of it nourished him. He would fall asleep to its buzzing, and it would awaken him when anyone approached who did not love him.

Eventually, Fúamnach came to visit Mider, and, to guarantee her safety, three of the Túatha Dé Danand came with her: Lug and the Dagdae and Ogmae. Mider upbraided Fúamnach and said that but for the guarantee of those who had come with her she would not have been permitted to leave; Fúamnach answered that she did not regret what she had done, that she preferred being good to herself to being good to anyone else, and that, wherever she went in Ériu, she would bring nothing but evil to Étaín, wherever and in whatever shape the latter might be. Fúamnach had brought from the druid Bresal Etarlám great spells and incantations with which to banish Étaín from Mider, for she knew that the scarlet fly that was entertaining Mider was Étaín: as long as he could watch the scarlet fly, Mider loved no woman, and he did not enjoy food or drink or music unless he could see it and listen to its music and its buzzing.

With her druidry, then, Fúamnach conjured up a lashing wind that blew Étaín out of Brí Léith, so that for seven years there was not a hill or a treetop or a cliff or a summit on which the fly might alight, only the rocks of the ocean and the waves; and it floated through the air until at last it alighted on the garment of the Macc Óc on the mound of the Bruig. The Macc Óc said 'Welcome, Étaín, troubled wanderer, you have endured great hardships through the power of Fúamnach. Not yet have you found happiness, your side secure in alliance with Mider. As for me, he has found me capable of action with hosts, the slaughter of a multitude, the clearing of wildernesses, the world's abundance for Ailill's daughter. An idle task, for your wretched ruin has followed. Welcome!' The Macc Óc welcomed the girl – that is, the scarlet fly. He took it against his breast in the fold of his cloak, and he brought it then to his house and his bower, the latter with its airy windows for coming and going and the scarlet veil he put round it. The Macc Óc carried that bower wherever he went, and he fell asleep by it every night, lifting the fly's spirit until its colour and cheer returned. The bower was filled with strange, fragrant herbs, and Étaín prospered with the scent and the colour of those healthful and precious herbs.

Fúamnach heard of the love and honour that the fly was shown by the Macc Óc, and she said to Mider 'Have your foster-son summoned, that I may make peace between the two of you, and I, meanwhile, will go in search of Étaín.' A messenger from Mider arrived at the Macc Óc's house, then, and the Macc Óc went to speak with him; Fúamnach, however, circled into the Bruig from another direction and unleashed the same wind against Étaín, so that the latter was driven out of the bower on the same wandering as before, seven years throughout Ériu. The lashing of the wind drove the fly on in wretchedness and weakness until it alighted on the roof of a house in Ulaid where people were drinking; there, it fell into a golden vessel that was in the hand of the wife of Étar, a warrior from Indber Cíchmane in the province of Conchubur. Étar's wife swallowed Étaín along with the drink in the vessel; Étaín was conceived in the woman's womb and was born as her daughter. One thousand and twelve years from her first begetting by Ailill until her last by Étar.

Thereafter Étaín was brought up by Étar at Indber Cích-mane, and fifty chieftains' daughters were reared along with her, and they were fed and clothed for the purpose of attending Étaín at all times. One day, when all the girls were bathing at the mouth of the river, they saw a rider coming towards them from the plain. His horse was broad and brown, prancing, with curly mane and curly tail. He wore a green cloak of the Síde, and a tunic with red embroidery, and the cloak was fastened with a gold brooch that reached to either shoulder.[5] A silver shield with a rim of gold was slung over his shoulder, and it had a silver strap with a gold buckle. In his hand he carried a five-pronged spear with a band of gold running from butt to socket. Fair yellow hair covered his forehead, but a band of gold restrained it so that it did not cover his face. The rider stopped a while on the river bank to look at Étaín, and all the girls fell in love with him. Then he recited this poem:

> Étaín is here today
> at Síd Ban Find west of Ailbe;
> among little boys she is,
> on the border of Indber Cíchmane.
>
> It is she who healed the king's eye
> from the well of Loch Dá Licc;
> it is she who was swallowed in the drink
> in the vessel of the wife of Étar.
>
> Because of her the king will chase
> the birds of Tethbae;
> because of her he will drown his two horses
> in the waters of Loch Dá Airbrech.
>
> Over her there will be much fighting
> against Echu of Mide;
> síde mounds will be destroyed,
> and many thousands will do battle.
>
> It is she who will be celebrated everywhere;
> it is she the king is seeking.
> Once she was called Bé Find.
> Now she is our Étaín.

The young warrior rode away, then, and they knew neither whence he had come nor where he had gone.

The Macc Óc went to speak with Mider, but he did not find Fúamnach there. Mider said to him 'Fúamnach has lied to us, and if she hears that Étaín is in Ériu, she will go to

do her harm.' 'Étaín has been at my house in the Bruig for
a while now,' said the Macc Óc, 'in the form in which she
was blown away from you, and it may be that Fúamnach
has gone there.' The Macc Óc returned to his house and
found the crystal bower without Étaín in it. He followed
Fúamnach's trail until he overtook her at Óenach Bodbgnai,
at the house of the druid Bresal Etarlám, and there he
attacked her and struck off her head and took it back with
him to Bruig na Bóinde.

*

Echu Airem became king of Ériu, and the five provinces of
the country submitted to him, and the king of each
province: Conchubur son of Ness, Mess Gegra, Tigernach
Tétbandach, Cú Ruí and Ailill son of Máta Murisc. Echu's
forts were Dún Frémaind in Mide and Dún Frémaind in
Tethbae; of all the forts in Ériu, Dún Frémaind in Tethbae
was the one he loved most.

The year after he became king, Echu ordered the men of
Ériu to hold the feis of Temuir, so that their taxes and
assessments for the next five years might be reckoned.[6] The
men of Ériu replied that they would not hold the feis of
Temuir for a king with no queen, for indeed Echu had had
no queen when he became king. Echu then sent messengers
to every province of Ériu to seek the fairest woman in the
land; and he said that he would have no wife but a woman
whom none of the men of Ériu had known before him.
Such a woman was found at Indber Cíchmane – Étaín
daughter of Étar – and Echu took her, for she was his
equal in beauty and form and race, in magnificence and
youth and high repute.

The three sons of Find son of Findlug were queen's sons:
Echu Feidlech, Echu Airem and Ailill Angubae. Ailill Angubae

fell in love with Étaín at the feis of Temuir, after she had slept with Echu Airem – he would gaze upon her constantly, and such gazing is a sign of love. Ailill reproached himself for what he was doing, but he could not desist: his desire was stronger than his will. He fell ill, then, for he would not dishonour himself by speaking with Étaín. When he sensed that he was dying, he had Echu's doctor Fachtna brought to him, and Fachtna said 'You have one of two deadly pangs that no doctor can cure: the pang of love and the pang of jealousy.' Ailill said nothing, for he was ashamed.

Ailill was left at Dún Frémaind in Tethbae to die, then, while Echu made a circuit of Ériu; and Étaín was left with him to perform the funeral rites: digging his grave, weeping over his body, slaying his cattle. Every day, she went to the house where he lay sick to talk to him, and he grew better, for when she was in the house he could look at her. Étaín observed this and meditated on it, and the next day, when they were together, she asked Ailill what had made him ill. 'My love for you,' he answered. 'A shame you did not tell me sooner,' she said, 'for had I known, you would long since have been well.' 'I can be well at once if you so desire,' said Ailill. 'Indeed, I do,' Étaín answered.

Every day, then, Étaín went to wash Ailill's head and cut his meat and pour water over his hands, and after thrice nine days he was well. He said to her, then, 'My healing yet wants one thing – when will I have that?' 'You will have it tomorrow,' she replied, 'but the sovereign must not be shamed in his own dwelling. Meet me tomorrow on the hill above the house.' Ailill remained awake all night, but at the hour of the meeting he fell asleep, and he did not wake until the third hour of the following day. Étaín went to the hill, and the man she saw there waiting for her was like Ailill in appearance; he lamented the weakness his ailment had brought about, and the words he spoke were the words Ailill would have used. Ailill himself woke at the third hour, and he was giving vent to his sorrow when Étaín returned to the house. 'Why so sad?' she asked. 'Because I made an appointment with you and was not there to meet you,' Ailill replied. 'Sleep overcame me, and I just now woke. It is clear that I am not yet well.' 'No matter,' said Étaín, 'for tomorrow is another day.'

Ailill remained awake that night in front of a huge fire, with water nearby for splashing over his face. At the appointed hour, Étaín went to meet him, and again she saw the man who was like Ailill; she returned home and found Ailill weeping. Three times Étaín went to the hill, and three times Ailill failed to meet her; always, the man who looked like Ailill met her. 'It is not you I am to meet,' she said. 'I come not to hurt or sin against the man I am to meet; I come rather to heal one who is worthy to be king of Ériu.' 'It would be more fitting for you to come to me,' replied the man, 'for when you were Étaín Echrade daughter of Ailill, I was your husband; I paid a great bride price for you by creating the plains and rivers of Ériu and by giving your weight in gold and silver to your father.' 'What is your name?' Étaín asked. 'Mider of Brí Léith.' 'And what is it that parted us?' 'The sorcery of Fúamnach and the spells of Bresal Etarlám.' Mider said to Étaín, then, 'Will you come with me?' 'I will not,' she answered. 'I will not exchange the king of Ériu for a man whose race and family I know nothing of.' 'It is I who made Ailill fall in love with you, so that his flesh and his blood fell from him; and it is I who quelled his desire to sleep with you, lest you be dishonoured. Will you come to my land with me if Echu bids you?' 'I will,' said Étaín.

She returned home, then, and Ailill said to her, 'Good our meeting here, for I have been healed, and you have not been dishonoured.' 'Wonderful that,' said Étaín. After that, Echu returned from his circuit; he rejoiced to find his brother alive, and he thanked Étaín for what she had done in his absence.

One beautiful summer day, Echu Airem king of Temuir rose and climbed on to the rampart of Temuir to look out over Mag mBreg, and he saw the plain vibrant with colour and bloom of every hue. And when he looked round the rampart, he saw a strange young warrior. The man wore a scarlet tunic; golden yellow hair fell to his shoulders, and his eyes were sparkling grey. In one hand he carried a five-pointed spear; in the other he held a shield studded with a white boss and gold gems. Echu was silent, for he did not remember the stranger's being in Temuir the previous evening, and at this hour the doors had not yet been opened.

The stranger approached Echu, and Echu said 'Welcome, young warrior whom I do not know.' 'It is for that I have come,' said the warrior. 'I do not recognize you,' said Echu. 'But I know you,' said the warrior. 'What is your name?' asked Echu. 'Not a famous one: Mider of Brí Léith.' 'What has brought you here?' Echu asked. 'The wish to play fidchell with you,' Mider replied.[7] 'Indeed, I am good at fidchell,' answered Echu. 'Let us see,' said Mider. 'The queen is asleep,' said Echu, 'and the fidchell set is with her in the house.' 'No worse the fidchell set I have with me,' said Mider. True that: the board was of silver and the men were of gold, a precious stone glittered in each corner of the board, and the bag for the men was woven in rounds of bronze.

Mider set up the pieces, then, and he said to Echu 'Let us play.' 'I will not play unless there is a stake,' Echu replied. 'What do you want to play for?' asked Mider. 'All the same to me,' answered Echu. 'If you win,' said Mider, 'I will give you fifty dark grey horses with dappled, blood-red heads, sharp-eared, broad-chested, wide-nostrilled, slender-footed, strong, keen, tall, swift, steady and yokable, and fifty enamelled bridles to go with them. You will have them at the third hour tomorrow.' Echu made the same wager; they played, and Mider lost his stake. He departed, then, taking his fidchell set with him.

The following day, at dawn, Echu rose and went out on to the rampart of Temuir, and he saw his opponent coming towards him. He did not know where Mider had gone the previous day or whence he came from now, but he saw the fifty dark grey horses with their enamelled bridles. 'Honourable this,' he said. 'What was promised is due,' answered Mider, and he went on 'Will we play fidchell?' 'Indeed,' said Echu, 'but there must be a stake.' 'I will give you fifty fiery boars,' said Mider, 'curly-haired, dappled, light grey underneath and dark grey above, with horses' hooves on them, and a blackthorn vat that can hold them all. Besides that, fifty gold-hilted swords. Moreover, fifty white red-eared cows and fifty white red-eared calves, and a bronze spancel on each calf. Moreover, fifty grey red-headed wethers, three-headed, three-horned. Moreover, fifty ivory-hilted blades. Moreover, fifty bright-speckled cloaks. But each fifty on its own day.'

Thereafter Echu's foster-father questioned him, asking how he had obtained such riches, and Echu answered 'It happened thus.' 'Indeed. You must take care,' replied his foster-father, 'for it is a man of great power who has come to you. Set him difficult tasks, my son.' When Mider came to him, then, Echu imposed these famous great labours: clearing Mide of stones, laying rushes over Tethbae, laying a causeway over Móin Lámrige, foresting Bréifne. 'You ask too much of me,' said Mider. 'Indeed, I do not,' replied

Echu. 'I have a request, then,' said Mider. 'Let neither man nor woman under your rule walk outside before sunrise tomorrow.' 'You will have that,' said Echu.

No person had ever walked out on the bog, but, after that, Echu commanded his steward to go out and see how the causeway was laid down. The steward went out into the bog, and it seemed that every man in the world was assembling there from sunrise to sunset. The men made a mound of their clothes, and that is where Mider sat. The trees of the forest, with their trunks and their roots, went into the foundation of the causeway, while Mider stood and encouraged the workers on every side. You would have thought that every man in the world was there making noise. After that, clay and gravel and stones were spread over the bog. Until that night, it had been customary for the men of Ériu to yoke oxen across the forehead, but that night it was seen that the people of the Síde placed the yoke across the shoulders. Echu thereafter did the same, and that is why he was called Echu Airem, for he was the first of the men of Ériu to place a yoke on the necks of oxen.[8] And these are the words that the host spoke as they were building the causeway: 'Place it here, place it there, excellent oxen, in the hours after sundown, very onerous is the demand, no one knows whose the gain, whose the loss in building the causeway over Móin Lámrige.' If the host had not been spied upon, there would have been no better road in the entire world; but, for that reason, the causeway was not made perfect.

Thereafter, the steward returned to Echu and described the great undertaking he had seen, and he said that in the entire world there was not the like of such power. As they were speaking, they saw Mider coming towards them, severely dressed and with an angry expression on his face. Echu was afraid, but he greeted Mider, and the latter replied 'It is for that I have come. It was harsh and senseless of you to impose such great difficulties and hardships upon me. I would have performed yet another task that would have pleased you, but I was angry with you.' 'I will not return anger for anger – rather, I will set your mind at ease,' said Echu. 'I will accept that,' said Mider. 'Will we play fidchell now?' 'What will the wager be?' asked Echu. 'Whatever stake the winner names,' said Mider. That day it was Mider who won. 'You have taken my stake,' said Echu. 'I could have done so earlier if I had wished,' replied Mider. 'What will you have from me?' asked Echu. 'My arms round Étaín and a kiss from her,' said Mider. Echu fell silent at that; finally, he said 'Return a month from today, and you will have that.'

The previous year, Mider had come to woo Étaín, but he had not been successful. The name by which he had called her then was Bé Find,[9] and this is how he had spoken to her:

> Bé Find, will you come with me
> to a wondrous land where there is music?
> Hair is like the blooming primrose there;
> smooth bodies are the colour of snow.
>
> There, there is neither mine nor yours;
> bright are teeth, dark are brows.
> A delight to the eye the number of our hosts,
> the colour of foxglove every cheek.
>
> The colour of the plain-pink every neck,
> a delight to the eye blackbirds' eggs;
> though fair to the eye Mag Fáil,
> it is a desert next to Mag Már.
>
> Intoxicating the ale of Inis Fáil;
> more intoxicating by far that of Tír Már.
> A wonderful land that I describe:
> youth does not precede age.

Warm, sweet streams throughout the land,
your choice of mead and wine.
A distinguished people, without blemish,
conceived without sin or crime.

We see everyone everywhere,
and no one sees us:
the darkness of Adam's sin
prevents our being discerned.

Woman, if you come to my bright people,
you will have a crown of gold for your head;
honey, wine, fresh milk to drink
you will have with me there, Bé Find.

Étaín had replied 'If you obtain me from my husband, I will go with you, but if you do not, I will stay.' After that, Mider went to Echu to play fidchell, and at first he lost in order that he might have reason to quarrel. That is why he fulfilled Echu's great demands, and that is why he afterwards proposed an undetermined stake.

Mider thus agreed to return after a month. Echu arranged for the best warriors and warbands in Ériu to assemble at Temuir, each band encircling the next, with Temuir in the middle and the king and queen in the centre of their house and the doors locked, for they knew it was a man of great power who would come. That night, Étaín was serving the chieftains, for serving drink was a special talent of hers. As they were talking, they saw Mider coming towards them in the centre of the house; he had always been beautiful, but that night he was more beautiful still. The hosts who saw him were astonished, and they fell silent, but Echu bade him welcome. 'It is that I have come for,' Mider said, 'that and what was promised me, for it is due. What was promised you was given.' 'I have not thought about it,' said Echu. 'Étaín herself promised me she would leave you,' said Mider, and at that, Étaín blushed. 'Do not blush, Étaín,' said Mider, 'for you have done no wrong. I have spent a year wooing you with the most beautiful gifts and treasures in Ériu, and I have not taken you without Echu's permission. If I have won you, I have done no evil.' 'I have said,' Étaín replied, 'that I will not go with you unless Echu sells me. For my part, you may take me if Echu sells me.' 'Indeed, I will not sell you,' said Echu, 'but he may put his arms round you here in the centre of the house.' 'That I will do,' said Mider. He shifted his weapons to his left hand and put his right hand round Étaín, and he bore her up through the skylight of the house. Ashamed, the hosts rose up round the king, and they saw two swans flying round Temuir and making for Síd ar Femuin.

Echu assembled the best men of Ériu, then, and went to Síd ar Femuin, that is, Síd Ban Find; and the men of Ériu advised him to unearth every síd in the land until the woman were found. They dug into Síd Ban Find until some-one came out and told them that the woman was not there. 'The king of the Síde of Ériu is the man who came to you. He is in his royal fort with the woman; go there.' Echu and his people went north and began to dig up Mider's síd; they were at it for a year and three months, and whatever they dug up one day would be filled back in the next. Two white ravens came forth from the síd, followed by two hounds, Scleth and Samair. After that, the men returned south to Síd Ban Find and again began to dig it up. Someone came out and said 'What do you have against us, Echu? We did not take your wife. No wrong has been done you. You dare not say anything harmful to a king.' 'I will not leave you,' said Echu, 'until you tell me how I may retrieve my wife.' 'Take with you blind dogs and cats, and leave them. That is what you must do each day.'

They returned north and did that. As they were tearing down Síd Breg Léith, they saw Mider coming towards them, and he said 'What do you have against me? You have not played fair with me, and you have imposed great hardships upon me. You sold your wife to me – do not injure me, then.' 'She will not remain with you,' said Echu. 'She will not, then,' replied Mider. 'Go home – by the truth of the one and the other, your wife will return to you by the third hour tomorrow. If that satisfies you, injure me no further.' 'I accept that,' said Echu. Mider secured his promise and departed.

At the third hour of the following day, they saw fifty women, all of the same appearance as Étaín and all dressed alike. At that, the hosts fell silent. A grey hag came before them and said to Echu 'It is time for us to return home. Choose your wife now, or tell one of these women to remain with you.' 'How will you resolve your doubt?' Echu asked his men. 'We have no idea how,' they answered. 'But I have,' said Echu. 'My wife is the best at serving in Ériu, and that is how I will know her.' Twenty-five of the women were sent to one side of the house, then, and twenty-five to the other side, and a vessel full of liquid was placed between them. The women came from one side and from the other, and still Echu could not find Étaín. It came down to the last two women: the first began to pour, and Echu said 'This is Étaín, but she is not herself.' He and his men held a council, and they decided 'This is Étaín though it is not her serving.' The other women left, then. The men of Ériu were greatly pleased with what Echu had done, and with the mighty accomplishments of the oxen and the rescue of the woman from the people of the Síde.

One fine day, Echu rose, and he was talking to his wife in the centre of the house when they saw Mider coming towards them. 'Well, Echu,' Mider said. 'Well,' said Echu. 'It is not fair play I have had from you,' said Mider, 'considering the hardships you imposed upon me and the troops you brought against me and all that you demanded of me. There is nothing you have not exacted from me.' 'I did not sell you my wife,' said Echu. 'Will you clear your conscience against me?' asked Mider. 'Not unless you offer a pledge of your own,' replied Echu. 'Are you content, then?' asked Mider. 'I am,' Echu replied. 'So am I,' said Mider. 'Your wife was pregnant when I took her from you, and she bore a daughter, and it is that daughter who is with you now. Your wife is with me, and you have let her go a second time.' With these words, Mider departed.

Echu did not dare unearth Mider's síd again, for he had pledged himself content. He was distressed that his wife had escaped and that he had slept with his own daughter; his daughter, moreover, became pregnant and bore a daughter. 'O gods,' he said, 'never will I look upon the daughter of my daughter.' Two members of his household took the girl, then, to throw her into a pit with wild beasts. They stopped at the house of Findlám, a herdsman of Temuir; this house was at Slíab Fúait, in the middle of a wilderness. There was no one in the house; the men ate there, and they threw the girl to the bitch and its pups that were in the house's kennel, and they left. When the herdsman and his wife returned and saw the fair-haired child in the kennel, they were astonished. They took her from the kennel and reared her, though they knew not whence she had come, and she prospered, for she was the daughter of a king and a queen. She was the best of women at embroidery: her eyes saw nothing that her hands could not embroider. She was reared by Findlám and his wife until, one day, Eterscélae's people saw her and told their king. Eterscélae took her away by force and made her his wife, and thus she became the mother of Conare son of Eterscélae.

The Destruction of Da Derga's Hostel

Introduction

'The Destruction of Da Derga's Hostel' is part impacted myth, part heroic saga and part literary tour de force. The name of the hosteller in the title is uncertain: some texts give Úa Dergae (the nephew of the red goddess) instead of Da Derga (the red god). In either case, the red deity is chthonic; and the mythic subtext deals with the slaying of a king, in a house of death, at Samuin. Although there is no mention of an iron house, the raiders' attempts to burn the hostel suggests that it is related to the iron houses in 'The Intoxication of the Ulaid' and 'The Destruction of Dind Rig'. Curiously, although Conare is slain – and that is the point of the tale – the hostel is never actually destroyed.

The opening episode, which describes the wooing of Étaín by Echu Feidlech, expands upon the story in the second section of 'The Wooing of Étaín'. At the point where Echu dies, however, something appears to be missing, even though there is no evidence of a lacuna. What follows in the manuscripts is very confused, even as to syntax, but it appears to be a garbled version of the incest episode at the end of 'The Wooing of Étaín', and we can probably assume that, originally, the child is abandoned because it is the offspring of the king's inadvertent union with his own daughter. The conception of Conare Már, like that of the Ulaid hero Cú Chulaind, is duple, the storyteller in both cases attempting to reconcile traditions of divine paternity with those of ordinary mortal fatherhood. Once Conare has been installed as king, the tale begins to edge into a kind of history – perhaps it recalls a significant battle or raid in Irish tribal warfare.

Throughout 'The Destruction of Da Derga's Hostel', Conare appears doomed: doomed to break his gessa (taboos), doomed to die for being the offspring of incest. Yet he is not entirely guiltless: the story suggests that he has shown poor judgement in excusing his foster-brothers from hanging and in interfering in the quarrel between his two clients. The structure of the tale is idiosyncratic; some may find the catalogue section tedious and the climax disappointingly perfunctory. Irish stories, in manuscript, do tend to become 'unbalanced': descriptive passages flower into luxuriant growths out of all proportion to their narrative importance (perhaps owing to the storyteller's showing off), while conclusions seem casually, even indifferently, thrown away (perhaps owing to the storyteller's or scribe's growing tired). But it is also true that descriptive catalogues of this sort were important to the Celts – both as literary set-pieces and as a matter of record – and that, in this case at least, the lack of attention given to the dénouement underlines its inevitability.

The Destruction of Da Derga's Hostel

There was once a famous, noble king of Ériu, and Echu Feidlech was his name. One day, as he was crossing the fairground of Brí Léith, he saw a woman at the edge of the well. She had a bright silver comb with gold ornamentation on it, and she was washing from a silver vessel with four gold birds on it and bright, tiny gems of crimson carbuncle on its rims. There was a crimson cloak of beautiful, curly fleece round her, fastened with a silver brooch coiled with lovely gold; her long-hooded tunic was of stiff, smooth, green silk embroidered with red gold, and there were wondrous animal brooches of gold and silver at her breast and on her shoulders. When the sun shone upon her, the gold would glisten very red against the green silk. Two tresses of yellow gold she had, and each tress was a weaving of four twists with a globe at the end. Men would say that hair was like the blooming iris in summer or like red gold after it had been burnished.

At the well, the woman loosened her hair in order to wash it, and her hands appeared through the opening of the neck of her dress. As white as the snow of a single night her wrists; as tender and even and red as foxglove her clear, lovely cheeks. As black as a beetle's back her brows; a shower of matched pearls her teeth. Hyacinth blue her eyes; Parthian red her lips. Straight, smooth, soft and white her shoulders; pure white and tapering her fingers; long her arms. As white as sea foam her side, slender, long, smooth, yielding, soft as wool. Warm and smooth, sleek and white her thighs; round and small, firm and white her knees. Short and white and straight her shins; fine and straight and lovely her heels. If a rule were put against her feet, scarcely a fault would be found save for a plenitude of flesh or skin. The blushing light of the moon in her noble face; an uplifting of pride in her smooth brows; a gleam of courting each of her two royal eyes. Dimples of pleasure each of her cheeks, where spots red as the blood of a calf alternated with spots the whiteness of shining snow. A gentle, womanly dignity in her voice; a steady, stately step, the walk of a queen. She was the fairest and most perfect and most beautiful of all the women in the world; men thought she was of the Síde, and they said of her: 'Lovely anyone until Étaín, Beautiful anyone until Étaín.'

A strong desire at once seized the king, and he sent a messenger on ahead to detain her. The king asked news of her, and when he had identified himself, he said 'Will there be a time for me to sleep with you?' 'It is that we have come for, under your protection,' she answered. 'Whence did you come and where do you go?' Echu asked. 'Not difficult that,' she replied. 'I am Étaín, daughter of Étar king of Echrade from the Síde. I have been here twenty years since I was born in the síd; men of the Síde, both kings and nobles, have sought me, but none obtained me, and that is because I have loved you with the love of a child since I was able to speak, both for your splendour and for the noble tales about you. I have never seen you, but I knew you by your description. It is you I wish to have.' 'Indeed, it is not a false friend whom you have sought from afar,' said Echu. 'You will be welcome, and you will have every one of your women, and I will be yours alone for as long as you desire.' 'My proper bridal gift first,' said Étaín, 'and then my desire.' 'You will have that,' said Echu, and her bridal price was given to her, seven cumals.

Then the king, Echu Feidlech, died.

*

After a time Cormac, who was king of Ulaid and a man of three gifts, abandoned Echu's daughter because she was barren save for the daughter she had borne after her mother had made a porridge for her. She had said to her mother 'A wrong you have done me, for it is a daughter I will bear.' 'No matter that,' her mother had replied, 'for a king will seek the girl.'

Cormac then took back the woman – Étaín – and it was his wish to kill the daughter of the woman he had abandoned. He did not allow her mother to rear her but ordered two servants to take her to a pit. As they were throwing her into the pit, she laughed and smiled at them, and a weakness overcame them. They took her, then, to the cattle shed of the herdsman of Eterscélae son of Íar king of Temuir; there they fostered her until she became a good embroiderer, and there was not in Ériu a king's daughter fairer than she. They wove her a house that had no door, only a window and a skylight. Eterscélae's people noticed this house, and it seemed to them that the herdsmen were taking food inside. One man looked through the skylight, then, and he saw a very fair, very beautiful woman inside. This news was related to the king, and people were sent immediately to destroy the house and take the woman without permission, for the king was barren, and it had been prophesied that a woman of unknown race would bear him a son.

That night, when the woman was in the house, she saw a bird coming to her through the skylight; it left its feather hood in the middle of the house and took her and said 'The king's people are coming to destroy this house and take you to him by force. But you will be with child by me and will bear a son, and his name will be Conare' (her name was Mess Búachalla), 'and he is not to kill birds.'

After that, she was taken to the king. Her fosterers went with her, and she was betrothed to the king; he gave seven cumals to her and seven to her fosterers. The fosterers were ennobled so that they became of the ruling class; thus, there are two men called Fedilmid Rechtade. The woman bore the king a son – Conare son of Mess Búachalla – and she requested of the king that the boy have three fosterages: the men who had fostered her and the two men called

Mane Milscothach and she herself. And she said to the men of Ériu 'Those of you who wish anything from the boy should contribute to the three households.'

Thus Conare was reared. The men of Ériu knew him from the day he was born, and three other boys were reared with him: Fer Lé and Fer Gar and Fer Rogain, all sons of the fían-champion Dond Désa, a man of supporters for the support of the boy.[1] Conare possessed three gifts – the gift of hearing and the gift of seeing and the gift of judgement – and he taught a gift to each of his foster-brothers. Whenever a meal was prepared for him, the four would go to it together; and even if three meals were prepared for him, every one of them would go to his meal. And all four had the same garments and weapons and colour of horses.

After that, the king, Eterscélae, died. The men of Ériu then assembled at the bull feast: a bull was killed, and one man ate his fill and drank its broth and slept, and an incantation of truth was chanted over him. Whoever this man saw in his sleep became king; if the man lied about what he saw in his sleep, he would die. Now four charioteers were playing by the Life, Conare and his three foster-brothers; and Conare's fosterers came to take him to the bull feast. The bull-feaster had in his sleep seen a naked man coming along the road to Temuir at daybreak and bearing a stone in his sling. 'I will follow you shortly,' Conare said.

Later, Conare left his foster-brothers playing and turned his chariot and charioteer towards Áth Clíath; there he saw huge, white-speckled birds, unusual as to size and colour. He turned and followed them until his horses grew tired, and the birds always preceded him by no more than the length of a spear cast. Then he took his sling and stepped from his chariot and followed the birds until he reached the ocean. The birds went on the waves, but he overtook them. The birds left their feather hoods, then, and turned on him with spears and swords; one bird protected him, however, saying 'I am Nemglan, king of your father's bird troop. You are forbidden to cast at birds, for, by reason of birth, every bird here is natural to you.' 'Until now, I did not know this,' said Conare. 'Go to Temuir tonight, for that would be more fitting,' Nemglan said. 'There is a bull feast there, and it will make you king. The man who naked comes along the road to Temuir at daybreak with a stone in his sling, it is he who will be king.'

Conare went forth, then, and on each of the four roads that led to Temuir there were three kings waiting with garments, for it had been prophesied that the king would come naked. He was seen on the road where his fosterers were waiting, and they put the clothing of a king round him and placed him in a chariot, and he took their hostages. The people of Temuir said 'It seems to us that our bull feast and our incantation of truth have been spoilt, for it is a young, beardless lad who has been brought to us.' But Conare replied 'No matter that. A young, generous king is no blemish, and I am not corrupt. It was the right of my father and grandfather to take hostages at Temuir.' 'Wonder of wonders!' said the hosts. They conferred the kingship of Ériu upon him, and he said 'I will inquire of wise men that I myself may be wise.'

All this Conare said just as the man on the waves had taught him to. This man had said to him 'Your bird-reign will be distinguished, but there will be gessa against it, and they are these:[2] You are not to go righthandwise round Temuir and lefthandwise round Brega. You are not to hunt the wild beasts of Cernae. You are not to venture out of Temuir every ninth night. You are not to pass the night in a house where firelight may be seen from within or from without after sunset. Three Deirgs are not to precede you into the house of Deirg. No plunder is to be taken in your reign. A company of one man or one woman is not to enter your house after sunset. You are not to interfere in a quarrel between two of your servants.'

There was great bounty, then, in Conare's reign: seven ships being brought to Indber Colptha in June of every year, acorns up to the knee every autumn, a surfeit over the Búas and the Bóand each June, and an abundance of peace, so that no one slew his neighbour anywhere in Ériu – rather, that neighbour's voice seemed as sweet as the strings of harps. From the middle of spring to the middle of autumn, no gust of wind stirred any cow's tail; there was no thunder, no stormy weather in Conare's reign.

Conare's foster-brothers, however, grumbled about losing the prerogatives of their father and their grandfather – theft and robbery and plunder and murder. Every year, they stole from the same farmer a pig and a calf and a cow, in order to see what punishment the king would mete out and what damage the theft would cause to his reign. Every year, the farmer went to the king to complain, and every year the king replied 'The three sons of Dond Désa are the thieves – go and speak with them.' But every time the farmer went to speak with the three sons, they attempted to kill him; and he did not return to the king for fear of angering him.

Thereafter wilfulness and greed overcame the three sons; they gathered sons of the lords of Ériu about them and went plundering. Three fifties of them were practising in Crích Connacht when Mane Milscothach's swineherd saw them, and he had never seen that before. He took to flight; they overheard him and followed. The swineherd cried out, then, and the people of each Mane came and seized the three fifties with their supernumeraries; they took these men to Temuir and appealed to the king, and he said 'Let each man slay his son, but let my foster-brothers be spared.' 'Indeed, indeed,' said everyone, 'that will be done.' 'Indeed not,' replied Conare. 'No lengthening of my life the judgement I have given. The men are not to be hanged – rather, let elders go with them that they may plunder Albu.'

This was done. The plunderers went to sea, and there they met the son of the king of the Bretain, Ingcél Cáech, the grandson of Conmac[3]; and they made an alliance with Ingcél that they might go and plunder with him. This is the destruction that Ingcél wrought: his father and his mother and his seven brothers were invited to the house of the king of his people, and all were slain by Ingcél in a single night. Then they crossed the sea to Ériu to seek a similar destruction, for that was owed to Ingcél.

In Ériu, there was complete peace during Conare's reign, save that battle was proposed in Túadmumu between two men named Coirpre, both foster-brothers of Conare, and the matter was not put right until Conare arrived. There was a geiss against his going to settle a quarrel before the quarrellers came to him, but he went all the same and made peace between them. He stayed five nights with each man, and there was also a geiss against that.

The quarrel having been settled, Conare made to return to Temuir. They passed Uisnech Mide, and after that, they saw forays being made from north and south and east and west, troops and hosts in turn, and naked men, and the land of the Uí Néill was a cloud of fire about them. 'What is this?' asked Conare. 'Not difficult that,' replied his people. 'When the land burns, it is easy to see that the law has been broken.' 'Where will we go?' asked Conare. 'Northeast,' said his people. So they went righthandwise round Temuir and lefthandwise round Brega, and Conare hunted the wild beasts of Cernae, but he did not perceive this until the hunt had ended. He thus became the king whom the spectres exiled.

After that, a great fear overcame Conare, for there were no roads they could take save Slige Midlúachra and Slige Chúaland. They took Slige Chúaland and went south along the coast of Ériu, and Conare asked 'Where will we spend the night?' 'If I may say it, Conare,' answered Macc Cécht son of Snade Teched, the champion of Conare son of Eterscélae, 'more often did the men of Ériu contest your company each night than were you at a loss for a guest house.' 'Judgement comes to all,' replied Conare. 'But I have a friend in this country, if we knew the way to his house.' 'What is his name?' asked Macc Cécht. 'Da Derga of the Lagin,' answered Conare. 'He came to me, indeed, seeking gifts, and he did not leave empty-handed. I gave him one hundred cows from my herd, one hundred close-fitting mantles, one hundred grey pigs, one hundred flashing battle weapons, ten gilded brooches, ten great vats for drinking, ten brown horses, ten servants, ten steeds, thrice nine hounds all equally white on silver chains, one hundred horses fleeter than herds of wild deer. Indeed, nothing was counted against him, and, were he to come again, he would receive still more. It would be odd if he were surly with me tonight.'

'Indeed, I know that house,' said Macc Cécht, 'and the road we are on goes to it, for the road goes through the house. There are seven entrances to the house, and seven apartments between each two entrances; there is only one door, however, and that is placed at the entrance against which the wind is blowing. With the great multitude that you have here, you can go on until you reach the centre of the house. If it is there that you go, I will go ahead and light a fire for you.'

After that, as Conare was making along Slige Chúaland, he perceived three horsemen up ahead making for the house. Red tunics and red mantles they wore, and red shields and spears were in their hands; they rode red horses, and their heads were red. They were entirely red, teeth and hair, horses and men. 'Who rides before us?' Conare asked. 'There is a geiss against three Deirgs preceding me into the house of Deirg.' Who will go after them and have them come back to me?' 'I will go,' said Lé Fer Flaith, Conare's son.

He went after them, then, lashing his horse, but they remained a spear-cast ahead; they did not gain on him, and he did not gain on them. He told them that they should not precede the king. He could not overtake them, but one of the three recited back to him this poem: 'Behold, lad, great tidings! Tidings from the hostel. A road for ships. A gleam of javelined men, fían-valorous in their wounding exploits. A great catastrophe. A fair woman upon whom the red embroidery of slaughter has settled. Behold!'

After that, they left him, and he could not detain them. He waited for the host and told his father what had been said. Conare was not pleased, and he said 'Go after them; offer them three oxen and three salted pigs, and tell them that as long as they are in my household there will be no one among them from the hearth to the wall.' The lad went back after them and offered them that; he did not overtake them, but one of the three recited back to him this poem: 'Behold, lad, great tidings! The great ardour of a generous king warms you, heats you. Through ancient enchantments a company of nine yields. Behold!'

After that, the lad turned back and repeated the poem to Conare. 'Go after them,' said the king, 'and offer them six oxen and six salted pigs and the leftovers the following day, and gifts as well; and tell them that as long as they are in my household there will be no one among them from the house to the wall.' The lad went after them, then, but he did not overtake them, and one of the three spoke this to him: 'Behold, lad, great tidings! Weary the horses we ride. We ride the horses of Dond Tétscorach of the Síde.⁵ Although we are alive, we are dead. Great omens! Cutting off of lives, satisfaction of crows, sustenance of ravens, din of slaughter, whetting of blades, shields with broken bosses after sunset. Behold!'

The men left him, then. 'I see that you have not detained them,' Conare said. 'Indeed, it is not I who has betrayed you,' replied Lé Fer Flaith, and he recited the last poem. They were no happier with that answer, and afterwards they felt great forebodings of terror because of it. 'All my gessa have overtaken me tonight,' said Conare, 'and that because of the banishment of my foster-brothers.' Meanwhile, the three Deirgs preceded him into the house and took their seats there, having tied their horses at the entrance.

Conare was still making for Áth Clíath when there overtook him a man with short, black hair and one eye and one hand and one foot. His hair was rough and bristling – if a sackful of wild apples were emptied over it, each apple would catch on his hair, and none would fall to the ground. If his snout were thrown against a branch, it would stick there. As long and thick as an outer yoke each of his shins; the size of a cheese on a withe each of his buttocks. In his hand a forked iron pole; a singed pig with short, black bristles on his back, and it squealed constantly. Behind him came a huge, black, gloomy, big-mouthed, ill-favoured woman; if her snout were thrown against a branch, the branch would support it, while her lower lip extended to her knee.

This man sprang towards Conare and greeted him, saying 'Welcome, popa Conare!⁶ It has long been known that you would come here.' 'Who is welcoming me?' Conare asked. 'Fer Calliu, and I bring a pig so that you will not have to fast tonight,' said the man. 'You are the best king who has ever come into the world.' 'What is the woman's name?' Conare asked. 'Cichuil,' the man replied. 'I will come any other night you please,' said Conare, 'only leave us tonight.' 'By no means,' replied the man, 'for I will come to you where you are tonight, fair popa Conare.'

He turned towards the house, then, with the singed, black-bristled pig squealing on his back and the huge, big-mouthed woman following. That violated another of Conare's gessa. There was a geiss, moreover, against plundering in Ériu during his reign; but plunder was being taken by the sons of Dond Désa, and there were five hundred in their band, not counting supernumeraries. One good warrior in the north was named Fén Tar Crínach, for he stepped over opponents the way a wagon passes over withered sticks. Yet there was a fían-band that was haughtier still: the seven sons of Ailill and Medb, each named Mane and each with a nickname – Mane Athramail and Mane Máthramail and Mane Mingor and Mane Márgor and Mane Andoe and Mane Milscothach and Mane Gaib Uile and Mane Mó Epirt. And all were plunderers. Mane Máthramail and Mane Andoe had fourteen score men, Mane Athramail had four hundred and fifty, Mane Milscothach had five hundred, Mane Gaib Uile had six hundred, Mane Mó Epirt had seven hundred and the others had five hundred each. There was also a valorous trio of the Uí Bríuin from Cúalu in Lagin, and all three were named Rúadchoin; they were plunderers, and they had twelve score men, and a frenzied troop besides. One third of the men of Ériu were marauders, then, in Conare's reign; he had sufficient strength and power to drive them out of Ériu and make them plunder elsewhere, but after that, they returned to the country.

When the plunderers of Ériu reached the shoulder of the sea, they met Ingcél Cáech and Éccell, two grandsons of Conmac of Bretain, on the back of the sea. A terrifying, ungentle man was Ingcél: he had a single eye in his head that was as broad as an oxhide and as black as a beetle, and there were three pupils in it. There were thirteen hundred men in his party, but the plunderers from Ériu were more numerous than that. The two bands were about to engage each other on the sea, but Ingcél said 'Do not do this – do not blot your honour. You have more men than I.' 'You will have equal combat,' said the plunderers of Ériu. 'I have a better thought,' said Ingcél. 'Let us make peace, for you have been cast out of Ériu, and we have been cast out of Albu and Bretain. Let us make a bargain: you will come with me to plunder in my country, and I will go with you to plunder in your country.'

Ingcél's advice was taken, and each side gave guarantees. The men of Ériu pledged Gér, Gabur and Fer Rogain as a guarantee that Ingcél would have the destruction of his choice in Ériu; the sons of Dond Désa would then have the destruction of their choice in Albu. Lots were cast to see where they would go first, and the lot fell to go with Ingcél. They returned to Albu, then, and wrought their destruction there; after that, they came back to Ériu.

At that time, Conare was proceeding along Slige Chúaland to the hostel. The raiders arrived along the coast of Brega, opposite Bend Étair, and they said 'Strike the sails, and form one fleet, lest you be seen from the land, and let one swift-footed man go ashore to see if we can save face with Ingcél by providing him with a destruction for the destruction he has given us.' 'Who will go to reconnoitre in the land?' asked Ingcél. 'Let it be someone with the three gifts: hearing and seeing and judgement.' 'I have the gift of hearing,' said Mane Milscothach. 'And I have the gifts of seeing and of judgement,' said Mane Andoe. 'Well that you should go, then,' said the raiders.

So nine men went to Bend Étair for what they might hear

73

and see. 'Hush!' said Mane Milscothach. 'What is that?' said Mane Andoe. 'I hear the noise of a king's horses,' answered Mane Milscothach. 'I see it through my gift of sight,' said his companion. 'What is it that you see?' asked Mane Milscothach. 'I see splendid horses, tall, beautiful, warlike, noble, slender-girthed, weary, nimble, keen, eager, ardent, and they on a course that shakes great areas of land. They cross many heights and wondrous waters and estuaries,' said Mane Andoe. 'What waters and heights and estuaries?' Mane Milscothach asked. 'Not difficult that: Indein, Cult, Culten, Mafat, Amatt, Iarmafat, Findi, Gosce and Guistine. Glittering spears above chariots, ivory-hilted swords against thighs, silver shields upon elbows, half red and half white. Garments of every colour upon them. I see also a special, pre-eminent herd: three fifties of dapple grey horses, small-headed, red-necked, sharp-eared, broad-hooved, large-nostrilled, red-chested, sweated, obedient, easily caught, swift on a raid, keen, eager and ardent, each with its own bridle of coloured enamel. I swear by what my people swear by,' said the far-sighted man, 'those are the steeds of a prosperous lord. In my judgement, it is Conare son of Eterscélae and the men of Ériu who are passing along the road.'

After that, Mane Milscothach and Mane Andoe returned to the raiders and told them what they had heard and seen. There was a multitude of the host on every side: three fifties of boats, and five thousand men in them, and ten hundred in every thousand. The sails were hoisted, and the boats moved towards the shore at Trácht Fuirbthen. As they were about to land, Macc Cécht began to light a fire in Da Derga's hostel; and the noise of the spark drove the three fifties of boats back out until they were once again on the shoulder of the sea. 'Hush!' said Ingcél. 'Explain that, Fer Rogain.' 'I do not know it,' said Fer Rogain, 'unless it is Luchdond, the satirist of Emuin Machae, clapping his hands when his food is taken away from him; or the screaming of Luchdond in Temuir Lúachra; or Macc Cécht setting off a spark while lighting a fire for the king of Ériu. When he lights a fire in the centre of the house, each spark can broil one hundred calves and a two-year-old pig.' 'May God not bring that man here tonight,' said the sons of Dond Désa, 'for it would be grievous.' 'It would be no sadder than the destruction I provided for you,' said Ingcél. 'I would be most satisfied if he came here.'

They put in to shore, then, and the noise that the three fifties of boats made shook Da Derga's hostel so much that the weapons on the racks all fell to the floor with a clatter. 'Explain that, Conare – what is that noise?' everyone asked. 'I do not know it,' said Conare, 'unless the earth has turned over; or the Leviathan that encircles the world has overturned it with his tail; or the ship of the sons of Dond Désa has landed. Alas that they are not here tonight, for they were dear foster-brothers and a beloved fían-band, and then we would not have to fear them.' After that, Conare arrived at the hostel's green. When Macc Cécht heard the din outside, he thought that warriors were attacking his people. He sprang for his weapons to help them, and to those outside his springing was like the thunder feat of three hundred.

The boat of the sons of Dond Désa held a champion, one powerful with arms, baleful at the prow of the boat, a lion implacable and terrifying, Ingcél Cáech grandson of Conmac. Wide as an oxhide the one eye in his head; seven pupils in it, and all black as a beetle. The size of a heifer's cauldron each of his knees; the size of a reaping basket each of his fists. The size of a cheese on a withe each of his buttocks; as long as an outer yoke each of his shins. And the five thousand landed at Trácht Fuirbthen, with ten hundred in every thousand.

Conare went into the hostel, then, and everyone took his seat, geiss or no geiss; the three Deirgs sat down, as did Fer Calliu, with his pig. Da Derga came to them after that, with three fifties of warriors: each man had long hair to the nape of his neck and a short green mantle reaching to his buttocks; each man wore short, speckled trousers and carried a great thorn club with a band of iron round it. 'Welcome, popa Conare,' said Da Derga. 'If the greater part of the men of Ériu were to accompany you, I would still feed them.'

As they were there in the hostel, a woman appeared at the entrance, after sunset, and sought to be let in. As long as a weaver's beam, and as black, her two shins. She wore a very fleecy, striped mantle. Her beard reached her knees, and her mouth was on one side of her head. She put one shoulder against the doorpost and cast a baleful eye upon the king and the youths about him, and Conare said to her from inside the house 'Well then, woman, what do you see for us, if you are a seer?' 'Indeed, I see that neither hide nor hair of you will escape from this house, save what the birds carry off in their claws,' the woman replied. 'It is not ill fortune that we prophesied, woman,' said Conare. 'Neither do you usually prophesy for us. What is your name?' 'Cailb,' she replied. 'A name with nothing to spare, that,' said Conare. 'Indeed, I have many other names,' she said. 'What are they?' asked Conare. 'Not difficult that,' she replied. 'Samuin, Sinand, Sesclend, Sodb, Saiglend, Samlocht, Caill, Coll, Díchoem, Díchuil, Díchim, Díchuimne, Díchuinne, Dárne, Dárine, Der Úane, Egem, Agam, Ethamne, Gnim, Cluche, Cethardam, Nith, Nemuin, Nóenden, Badb, Blosc, Bloar, Úaet, Mede, Mod.' And she recited these in one breath, and standing on one foot, at the entrance to the house.

'What do you want, then?' Conare asked. 'Whatever

pleases you,' she answered. 'There is a geiss against my admitting a single woman after sunset,' said Conare. 'Geiss or not,' replied the woman, 'I will not go until I have had hospitality from this house tonight.' 'Tell her,' said Conare, 'that she will be sent an ox and a salted pig and the leftovers if only she will go elsewhere tonight.' 'Indeed, if the king cannot spare a meal and a bed in his house for one woman, if the hospitality of the sovereign in this hostel is no more, then something will be gotten from someone else, someone of honour,' answered the woman. 'Savage her reply,' said Conare. 'Let her in, then, despite the geiss against it.' After this conversation with the woman, and her prophecy of doom, a great fear came over the host, but no one knew why.

The raiders, meanwhile, reached land and advanced as far as Lecca Cind Slébe. The hostel was always open, and that is why it was called a hostel, for it was like the mouth of a man when he yawns. Each night, Conare kindled a huge fire, a boar in the forest. Seven outlets it had, and when a log was taken from its side, the extent of the flames at each outlet was that of a burning oratory. Seventeen of Conare's chariots stood at each entrance to the house, and the great light inside was visible to the watchers outside through the wheels of those chariots.

'Explain that, Fer Rogain,' said Ingcél. 'What is that great light yonder?' 'I do not know it,' said Fer Rogain, 'unless it is the fire of a king.' 'May God not bring that man here tonight. It is grievous,' said the sons of Dond Désa. 'What are the properties of his reign in Ériu?' Ingcél asked. 'His reign is good,' replied Fer Rogain. 'Since he became king, no cloud has obscured the sun from the middle of spring to the middle of autumn. Not a drop of dew falls from the grass until noon; no gust of wind stirs a cow's tail until evening. No wolf takes more than one bull calf from every enclosure during the year, and seven wolves remain by the wall of his house as a guarantee of this agreement; there is a further guarantee, moreover, and that is Macc Locc, who pleads their case in Conare's house. Each man's voice seems to his neighbour as melodious as the strings of harps, and that because of the excellence of law and peace and goodwill throughout Ériu. It is in Conare's reign that we have the three crowns of Ériu: the crown of corn, the crown of flowers and the crown of acorns. May God not bring that man here tonight. It is grievous. It is a pig that falls before acorns. It is a child who is aged. It is grievous his shortness of life.'

'I would be most satisfied if he came here,' said Ingcél. 'It would be one destruction for another. This destruction would be no more difficult for me than was the destruction of my mother and my father and my seven brothers and the king of the country that I did for you as my part of the bargain.' 'True, true,' said the evil-doers who had accompanied the raiders. The raiders started out from Trácht Fuirbthen, then, and each man took with him a stone for the making of the cairn, for this is the distinction that the fíana instituted between a destruction and a rout: they erected a pillar stone for a rout but built a cairn for a destruction. Since this was to be a destruction, the raiders made a cairn, and they built it far from the house lest they be seen or heard.

After that, the raiders held a council, in the place where they had made the cairn. 'Well then,' said Ingcél to those who knew the country, 'what is nearest to us?' 'Not difficult that: the hostel of Da Derga, the royal hospitaller of Ériu,' these men answered. 'A good chance, then, that chieftains will be seeking their fellows in that hostel tonight,' said Ingcél. It was decided, then, that one of the plunderers should go and look to see how things were in the house.

'Who should go to look?' it was asked. 'Who but I?' said Ingcél. 'For it is to me that the debt is owed.'

Ingcél then went to spy upon the hostel with one of the three pupils in his eye, and he adjusted his eye so as to cast a baleful look upon the king and the youths about him, and he looked through the wheels of the chariots. He was perceived from the house, however, and so he hurried away until he rejoined the raiders. They had formed circles, one about the other, in order to hear the news, and in the centre of the circles were the six chieftains: Fer Gel, Fer Gar, Fer Rogel, Fer Rogain, Lomnae Drúth and Ingcél Cáech.

'What is there, Ingcél?' asked Fer Rogain. 'Whatever it is,' answered Ingcél, 'the customs are regal, the tumult is that of a host and the noise is that of princes. Whether or not there is a king there, I will take the house in payment of the debt, and I will plunder there.' 'We leave it to you, Ingcél,' said Conare's foster-brothers, 'save that we should not destroy the house until we know who is inside.' 'Did you look the house over well, Ingcél?' Fer Rogain asked. 'My eye made a quick circuit, and I will accept it in payment just as it is,' said Ingcél. 'Although you take the house, it is yours by right,' said Fer Rogain. 'Our foster-father is inside, the high king of Ériu, Conare son of Eterscélae. Whom did you see in the champion's seat, the one facing the king?' 'I saw a huge, bright-faced man,' said Ingcél, 'with clear, shining eyes and straight teeth and a face narrow below and broad above. Fair, flaxen, golden hair he had, and a proper hood over it, and a silver brooch in his mantle. In his hands a gold-hilted sword and a shield with five concentric circles of gold and a five-pointed spear. A fair, ruddy complexion he had, with no beard, and a modest bearing. On his left and on his right and in front of him I saw three men, and you would think that all nine had the same father and the same mother. They were of the same age, and all were equal in appearance and handsomeness. All had long hair and green mantles with gold pins; all bore in their hands round shields of bronze and ridged spears and ivory-hilted swords. All performed the same trick: each man would take the point of his sword between his two fingers and wind it about his fingers, and the sword would straighten out by itself afterwards. Explain that, Fer Rogain.'

'Not difficult that,' said Fer Rogain. 'Cormac Cond Longes son of Conchubur he, the best warrior to hold a shield in Ériu. Of modest bearing he. Little does he fear tonight. A warrior in weaponry, a hospitaller in husbandry. Of the men about him, three are named Dúngus, three Dáelgus and three Dángus, and they are the nine companions of Cormac Cond Longes. Never have they slain men at a disadvantage, and never have they spared men at an advantage. Good the warrior in their midst, that is, Cormac. I swear by what my people swear by, nine tens will fall by Cormac at the first onslaught, and nine tens by his companions; and there will also fall a man for each weapon and a man for each man. Cormac will match the performance of any man at the entrance to the hostel; he will boast of victories over kings and royal heirs and plundering chieftains, and though his companions be wounded, he himself will escape.'

'Woe to him who carries out this destruction,' said Lomnae Drúth, 'if only because of that one man, Cormac Cond Longes. I swear by what my people swear by, if I ruled the council, I would not attempt the destruction, if only because of that one man and because of his gentleness and excellence.' 'You do not rule it,' said Ingcél. 'Clouds of blood will come to you. Gér's word will seize the two cheeks of Gabur; it will be brought against him by the oath of an angry Fer Rogain. Your voice has begun to break, Lomnae. They have known you to be an evil warrior. Clouds of blood ... An easier death for a house full of hosts death by iron weapons . . . Neither old man nor storyteller will say that I retreated from this destruction; they will say that it was I who carried it out.'

'Do not impugn our honour, Ingcél,' said Gér and Gabur and Fer Rogain. 'The destruction will be wrought, unless the earth breaks under us and swallows us.' 'Indeed, it is yours by right,' said Lomnae Drúth son of Dond Désa. 'You will suffer no loss – you will bear off the head of a king from another tribe, and you will cut off another head, and you and your two brothers, Éccell and Dartaid, will escape the destruction. It will be more difficult for me, however. Woe to me before everyone, woe to me after everyone. Afterwards, my head will be tossed about between the chariot shafts, where devilish enemies will meet; it will be thrown into the hostel thrice, and it will be thrown back out thrice. Woe to them that go, woe to them with whom they go, woe to them to whom they go. Doomed they that go, doomed they to whom they go.'

'Nothing can touch me,' said Ingcél, 'not my mother, not my father, not my seven brothers, not the king of my country, whom I slew – there is nothing I will not endure from now on.' 'Though blood flow through you, the destruction will be wrought by you tonight,' said Gér and Gabur and Fer Rogain. 'Woe to him who delivers the hostel into the hands of its enemies,' said Lomnae Drúth. 'After that, what did you see?'

'I saw an apartment with three men in it,' said Ingcél, 'three huge, brown men with brown hair equally long in front and at the back. They wore short black capes that reached to their elbows, and the capes all had long hoods. In their hands they held large, black swords and black shields and broad, dark, glittering spears; and each spear shaft was as thick as the lifting bar of a cauldron. Explain that, Fer Rogain.'

'Difficult that to explain,' said Fer Rogain. 'I know no trio in Ériu like that, unless they are the three Cruithnig who forsook their country and came into Conare's household: Dub Longes son of Trebúait and Trebúait grandson of Lonsce and Curnach grandson of Fíach. They are the three best warriors to have taken arms among the Cruithnig. Nine tens will fall by them at the first onslaught, and a man for each weapon, and a man for each man. They will match the performance of any trio in the hostel; they will boast of victories over kings and royal heirs and plundering chieftains, and, though wounded, they will escape afterwards. Woe to him who carries out this destruction, if only because of those three.' 'I swear by the god my people swear by,' said Lomnae Drúth, 'if my advice were taken, the destruction would not be attempted.' 'You do not rule me,' said Ingcél. 'Clouds of blood will come.' 'After that, what did you see?' asked Lomnae Drúth.

'I saw an apartment with nine men in it; all had fair, yellow hair and all were equally handsome, and they wore mantles of various hues,' said Ingcél. 'Overhead there were nine pipes, all four-toned and ornamented; and the light from the ornamentation was sufficient for the royal house. Explain that, Fer Rogain.'

'Not difficult that,' said Fer Rogain. 'They are the nine pipers that came to Conare from Síd Breg because of the famous tales about him; their names are Bind, Robind, Ríanbind, Nibe, Dibe, Dechrind, Umal, Cumal and Cíalgrind. They are the best pipers in the world. Nine tens will fall by them at the first onslaught, and a man for each weapon, and a man for each man. They will match the performance of anyone in the hostel; each of them will boast of victories over kings and royal heirs and plundering chieftains, and they will escape afterwards, for combat with them is combat with a shadow. They will slay and will not be slain, for they

82

are of the Síde.' 'Woe to him who carries out this destruction, if only because of those nine men,' said Lomnae Drúth. 'You do not rule me,' said Ingcél. 'Clouds of blood will come to you.' 'After that, what did you see?' asked Lomnae Drúth.

'I saw an apartment with one man in it,' said Ingcél. 'His hair was rough and bristling – if a sackful of apples were emptied over it, each apple would catch on his hair, and none would fall to the ground. He wore a very fleecy cloak. Every quarrel that arose over seat or couch was submitted to his judgement; and when he spoke, a needle falling in the house could be heard. A great, dark staff overhead, like a mill wheel with its paddles and its fastener and its spike. Explain that, Fer Rogain.'

'Not difficult that,' said Fer Rogain. 'Taidle Ulad that one, the steward of Conare's household. It is necessary to listen to his judgements, for he has power over seat and couch and food. It is his household staff that is overhead. That man will fall by you. I swear by what my people swear by, his dead will outnumber the living at the destruction; three times his number will fall, and he will fall himself.' 'Woe to him who carries out this destruction, if only because of that one man,' said Lomnae Drúth. 'You do not rule me,' said Ingcél. 'Clouds of blood will come to you.' 'After that, what did you see?' asked Lomnae Drúth.

'I saw an apartment with three men in it, three ill-favoured, close-cropped men, and the largest of them was in the centre,' said Ingcél. 'Clamorous, sweated, hard-bodied, fierce, dealing mighty blows that can slay nine hundred in battle. He had a dun-coloured wooden shield with a hard serrated edge of iron, and on its front there was room for four bands of ten weaklings each. The boss was very strong; it was as deep as a yawning cauldron that could hold four oxen placed over four pigs of medium age. Alongside him two five-benched boats, each large enough to hold three

83

parties of ten men. A glittering red spear he had, fitted to his grip and resting on a powerful shaft; it extended from the floor to the ceiling. Its iron point was dark and dripping; a full four feet between any two of its points. A full thirty feet from the dark point of his death-dealing sword to its iron hilt, and it emitted fiery sparks that lit up the house's mead circuit from floor to roof. A powerful form I saw – after looking at those three, I nearly died from fright. There is nothing stranger. Two cropped heads next to the one with hair; two lakes next to a mountain, two surfaces of blue sea; two hides next to an oak; two small boats full of thorns floating upon a wheel cover. And there seemed to be a slender stream of water upon which the sun was shining, with a trickle down from it, and a hide rolled up behind it, and the pillar of a royal house in the shape of a great lance overhead. A great load for any team of oxen that shaft. Explain that, Fer Rogain.'

'Not difficult that,' said Fer Rogain. 'Macc Cécht son of Snade Teched that one, the champion of Conare son of Eterscélae. A good warrior Macc Cécht. Asleep he was, prostrate in his apartment, when you saw him. The two cropped heads next to the one with hair that you saw, those were his two knees drawn up next to his head. The two lakes next to the mountain that you saw, those were his two eyes next to his nose. The two hides about the oak that you saw, those were his two ears about his head. The two small boats upon the wheel cover that you saw, those were his shoes upon his shield. The slender stream of water upon which the sun shone, and the trickle down from it, that was the flickering of his sword. The hide that you saw rolled up behind it, that was the scabbard for his sword. The pillar of the royal house that you saw, that was his lance; when he brandishes it, the two ends meet, and he casts it whenever he pleases. The two surfaces of blue sea that you saw, those were his eyebrows, matched exactly on his handsome, ruddy countenance. A good warrior Macc Cécht! Six hundred will fall by him at the first onslaught, and a man for each weapon, and a man for himself, and he will match the performance of any man in the hostel; he will boast of victories over kings and royal heirs and plundering chieftains, and, though wounded, he will escape afterwards. When he encounters you in the hostel, as numerous as hailstones or blades of grass or stars in the sky will be your cloven heads and cloven skulls and heaps of entrails that he crushes after he has scattered you about the ridges.'

The raiders retreated over three ridges, then, trembling and in fear of Macc Cécht; and Gér, Gabur and Fer Rogain reaffirmed their pledges. 'Woe to him who carries out this destruction, if only because of this one man,' said Lomnae Drúth. 'Your heads will leave your bodies.' 'You do not rule me,' said Ingcél. 'Clouds of blood will come to you.' 'Indeed, Ingcél, the destruction is yours by right,' said Lomnae Drúth. 'You will suffer no loss. It will be more difficult for me, however.' 'No lie that,' said Ingcél. 'After that, what did you see?' asked Lomnae Drúth.

'I saw an apartment with three callow youths in it,' said Ingcél. 'They wore silken mantles with gilded brooches; they had manes of yellow gold hair, and when they engage in combat, their manes extend to the front of the apartment. Moreover, when they raise their eyes, their hair rises until no part of it is below the lobes of their ears. As fleecy as a ram their cloaks. Five concentric circles of gold and the candle of a royal house above each youth, and there is not a man in the house who can match them for voice and words and deeds. Explain that, Fer Rogain.'

Fer Rogain wept, so that his cloak was wet about his face, and for a third of the night not a word was to be had from him. 'Little people,' he said, 'what I do is proper. Oball and

Obléne and Coirpre Músc those three youths, the three sons of the king of Ériu.' 'Woe to us if that is the case,' said the sons of Dond Désa. 'Good the trio in that apartment. They have the bearing of young girls, the hearts of friars, the courage of bears and the ferocity of lions. Anyone who is in their company and in their bed will neither sleep nor eat in comfort for nine days after escaping from them. Good are the warriors of their people. Three tens will fall by them at the first onslaught, and a man for each weapon, and a man for each of them, and they will match the performance of anyone in the hostel; they will boast of victories over kings and royal heirs and plundering chieftains, and, though wounded, they will escape afterwards, and two of you will fall by them.' 'Woe to him who carries out this destruction, if only because of those three,' said Lomnae Drúth. 'You do not rule me,' said Ingcél. 'Clouds of blood will come to you.' 'After that, what did you see?' asked Lomnae Drúth.

'I saw an apartment with three men in it,' said Ingcél, 'three strange, horrible men with three heads each. Three fearsome Fomóri, without the form of human beings. The raging sea has given them features that are not easy to recognize: each head has three full rows of teeth, from ear to ear. Noble stewards of households each, and each with one hundred exploits. Their swords hew through the host about Borg Buredach in the assembly at Da Derga's hostel. Explain that, Fer Rogain.'

'Difficult that,' said Fer Rogain. 'I know no trio in Ériu or anywhere else like that, unless they are the trio whom Macc Cécht brought single-handedly out of the land of the Fomóri. There could not be found among the Fomóri even one man to face him, so he took the trio to Conare's house as a guarantee that the Fomóri would not spoil milk or grain in Ériu beyond their lawful allowance, and that so long as Conare reigned. They are not pleasant to look at, indeed, with their three rows of teeth from one ear to the other. An ox with a salted pig would be a typical meal for each of them, and that meal, when eaten, would be visible down to their navels. Bones without joints the three have. I swear by the god my people swear by, when they destroy, the dead outnumber the living. Six hundred warriors will fall by them at the first onslaught, and each of them will kill with no more than a bite or a kick or a blow, for they are hostages placed against the wall lest they do any misdeed, and therefore they are not allowed to have weapons in the hostel. I swear by the god my people swear by, if they had weapons now, they would kill two thirds of us.' 'Woe to him who carries out this destruction, for it will not be a contest against the weak,' said Lomnae Drúth. 'You do not rule me,' said Ingcél. 'Clouds of blood will come to you.' 'After that, what did you see?' asked Lomnae Drúth.

'I saw an apartment with three men in it,' said Ingcél, 'three huge, dark men. They wore dark garments and heavy ankle bracelets, and each of their limbs was as thick as a man's waist. Their heads were broad and covered with dark, curly hair, and they wore cloaks of speckled red. Dark shields they had, with curved animal clasps of gold, and five-pointed javelins and ivory-hilted swords. This is the trick they would perform with their swords: they would throw the swords up in the air, and the scabbards after, and the swords would return to the scabbards before the scabbards could strike the ground. Then they would throw the scabbards up in the air, and the swords after, and the scabbards would envelop the swords before the swords could strike the ground. Explain that, Fer Rogain.'

'Not difficult that,' said Fer Rogain. 'Mál son of Telband and Muinremur son of Gerrgend and Birrderg son of Rúad they, three royal heirs, three valorous heroes, the three best men to stand behind weapons in Ériu. One hundred warriors will fall by them at the first onslaught, and a man for each weapon, and a man for each of them, and they will match the performance of any trio in the hostel; they will boast of victories over kings and royal heirs and plundering chieftains, and, though wounded, they will escape afterwards. On their account alone, the destruction of the hostel should not be carried out.' 'Woe to him who carries out this destruction,' said Lomnae Drúth. 'Better a victory won by protecting them than a victory of wounding. Who spares them may survive; who wounds them, woe to him.' 'You do not rule me,' said Ingcél. 'Clouds of blood will come to you.' 'After that, what did you see?' asked Lomnae Drúth.

'I saw a man in an ornamented apartment,' said Ingcél, 'and he is the handsomest of the heroes of Ériu. He had a fleecy crimson cloak about him. As bright as snow one cheek, as speckled red as foxglove the other; as blue as hyacinth one eye, as black as a beetle's back the other. His fair, yellow hair would fill a reaping basket, and it was as fleecy as the wool of a ram. If a sackful of red nuts were emptied over his hand, not a single nut would reach the ground. In his hands, a gold-hilted sword, a blood-red shield studded with rivets of white gold and gold plates, and a long, three-ridged spear with a shaft the thickness of an outer yoke. Explain that, Fer Rogain.'

'Not difficult that,' said Fer Rogain, 'for the men of Ériu know that child. He is Conall Cernach son of Amorgen, and just now he has fallen in with Conare, for Conare loves him above all others, and that because the two are so similar in shape and form. A good warrior Conall Cernach. The blood-red shield on his back is so studded with rivets of white gold that it is speckled, and thus the Ulaid have named it the Bricriu of Conall Cernach. I swear by what my people swear by, many a drop of red blood will splatter that shield tonight at the entrance to the hostel. There are seven entrances to the house, and Conall Cernach will meet us at each one, and he will not be absent from any; and his ridged spear will serve the drink of death to many. Three hundred will fall by him at the first onslaught, and a man for each weapon, and a man for himself, and he will match the performance of any man in the hostel; he will boast of victories over kings and royal heirs and plundering chieftains, and, though wounded, he will escape afterwards. When he encounters you in the hostel, as numerous as hailstones or blades of grass or stars in the sky will be your cloven heads and cloven skulls and heaps of entrails that he crushes after he has scattered you about the ridges.' 'Woe to him who carries out this destruction,' said Lomnae Drúth. 'You do not rule me,' said Ingcél. 'Clouds of blood will come to you.' 'After that, what did you see?' asked Lomnae Drúth.

'I saw an apartment, the most beautifully decorated one in the house, with hangings and ornaments of silver, and three men in it,' said Ingcél. 'The men on either side were fair with their flaxen hair and their cloaks; they were as white as snow, and their cheeks blushed pleasingly. Between them a callow youth with the ardour and deeds of a lord and the advice of a seer. The cloak he wore was like mist on the first day of summer: its colour and appearance changed from moment to moment, and each colour was lovelier than the one before. Moreover, there was a wheel of gold over the front of the cloak, and it reached from his chin to his navel. His hair was the colour of refined gold. Of all the forms I have seen in the world, his is the most beautiful. At his side, there was a gold-hilted sword; a hand's length of it was visible, and the light reflected from that part of the sword would enable a man out in front of the house to discern a fleshworm. Sweeter the music of that sword than the sweet sound of the golden pipes that drone in the royal house.

'This is what I said upon seeing him,' Ingcél continued.
' "I see a lofty, noble reign, and a noisy flowering that
blooms with an abundant spring tide. A furious ardour of
fair forms is assembled. I see a noble, restrained king who
rules by right and by consent, from partition to wall. I see
the diadem of a fair prince, proper to the dignity of a ruling
lord. A gleam of light his lordly countenance. I see his two
shining cheeks, as white and glistening and noble-hued as
snow. His two eyes are blue grey and brighter than hyacinth.
Firm his brow between a hedge of black eyelashes. I see a
crown encircling his head, the colour of beautiful gold over
his yellow, curly hair. I see his cloak red, multihued, of
excellent braided silk. I see a huge brooch, ornamented with
gold, that shines with the vigour of the full moon. I see a
circle of crimson gems in a bowl-like cluster. Beautiful his
head between his straight, bright shoulders. I see a tunic of
splendid linen, silken its sheen, refracted and many-coloured
its hue. A grazing for the eyes of a multitude this man. He
maintains justice among his people. He delivers from the
enemy braided silk ornamented with gold from ankle to
knee. I see his sword, its hilt ornamented with gold, in its
scabbard of white silver; the latter, with its five concentric
circles, retains its excellence. I see his bright, lime-whitened
shield overhead; it scorns throngs of enemies. His spear of
sparkling gold would illumine a feast, and its shaft is of
ornamented gold. His right hand that wards off is the hand
of a king. He raises his spear firmly, as a king would, twist-
ing its stiffness. Three hundred perfect men about this
generous king. He overtakes like the scald-crow in battle,
in the sorrowful hostel."

'The young lad was sleeping, then, his feet in the lap of
the one man and his head in the lap of the other,' Ingcél
continued. 'He awoke from his sleep, then, and recited this
poem: "The cry of Ossar. Ossar the hound. A shout of youths

going up from the marsh of Tule Gossi. A cold wind across a dangerous blade. A night for destroying a king. It is heard again, the cry of Ossar, Ossar the hound. Battle is declared. The end of a people. The destruction of a hostel. Saddened fíana. Wounded men. A fearful wind. The carrying off of spears. Pain against unfair odds. The fall of a house. Temuir desolate. Unknown heirs. Weeping over Conare. Destruction of corn. A shout. A cry. The destruction of the king of Ériu. Chariots whirling about. Hardship for the king of Temuir." The third time he said:[7] "The cry of Ossar. Ossar the hound. A combat of heroes. Youths in slaughter. Slaughter will be done. Champions will be destroyed. Men will bend. Warriors will be despoiled. A bellowing encounter. Shouts raised. Concern shown. An abundance of spectres. A prostrate host. The overthrowing of enemies. A combat of men on the Dothra. Hardship for the king of Temuir. Men cut down in youth." Explain that, Fer Rogain – who recited that poem?'

'Not difficult that,' said Fer Rogain. 'Indeed, it is not a moon without a king. The most splendid and distinguished and handsome and powerful king who has ever come into the world that one – the kindest and gentlest and most humble as well. Conare Már son of Eterscélae is his name, and he is the high king of Ériu. There is no flaw in him, not as to form or shape or clothing, or size or arrangement or proportion, or eye or hair or whiteness, or wisdom or pleasingness or eloquence, or weapons or equipment or attire, or splendour or abundance or dignity, or bearing or prowess or ancestry. Great the youth of this man, who seems simple and sleepy until he undertakes a feat of arms; but if his ardour and fury are aroused while the fíana of Ériu and Albu are about him in his house, then there will be no destruction of the hostel. Six hundred will fall by him before he reaches his weapons, and once he has obtained his weapons, six hundred more will fall at the first onslaught. I swear by the god my people swear by, if his drink is not taken from him, he will reach men from Tond Chlidnai to Tond Essa Rúaid, even though he is alone in the house. There are nine entrances to the house, and at each entrance one hundred heroes will fall, and when everyone has stopped fighting, it is then that he will be performing feats of arms. If he encounters you outside the hostel, as numerous as hailstones or blades of grass or stars in the sky will be your cloven heads and cloven skulls and heaps of entrails that he crushes after he has scattered you about the ridges. But I do not believe that he will succeed in leaving the house. Dear to him are the two men in his apartment, his two foster-brothers, Driss and Sníthe. Three fifties of heroes will fall by each man at the entrance to the hostel, and no farther than a foot away, on this side and that, will they fall.' 'Woe to him who carries out this destruction, if only because of those two men and the prince who is between them, the high king of Ériu, Conare Már son of Eterscélae,' said Lomnae Drúth. 'It would be grievous to extinguish that reign.' 'You do not rule me,' said Ingcél. 'Clouds of blood will come to you.' 'Indeed, Ingcél, the destruction is yours by right,' said Lomnae Drúth. 'You will come to no harm. It will be harder on me, however.' 'No lie that,' said Ingcél. 'After that, what did you see?' asked Lomnae Drúth.

'I saw twelve men gathered round the apartment in a circle,' said Ingcél, 'and they had silver swords. Fair yellow manes they had, and bright tunics, and all were equal in form and shape and appearance. All had ivory-hilted swords in their hands, and they did not put them down unless they were holding horsewhips as they gathered round the apartment. Explain that, Fer Rogain.'

'Not difficult that,' said Fer Rogain. 'The guards of the king of Temuir they: the three Londs of Life, the three Arts of Áth Clíath, the three Bodars of Búaignige and the three

Trénfers of Cuilne. I swear by the god my people swear by, when they destroy, the dead outnumber the living. Twelve hundred will fall by them at the first onslaught, and a man for each weapon, and a man for each of them, and they will match the performance of any band in the hostel; they will boast of victories over kings and royal heirs and plundering chieftains, and, though wounded, they will escape afterwards.' 'Woe to him who carries out this destruction, if only because of those twelve,' said Lomnae Drúth. 'You do not rule me,' said Ingcél. 'Clouds of blood will come to you.' 'After that, what did you see?' asked Lomnae Drúth.

'I saw a red-freckled lad in a crimson cloak,' said Ingcél, 'and he was weeping in the house. Wherever the thirty hundred men were, each of them would take the lad to his breast. He was sitting on a bright silver chair in the middle of the house and sobbing, and the household were sorrowful from listening to him. The lad had three colours of hair: green, yellow crimson and pure gold. I do not know whether each hair is multihued or whether he has three different hairs. But I do know that there is something he fears tonight. I saw three fifties of lads in silver chairs round him, and those red-freckled lads had fifteen reeds in their hands, with a thorn spike at the top of each reed. We were fifteen men, and our fifteen right eyes were being blinded by him, and one of the seven pupils in my eye was being blinded by him. Explain that, Fer Rogain.'

'Not difficult that,' said Fer Rogain, and he wept until tears of blood poured forth. 'Wretched that one, for he has been named by the men of Ériu against the men of Albu as a champion of hospitality and shape and form and horsemanship. It is grievous. He is a pig that falls before acorns. The making of a king, he is the best ever to come into Ériu. The infant son of Conare, Lé Fer Flaith is his name, and he is seven years old. I think it not unlikely that he is foredoomed, and that by reason of the various hues of his hair. The three fifties of lads round him are his special household.' 'Woe to him who carries out this destruction, if only because of this one lad,' said Lomnae Drúth. 'You do not rule me,' said Ingcél. 'Clouds of blood will come to you.' 'After that, what did you see?' asked Lomnae Drúth.

'I saw six men before the same apartment,' said Ingcél. 'Fair yellow manes they had, and green cloaks, and tin brooches for the cloaks. All were mounted like Conall Cernach. Each man could put his cloak round the other as quickly as a mill wheel; the eye could scarcely follow it. Explain that, Fer Rogain.'

'Not difficult that,' said Fer Rogain. 'The six servers of the king of Temuir they: Úan, Bróen, Banda, Delt, Drúcht and Dathen. That trick does not interfere with their serving, and neither does their intelligence. They are the chieftains of the youth in the hostel. Three champions, equally matched, will fall by them, and they will match the performance of any six men in the hostel, and they will escape afterwards, for they are of the Síde. They are the best servers in Ériu.' 'Woe to him who carries out this destruction, if only because of those six,' said Lomnae Drúth. 'You do not rule me,' said Ingcél. 'Clouds of blood will come to you.' 'After that, what did you see?' asked Lomnae Drúth.

'I saw a strapping fellow before the same apartment in the centre of the house,' said Ingcél. 'A shameful haircut he had, and every hair on his head was as white as a mountain bog. Gold earrings on his ears, and a cloak of many colours about him; nine swords in his hands, and nine silver shields and nine apples of gold. He threw up the swords and shields and apples, and only one remained in his hand, but none fell to the ground, and their movement was like that of bees going past one another on a beautiful day. When I saw him, he was at his most splendid; but as I looked, everything fell to the floor, and a great clatter arose about him. The ruler said to the trickster, then, "We have known each other since I was a lad, and never before has that trick failed you." "Alas, alas, fair popa Conare," the trickster replied, "it was proper that this should happen, for a keen, baleful eye is staring at me. A man with three pupils is watching the passing of three companies, and his watching is nothing at all for him. Baleful that. A battle will be fought; it will be remembered until the day of Judgement, and there will be evil at the entrance to the hostel." After that, he took his swords in hand, and his silver shields and his apples of gold, and everything fell on the floor again, and there was a great clatter. He put everything away, then, and abandoned his feat and said "Fer Calliu, rise now, do not permit the slaughter of your pig. Find out who is at the entrance to the house doing injury to the men of the hostel." "Fer Cúailge, Fer Lé, Fer Gar, Fer Rogel and Fer Rogain are there," said Fer Calliu. "They have announced a deed that was not expected, Conare's forgiveness by the five sons of Dond Désa, his five beloved foster-brothers." Explain that, Fer Rogain – who recited that poem?'

'Not difficult that,' said Fer Rogain. 'That one was Tulchaíne, the royal fool of the king of Temuir, Conare's trickster, a man of great power. Three nines will fall by him at the first onslaught, and he will match the performance of anyone in the hostel, and, though wounded, he will escape afterwards.' 'On his account alone, there should be no destruction. Happy the man who spares him,' said Lomnae Drúth. 'You do not rule me,' said Ingcél. 'Clouds of blood will come to you.' 'After that, what did you see?' asked Lomnae Drúth.

'I saw nine men before the same apartment,' said Ingcél. 'Fair yellow manes they had, and short trousers and speckled red tunics and shields lest they be struck. A sword with an ivory hilt in the hand of each man, and anyone who entered the house would be struck with those swords. No one dared enter the house without their permission. Explain that, Fer Rogain.'

'Not difficult that,' said Fer Rogain. 'Those are the three Mochmaitnechs of Mide, the three Búadeltachs of Brega and the three Sostachs of Slíab Fúait. Nine tens will fall by them at the first onslaught, and they will match the performance of anyone in the hostel, and, though wounded, they will escape afterwards.' 'Woe to him who carries out this destruction, if only because of those nine,' said Lomnae Drúth. 'You do not rule me,' said Ingcél. 'Clouds of blood will come to you.' 'After that, what did you see?' asked Lomnae Drúth.

'I saw another apartment, with two men in it,' said Ingcél. 'Stout and strong they were, with short trousers, and they were dusky red; short hair at the back of their heads and long hair on top. Each was as quick as a mill wheel going past the other, the one going to the apartment, the other to the hearth. Explain that, Fer Rogain.'

'Not difficult that,' said Fer Rogain. 'Nía and Bruithne they, Conare's two servers, the best pair in Ériu. That is why they are swarthy and why their hair stands up – because they visit the fire so often. No pair in the world are better servers than they. Three nines will fall by them at the first onslaught, and a man for each weapon, and a man for each man, and they will match the performance of any pair in the hostel; they will boast of victories over kings and royal heirs and plundering chieftains, and, though wounded, they will escape afterwards.' 'Woe to him who carries out this destruction, if only because of those two,' said Lomnae Drúth. 'You do not rule me,' said Ingcél. 'Clouds of blood will come to you.' 'After that, what did you see?' asked Lomnae Drúth.

'I saw the apartment next to Conare's,' said Ingcél. 'Three chief warriors were there, and they were just turning grey. They wore dark grey shirts, and each of their limbs was as thick as a man's waist; each man had a huge, black sword, as long as a weaver's beam, that could split a hair floating on the water. The man in the centre had a great lance, with fifty rivets through it, and its shaft would be a load for a team of oxen. He brandished the lance until sparks as big as eggs all but flew from it, and then he struck the butt against his palm three times. Before them was a great food cauldron, large enough for a bullock, with an appalling dark liquid in it, and the man dipped the lance into the liquid. If the lance was not quenched quickly, it blazed up over its shaft — you would have thought there was a roaring fire in the upper part of the house. Explain that, Fer Rogain.'

'Not difficult that,' said Fer Rogain. 'Three heroes they, the three best that ever took weapons in Ériu: Senchae son of Ailill, Dubthach Dóeltenga and Goibniu son of Lorgnech. And the lance that was in the hand of Dubthach, that was the Lúin of Celtchair son of Uthechar that was found at the battle of Mag Tured. Whenever the blood of enemies is about to flow from the lance, a cauldron full of venom is required to quench it; otherwise, the lance will blaze up in the fist of the man carrying it, and it will pierce him or the lord of the royal house. Each thrust of this lance will kill a man, even if it does not reach him; if the lance is cast, it will kill nine men, and there will be a king or royal heir or plundering chieftain in their number. I swear by what my people swear by, the Lúin of Celtchair will serve drinks of death to a multitude tonight. Three hundred will fall by these three at the first onslaught, and a man for each weapon, and a man for each man, and they will match the performance of any trio in the hostel; they will boast of victories over kings and royal heirs and plundering chieftains, and, though wounded, they will escape afterwards.' 'Woe to him who carries out this destruction, if only because of those three,' said Lomnae Drúth. 'You do not rule me,' said Ingcél. 'Clouds of blood will come to you.' 'After that, what did you see?' asked Lomnae Drúth.

'I saw an apartment with three men in it,' said Ingcél. 'Three strong, powerful men – a man passing by would not eye their dark, uncouth faces for fear of the terror that would result. Rough-haired garments all about them, and no other clothing on them from head to toe. Their horrible, horselike manes reached their sides. Furious warriors, they were quick to their swords, and they struck stoutly against enemies. Each bore an iron flail with seven chains; each chain was twisted into three strands, and each had at its end a knob as heavy as a bar for lifting ten pieces of burning metal. Huge oxhides they wore, and the four-cornered clasps that fastened them were as thick as a man's thighs, and the hair from the hides went through them. Each man had an iron staff as long and thick as an outer yoke; each staff had nine chains of iron, and each chain had a pestle of iron as long and thick as an outer yoke. These men were dejected, and they were horrible to behold; no one in the house was not aware of them. Explain that, Fer Rogain.'

Fer Rogain fell silent. 'Difficult that,' he said. 'I know no trio in Ériu like that, unless they are the three churls whom Cú Chulaind spared at Forbas Fer Fálgai; they slew fifty warriors while under his protection, and he protected them because of their strangeness. These are their names: Srúb Dare son of Dorn Bude, Conchend Cind Mage and Fíad Sceme son of Scippe. Three hundred will fall by them at the first onslaught, and they will match the performance of any trio in the hostel; if they encounter you, your fragments will pass through a corn sieve after they have destroyed you with their iron flails.' 'Woe to him who carries out this destruction, if only because of those three,' said Lomnae Drúth. 'You do not rule me,' said Ingcél. 'Clouds of blood will come to you.' 'After that, what did you see?' asked Lomnae Drúth.

'I saw another apartment, with one man in it,' said Ingcél, 'and two lads before him, both with long hair, the one as dark as the other was fair. The warrior had blood-red hair and a blood-red mantle, and his cheeks were ruddy. Very beautiful blue eyes he had, and a green cloak about him, and a hooded white tunic with red embroidery, and an ivory-hilted sword in his hand. He supplied food and drink to every apartment in the hostel and waited upon the host. Explain that, Fer Rogain.'

'Not difficult that,' said Fer Rogain. 'I know that man – Da Derga. It is he who built the hostel. Since he became a hospitaller, the entrances to the hostel have never been closed, save in the direction from which the wind blows; since he became a hospitaller, his cauldron has never gone from the fire, and it boils food for the men of Ériu. The two lads before him are his foster-sons, the children of the king of the Lagin, Muredach and Coirpre. Three tens will fall by this trio at the entrance to the house, and they will boast of victories over kings and royal heirs and plundering chieftains, and they will escape afterwards.' 'Happy he who spares those children,' said Lomnae Drúth. 'Better a victory of sparing them than a victory of wounding them. They should be spared, if only because of that man, for he would be capable of protecting them.' 'You do not rule me,' said Ingcél. 'Clouds of blood will come to you.' 'After that, what did you see?' asked Lomnae Drúth.

'I saw an apartment with three men in it,' said Ingcél. 'Three blood-red cloaks about them, and blood-red tunics, and blood-red hair on their heads – they were blood red to the teeth. Three blood-red shields hung overhead, along with three blood-red spears; three blood-red horses were bridled at the entrance to the house. Explain that, Fer Rogain.'

'Not difficult that,' said Fer Rogain. 'They are the three nephews that lied in the síd. The punishment inflicted upon them by the king of the Síde is that they be destroyed three times by the king of Temuir. Conare son of Eterscélae is the last king by whom they are to be destroyed. These men will escape you. To fulfil their destruction they have come, but they will wound no one, and they will not be wounded.' 'After that, what did you see?' asked Lomnae Drúth.

'I saw three men in the centre of the house, near the door,' said Ingcél. 'Three barbed staffs were in their hands. As fast as a rabbit each of them round the others and towards the door. Short, speckled trousers on them, and grey cloaks. Explain that, Fer Rogain.'

'Not difficult that,' said Fer Rogain. 'The three door-keepers of the king of Temuir they: Echuir and Tochur and Tegmong, the sons of Ersa and Comla. Three champions, equally matched, will fall by them, and their performance will equal that of any trio in the hostel, and, though wounded, they will escape afterwards.' 'Woe to him who carries out this destruction, if only because of those three,' said Lomnae Drúth. 'You do not rule me,' said Ingcél. 'Clouds of blood will come to you.' 'After that, what did you see?' asked Lomnae Drúth.

'I saw at the front fire,' said Ingcél, 'a black-haired man with one eye and one arm and one leg; he was carrying a singed, black-bristled pig towards the fire, and it was squealing. With him he had a large, large-lipped woman. Explain that, Fer Rogain.'

'Not difficult that,' said Fer Rogain. 'Fer Calliu was the man with the pig, and the woman is his wife, Cichuil. They are the instruments by which you may lawfully destroy

Conare tonight. Woe to the face that blushes between them. Indeed, Fer Calliu and his pig are geiss to Conare.' 'Woe to him who carries out this destruction, if only because of those two,' said Lomnae Drúth. 'You do not rule me,' said Ingcél. 'Clouds of blood will come to you.' 'After that, what did you see?' asked Lomnae Drúth.

'I saw an apartment with three nines in it,' Ingcél said. 'Fair yellow hair they had, and all were equally handsome. Each had a black cape with a white hood and a blood-red crest and an iron brooch; each bore a very large, black sword that could split a hair floating on the water, and each had a shield with serrated edges. Explain that, Fer Rogain.'

'Not difficult that,' said Fer Rogain. 'The three sons of Baithse of the Bretain they, three plunderers. Three nines will fall by them at the first onslaught, and they will match the performance of any trio in the hostel, and they will escape afterwards.' 'Woe to him who carries out this destruction, if only because of those three,' said Lomnae Drúth. 'You do not rule me,' said Ingcél. 'Clouds of blood will come to you.' 'After that, what did you see?' asked Lomnae Drúth.

'I saw three fools at one end of the fire,' said Ingcél, 'all wearing dun mantles. If the men of Ériu were assembled in one place, and if the bodies of his father and his mother were before each man, no one could help but laugh. If there were thirty hundred in the house, none would manage to sit or lie down because of those three. When the king's eye lights upon them, it laughs with each glance. Explain that, Fer Rogain.'

'Not difficult that,' said Fer Rogain. 'Mlithe and Máel and Admlithe they, the three fools of the king of Ériu. A man will fall by each of them, and they will match the performance of any trio in the hostel, and they will escape afterwards.' 'Woe to him who carries out this destruction, if only because of those three,' said Lomnae Drúth. 'You do not rule me,' said Ingcél. 'Clouds of blood will come to you.' 'After that, what did you see?' asked Lomnae Drúth.

'I saw an apartment with three men in it,' said Ingcél. 'Three swirling grey cloaks about them. A cup of water before each man, and a bunch of watercress in each cup. Explain that, Fer Rogain.'

'Not difficult that,' said Fer Rogain. 'Dub and Dond and Dobar they, the three cupbearers of the king of Temuir. They are the sons of Lá and Aidche.' 'Woe to him who carries out this destruction, if only because of those three,' said Lomnae Drúth. 'You do not rule me,' said Ingcél. 'Clouds of blood will come to you.' 'After that, what did you see?' asked Lomnae Drúth.

'I saw a man who was blind in his left eye and destructive in his right,' said Ingcél. 'He was carrying a pig's head towards the fire, and it was squealing. Explain that, Fer Rogain.'

'Not difficult that,' said Fer Rogain. 'Nár Thúathcáech that one, the swineherd of Bodb, from Síd ar Femuin. He has never attended a feast where he did not shed blood.' 'Woe to him who carries out this destruction, if only because of that one man,' said Lomnae Drúth. 'You do not rule me,' said Ingcél. 'Clouds of blood will come to you. Rise, now, fíana, and let us make for the house.'

At that, the plunderers rose and made for the house, and they raised a loud shout. 'Hush!' said Conare. 'What is that?' 'Fíana encircling the house,' said Conall Cernach. 'There are youths here to meet them,' said Conare. 'They will be needed tonight,' said Conall Cernach. Lomnae Drúth preceded the plunderers into the hostel, and the doorkeepers cut off his head. The head was thrown into the hostel three times, and it was thrown back out three times, just as Lomnae Drúth had prophesied.

Six hundred fell by Conare before he could reach his weapons. The hostel was fired three times and extinguished three times, and it was conceded that the destruction would not be carried out until Conare had performed some feat of arms. After that, Conare obtained his weapons, and six hundred fell at the first onslaught, and the plunderers were routed. 'I told you,' said Fer Rogain, 'that if the fíana of Ériu and Albu were about the house, the destruction would nonetheless not be carried out until Conare's heat and ardour were quenched.' 'He has only a short time,' said the druids who had accompanied the plunderers, and they caused a weakness for drink to overcome him. Conare entered the house and said 'Drink, popa Macc Céchtl' 'Indeed, I have never taken an order to bring you drink before,' said Macc Cécht. 'You have servers and cupbearers to bring you drink. The order I have taken up to now has been to guard you from the fíana of Ériu and Albu who have encircled the hostel – I will protect you from them, and not a single spear will pierce your body. Seek drink from your servers and your cupbearers.'

After that, Conare sought drink from his servers and cupbearers. 'There is none,' they said. 'All the liquid in the house was spent extinguishing the fire.' The river Dothra flowed through the house, but they found no drink for him there. Conare sought drink once more, saying 'Drink for me, Macc Cécht, my foster-son. I do not care if death follows, for I will die anyway.' Conare sought drink a third time, and at that, Macc Cécht went to the chieftains of Ériu, and he offered the warriors in the house the choice of protecting the king or fetching drink for him. Conall Cernach answered from within the house: 'We will protect the king. You go to fetch drink, since it is you he asked.'

Macc Cécht went to fetch drink, then; he put Lé Fer Flaith son of Conare under one arm, and under the other he put Conare's gilt cup, which was large enough for an ox to boil over the fire, and he took his sword and his shield and his two spears and a bar of iron that was under the king's cauldron. At the entrance to the hostel he dealt nine blows with the iron bar, and each blow felled nine men. He did the edge feat with his sword about his head and so cut a path out of the house. Macc Cécht went on to Tipra Cuirp, which was nearby, in Crích Chúaland; he had Conare's cup in his hand, but he could not fill it there. Before morning he had gone round the major rivers of Ériu: Búas, Bóand, Bandai, Berbai, Nem, Laí, Laígdai, Sinand, Síuir, Slicech, Samuir, Findi and Ruirthech. But he could not fill the cup. He went on until he reached Úarán Garaid in Mag Aí, having first gone round the waters and the chief lakes of Ériu – Dergderc, Luimnech, Loch Ríb, Loch Febail, Loch Mesca, Loch nOrbsen, Loch Laíg, Loch Cúan, Loch nEchach, Márloch – and still failing to fill the cup. Úarán Garaid did not hide from him, so he filled the cup and put the lad under his arm. He returned, then, and reached the hostel before morning.

When Macc Cécht reached the third ridge from the house, he saw two men striking Conare's head off. He struck the head from one of the two men, but the second made to escape with Conare's head. On the floor of the hostel, near the entrance, there happened to be a pillar stone at Macc Cécht's feet. He cast this stone at the second man; it struck the man in the small of the back, and his back broke. Macc Cécht struck off the man's head. Then he poured the cup of water into Conare's throat, and Conare's head recited this poem:

A good man Macc Cécht!
Welcome, Macc Cécht!
He brings drink to a king.
He does well.

After that, Macc Cécht went after the rout. Only a very few
– nine – had fallen round Conare, and scarcely a single
messenger had escaped to bear the news to the plunderers
who were about the house. Where there had been five
thousand, and ten hundred in every thousand, there escaped
no more than one fifth, apart from Ingcél and his brothers,
Éccell and Dartaid.

At the end of the third day, Macc Cécht was among the
wounded on the field of slaughter, and he saw a woman
going by. 'Stay awhile, woman,' he said. 'I dare not go to
you,' she answered, 'for fear and horror of you.' 'That time
has passed, woman,' said Macc Cécht. 'I give you the truth
of my honour and my protection.' The woman went to him,
then. 'I do not know if it is a fly or an ant or a midge that
nips at my wound,' Macc Cécht said. 'Indeed, it is an ant
of the ancient earth,' said the woman.[8] 'I swear by the god
my people swear by,' said Macc Cécht, 'I thought it no more
than a fly or a midge.' Then he died on the field of slaughter.

Conall Cernach escaped, though three fifties of spears had
gone through his shield hand; he went to his father's house,
bearing fragments of his sword and his shield and his two
spears in his hand. He met his father at the entrance to the
courtyard at Tailtiu. 'Swift the dogs that have chased you,
my son,' said his father. 'It was a combat with young heroes,
old warrior,' said Conall. 'Have you news of Da Derga's
hostel? Does your lord live?' asked his father. 'He does
not,' Conall replied. 'I swear by the god my people swear by,
it is a coward who would come away alive and leave his
lord with the enemy,' said the father. 'My wounds are not
white, old warrior,' said Conall. He showed his father his

shield arm and the three fifties of wounds that had been inflicted upon it. His shield had protected that hand, but it had not protected his right hand. That had been attacked over two thirds of its length; it had been hacked and cut and wounded and riddled, but the sinews had not permitted it to fall off. 'That hand injured many tonight, and it was much injured,' said Amorgen. 'True, old warrior,' said Conall Cernach. 'There are many to whom it served drinks of death at the entrance to the hostel tonight.'

The Dream of Óengus

Introduction

'The Dream of Óengus' is a continuation of the opening episode of 'The Wooing of Étaín', wherein Bóand and the Dagdae sleep together and Óengus is born. Although the story survives only in a relatively late source, the fifteenth-century Egerton 1782 manuscript, it is mentioned in the Book of Leinster, in a list of preliminary tales to 'The Cattle Raid of Cúailnge'.

Even so, 'The Dream of Óengus' does not appear to be especially old. The themes are familiar to Celtic literature: love before first sight (as in the Welsh tale 'How Culhwch Won Olwen'), the initiative of the otherworld woman (as by Rhiannon in 'Pwyll Lord of Dyved' and by Macha in 'The Labour Pains of the Ulaid'), the wasting away of the mortal lover (Gilvaethwy in 'Math Son of Mathonwy', Ailill Angubae in 'The Wooing of Étaín'), the unwillingness of the woman's father (as in 'How Culhwch Won Olwen' and 'The Wooing of Étaín') and the transformation of the lovers into swans (Mider and Étaín). And Bóand and the Dagdae are scarcely recognizable as people of the Síde: Bóand is unable to help her son at all, and the Dagdae has to ask assistance from the king of the Síde of Mumu. The meeting and transformation of Óengus and Cáer Ibormeith at Samuin, a time of changes, does evince a genuinely ancient Celtic motif; and the tone of

107

the story, while romantic, is still restrained. The link to 'The Cattle Raid of Cúailnge', however, is pure artifice.

One puzzling feature of this story is Óengus's failure to reveal the cause of his illness. In the Welsh story 'Math Son of Mathonwy', Gilvaethwy falls in love with Math's virgin footholder; in the second section of 'The Wooing of Étaín', Ailill falls in love with his brother's wife. Both men fall ill from love, but neither will reveal his guilty secret, and it may be that this idea of silence was transferred, inappropriately (since Óengus has no cause for guilt), as part of the overall theme of wasting sickness.

'The Dream of Óengus' is the ultimate source of Yeats's poem 'The Dream of Wandering Aengus'.

The Dream of Óengus

Óengus was asleep one night when he saw something like a young girl coming towards the head of his bed, and she was the most beautiful woman in Ériu. He made to take her hand and draw her to his bed, but, as he welcomed her, she vanished suddenly, and he did not know who had taken her from him. He remained in bed until the morning, but he was troubled in his mind: the form he had seen but not spoken to was making him ill. No food entered his mouth that day. He waited until evening, and then he saw a timpán in her hand, the sweetest ever, and she played for him until he fell asleep. Thus he was all night, and the next morning he ate nothing.

A full year passed, and the girl continued to visit Óengus,

so that he fell in love with her, but he told no one. Then he fell sick, but no one knew what ailed him. The physicians of Ériu gathered but could not discover what was wrong, so they sent for Fergne, Cond's physician, and Fergne came. He could tell from a man's face what the illness was, just as he could tell from the smoke that came from a house how many were sick inside. Fergne took Óengus aside and said to him 'No meeting this, but love in absence.' 'You have divined my illness,' said Óengus. 'You have grown sick at heart,' said Fergne, 'and you have not dared to tell anyone.' 'It is true,' said Óengus. 'A young girl came to me; her form was the most beautiful that I have ever seen, and her appearance was excellent. A timpán was in her hand, and she played for me each night.' 'No matter,' said Fergne, 'love for her has seized you. We will send to Bóand, your mother, that she may come and speak with you.'

They sent to Bóand, then, and she came. 'I was called to see to this man, for a mysterious illness had overcome him,' said Fergne, and he told Bóand what had happened. 'Let his mother tend to him,' said Fergne, 'and let her search throughout Ériu until she finds the form that her son saw.' The search was carried on for a year, but the like of the girl was not found, so Fergne was summoned again. 'No help has been found for him,' said Bóand. 'Then send for the Dagdae, and let him come and speak with his son,' said Fergne. The Dagdae was sent for and came, asking 'Why have I been summoned?' 'To advise your son,' said Bóand. 'It is right that you help him, for his death would be a pity. Love in absence has overcome him, and no help for it has been found.' 'Why tell me?' asked the Dagdae. 'My knowledge is no greater than yours.' 'Indeed it is,' said Fergne, 'for you are king of the Síde of Ériu. Send messengers to Bodb, for he is king of the Síde of Mumu, and his knowledge spreads throughout Ériu.'

Messengers went to Bodb, then, and they were welcomed; Bodb said 'Welcome, people of the Dagdae.' 'It is that we have come for,' they replied. 'Have you news?' Bodb asked. 'We have: Óengus son of the Dagdae has been in love for two years,' they replied. 'How is that?' Bodb asked. 'He saw a young girl in his sleep,' they said, 'but we do not know where in Ériu she is to be found. The Dagdae asks that you search all Ériu for a girl of her form and appearance.' 'That search will be made,' said Bodb, 'and it will be carried on for a year, so that I may be sure of finding her.' At the end of the year, Bodb's people went to him at his house in Síd ar Femuin and said 'We made a circuit of Ériu, and we found the girl at Loch Bél Dracon in Cruitt Clíach.' Messengers were sent to the Dagdae, then; he welcomed them and said 'Have you news?' 'Good news: the girl of the form you described has been found,' they said. 'Bodb has asked that Óengus return with us to see if he recognizes her as the girl he saw.'

Óengus was taken in a chariot to Síd ar Femuin, then, and he was welcomed there; a great feast was prepared for him, and it lasted three days and three nights. After that, Bodb said to Óengus 'Let us go, now, to see if you recognize the girl. You may see her, but it is not in my power to give her to you.' They went on until they reached a lake; there, they saw three fifties of young girls, and Óengus's girl was among them. The other girls were no taller than her shoulder; each pair of them was linked by a silver chain, but Óengus's girl wore a silver necklace, and her chain was of burnished gold. 'Do you recognize that girl?' asked Bodb. 'Indeed, I do,' Óengus replied. 'I can do no more for you, then,' said Bodb. 'No matter, for she is the girl I saw. I cannot take her now. Who is she?' Óengus said. 'I know her, of course: Cáer Ibormeith daughter of Ethal Anbúail from Síd Úamuin in the province of Connachta.'

After that, Óengus and his people returned to their own land, and Bodb went with them to visit the Dagdae and Bóand at Bruig ind Maicc Óic. They told their news: how the girl's form and appearance were just as Óengus had seen; and they told her name and those of her father and grandfather. 'A pity that we cannot get her,' said the Dagdae. 'What you should do is go to Ailill and Medb, for the girl is in their territory,' said Bodb.

The Dagdae went to Connachta, then, and three score chariots with him; they were welcomed by the king and queen there and spent a week feasting and drinking. 'Why your journey?' asked the king. 'There is a girl in your territory,' said the Dagdae, 'with whom my son has fallen in love, and he has now fallen ill. I have come to see if you will give her to him.' 'Who is she?' Ailill asked. 'The daughter of Ethal Anbúail,' the Dagdae replied. 'We do not have the power to give her to you,' said Ailill and Medb. 'Then the best thing would be to have the king of the síd called here,' said the Dagdae. Ailill's steward went to Ethal Anbúail and said 'Ailill and Medb require that you come and speak with them.' 'I will not come,' Ethal said, 'and I will not give my daughter to the son of the Dagdae.' The steward repeated this to Ailill, saying 'He knows why he has been summoned, and he will not come.' 'No matter,' said Ailill, 'for he will come, and the heads of his warriors with him.'

After that, Ailill's household and the Dagdae's people rose up against the síd and destroyed it; they brought out three score heads and confined the king at Crúachu. Ailill said to Ethal Anbúail 'Give your daughter to the son of the Dagdae.' 'I cannot,' he said, 'for her power is greater than mine.' 'What great power does she have?' Ailill asked. 'Being in the form of a bird each day of one year and in human form each day of the following year,' Ethal said. 'Which year will she be in the shape of a bird?' Ailill asked. 'It is not for me to

111

reveal that,' Ethal replied. 'Your head off,' said Ailill, 'unless you tell us.' 'I will conceal it no longer, then, but will tell you, since you are so obstinate,' said Ethal. 'Next Samuin she will be in the form of a bird; she will be at Loch Bél Dracon, and beautiful birds will be seen with her, three fifties of swans about her, and I will make ready for them.' 'No matter that,' said the Dagdae, 'since I know the nature you have brought upon her.'

Peace and friendship were made among Ailill and Ethal and the Dagdae, then, and the Dagdae bade them farewell and went to his house and told the news to his son. 'Go next Samuin to Loch Bél Dracon,' he said, 'and call her to you there.' The Macc Óc went to Loch Bél Dracon, and there he saw the three fifties of white birds, with silver chains, and golden hair about their heads. Óengus was in human form at the edge of the lake, and he called to the girl, saying 'Come and speak with me, Cáer!' 'Who is calling to me?' asked Cáer. 'Óengus is calling,' he replied. 'I will come,' she said, 'if you will promise me that I may return to the water.' 'I promise that,' he said. She went to him, then; he put his arms round her, and they slept in the form of swans until they had circled the lake three times. Thus, he kept his promise. They left in the form of two white birds and flew to Bruig ind Maicc Óic, and there they sang until the people inside fell asleep for three days and three nights. The girl remained with Óengus after that. This is how the friendship between Ailill and Medb and the Macc Óc arose, and this is why Óengus took three hundred to the cattle raid of Cúailnge.

The Cattle Raid of Fróech

Introduction

'The Cattle Raid of Fróech' has a peculiar title. Fróech's 'cattle raid' is nothing more than the recovery of his own cattle (and his wife) from beyond the Alps; moreover, this exploit, which has a late look to it, is tacked on to the main tale, which could better have been called 'The Wooing of Findabair'. And the tale itself is unusual, for it is a mythological story – and with the personae of the Mythological Cycle – pressed into the service of the Ulster Cycle, as a preliminary tale to 'The Cattle Raid of Cúailnge'. It begins in the realm of the Síde, with Fróech going to ask presents of his aunt, Bóand (compare Fróech's cattle with the hounds of Arawn in 'Pwyll Lord of Dyved': white animals with red ears are always from the otherworld); immediately, the setting shifts to the heroic warrior-world of Connachta, though Fróech returns to the Síde for healing after his battle with the water monster.

The theme of 'The Cattle Raid of Fróech', that of the young hero who must win his love away from her unwilling father, appears also in 'The Wooing of Étaín' and 'The Dream of Óengus'; it is a degraded form of the familiar regeneration motif. The mythic – actually folkloric, in this manifestation – pattern imposes an uncharacteristic degree of villainy on Ailill and Medb. (Also uncharacteristic is the dominance of Ailill – elsewhere in the Ulster Cycle it is Medb who is the strong partner.) Our version of the tale, however, is neither mythic nor heroic so much as literary and psychological. More attention is paid to motivation here than in any other early Irish story: Medb is guilt-stricken at having neglected Fróech's retinue, Findabair refuses to elope with Fróech but admonishes him to bargain for her, Fróech rejects the bride price as excessive even for Medb, Ailill tricks Fróech into entering the water monster's lake and seems to regret the ruse only because Fróech survives it, Findabair asserts her independence of her father after he has accused her of giving her ring (and by implication herself) to Fróech. Even the dialogue is unusually subtle. Oddly, though, Fróech's lie about how he received the ring is never challenged – is this an extraordinarily ironic touch, or did the storyteller simply forget that Findabair actually does give Fróech the ring? – and Findabair, even after producing the ring on the salmon platter, is not allowed to go away at once with Fróech.

The Cattle Raid of Fróech

Fróech son of Idath of the Connachta was the son of Bé Find of the Síde, and Bé Find was a sister of Bóand.¹ Fróech was the handsomest warrior in Ériu and Albu, but he did not live long. His mother gave him twelve cows from the síd; they were white, with red ears. Although he had no wife, his household prospered for eight years. Fifty kings' sons were the number of his household, all equal in age and form and appearance.

Findabair, the daughter of Ailill and Medb, fell in love with Fróech after hearing stories about him, for Ériu and Albu were full of his fame and his stories. Fróech was told of this at his house, and it fell to him to go and speak with the girl. He discussed the matter with his people, and they said 'Go to your mother's sister, that she may give you some of the wondrous garments and gifts of the Síde.'

Fróech went then to his mother's sister, to Bóand, in Mag mBreg. He brought back fifty blue mantles; each was the colour of a beetle's back, with four dark grey corners and a brooch of red gold. Fifty tunics of brilliant white, with animal embroidery of gold. Fifty silver shields with gold rims, and fifty candles of a king's house in the hand of each man, with fifty rivets of white gold in each candle, and fifty coils of refined gold about each.[2] The spear butts were of carbuncle, the spear blades of precious stones, and these would light up the night like the rays of the sun. Fifty men with gold-hilted swords, and fifty dapple grey horses; for each horse a bridle bit of gold, a silver breastplate with little gold bells, a crimson saddlecloth with silver threads, an animal-head pin of gold and silver, and a horsewhip of white gold with a gold hook at the end. Seven hounds on silver chains, with an apple of gold between each two hounds. Shoes of bronze, and no colour that was not on them. Seven horn-blowers, with horns of gold and silver and clothes of many colours, with shining mantles and the golden yellow hair of the Síde. Three fools preceding, each with a silver gilded diadem and a shield with an engraved spiral ornament and polished strips of bronze inlaid along the sides. Three harpers in royal garb about each fool.

That company set out for Crúachu, then, and the watchman at the fort perceived them as they entered Mag Crúachan. 'I see a great company approaching the fort,' he said. 'Since Ailill and Medb became sovereigns, no nobler or handsomer company have ever arrived, and no such company ever will arrive. The wind that blows from them is such that my head might as well be in a vat of wine. One warrior performs a feat the like of which I have never seen: he casts his javelin on ahead of him, and before it can strike the ground, seven hounds with their silver chains have caught it.'

At that, the hosts came out of the fort of Crúachu to see the company, and there was such a crowd that the people suffocated, and sixteen men died looking. The company dismounted at the door of the fort. They unbridled their horses and unleashed their hounds; they hunted seven deer to Ráith Crúachan, and seven foxes and seven hares and seven wild boars, and the warriors slew these on the green of the fort. After that, the hounds leapt into the river Brei and caught seven otters and brought them up to the entrance of the royal dwelling.

The company sat down, then, and messengers came from the king to ask them who they were and whence they came; the company gave their true names, and their leader said he was Fróech son of Idath. The steward related that to the king. 'Welcome!' said Ailill and Medb. 'A splendid warrior Fróech,' said Ailill. 'Let him enter the courtyard.'

A fourth of the house, then, was set aside for the company. This was the arrangement of the house: seven rows, and seven apartments round about the house from the fire to the wall. Each apartment had a façade of bronze, divided laterally by specially ornamented red yew, and there were three strips of bronze at the base of each apartment. Seven rods of copper ran from the house vat to the ceiling. The house was built of pine, with a shingled roof; there were sixteen windows in the house, with a copper shutter for each window, and there was a copper grating for the skylight. In the exact centre of the house was the apartment of Ailill and Medb. It had copper pillars and was ornamented everywhere with bronze; two borders of gilded silver went about it, while a silver moulding from the headboard rose to the crossbeams.

The company made a circuit of the house, from one entrance to the next; they hung up their weapons and sat down and were made comfortable. 'Welcome!' said Ailill and Medb. 'It is for that we have come,' said Fróech. 'Then your journey will not be for nothing,' said Medb. Ailill and Medb played fidchell after that, and Fróech began to play with one of his own people. Beautiful his fidchell set: the board was of white gold, and the edges and corners were of gold, while the pieces were of gold and silver, and a candle of precious stone provided light. 'Have food prepared for the youths,' said Ailill. 'I have no wish,' answered Medb, 'but to go and play fidchell with Fróech.' 'Do that, then; it is fine with me,' said Ailill. Medb and Fróech played fidchell after that.

Meanwhile, Fróech's people were roasting the game. 'Let the harpers play for us,' said Ailill to Fróech. 'Indeed, let them,' said Fróech. The harp bags were of otterskin and were decorated with Parthian leather ornamented with gold and silver. The kidskin about the harps was white as snow and had dark grey eyes in the middle; the coverings of linen about the strings were white as swans' down. The harps were of gold and silver and white gold, with the forms of snakes and birds and hounds in gold and silver on them; and as the strings moved, these forms would make circuits round the men.

The harpers played, then, and twelve men died of weeping and sorrow. The three harpers were fair and melodious, for they were the fair ones of Úaithne, three brothers, Goltrade and Gentrade and Súantrade, and Bóand of the Síde was their mother. They were named after the music that Úaithne, the Dagdae's harper, played. At first, the music was sad and mournful because of the sharpness of the pains; then it was

117

joyful and happy because of the two sons; finally, it was quiet and peaceful because of the heaviness of the birth of the last son, and he was named for the last third of the music. After that, Bóand woke from her sleep. 'Receive your three sons, O passionate Úaithne,' she said, 'for the music of sleep and laughter and sorrow will reach the cattle and women of Ailill and Medb that bring forth young. Men will die from hearing their music.'

The harpers ceased to play, then. 'It is a champion who has come,' said Fergus. 'Divide for us,' said Fróech, 'the food that has been brought into the house.' Lothur strode to the centre of the house and divided their food for them: he divided each piece in his palm with his sword, but neither skin nor flesh was ever touched. From the time that he became carver, no food in his hand was ever lost.

Medb and Fróech spent three days playing fidchell, by the light of the precious stones in Fróech's company. 'I have been good to you,' Fróech said to Medb, 'for I have not beaten you at fidchell, lest you be dishonoured.' 'The longest day I have ever spent in the fort this,' said Medb. 'Certainly,' said Fróech, 'for we have been here three days and three nights.'

With that Medb rose and went to Ailill, for she was ashamed that the youths had had no food. 'A great evil we have done,' she said, 'not to have fed the youths who have come from so far.' 'You preferred to play fidchell,' replied Ailill. 'That ought not to have prevented the distribution of food to his people in the house,' said Medb. 'We were here three days and three nights, but we did not perceive night because of the brilliance of the precious stones.' 'Tell them,' said Ailill, 'to leave off their amusements until their food is distributed.' The food was distributed, then, and everyone was good to them, and they stayed and feasted for three days and three nights.

After that, Fróech was summoned to the house of council,

and he was asked what had brought him. 'We would like to visit you,' he replied. 'Indeed, the household enjoys your company,' said Ailill. 'Better more of you than less.' 'We will stay about a week, then,' said Fróech. The company remained a fortnight in the fort; they hunted about the fort every day, and the Connachta would come to watch.

Fróech was distressed not to have spoken with Findabair since it was the need to do so that had brought him. One day, he rose at dawn to bathe in the river, and she and her serving maid came to bathe also. Fróech took her hand and said 'Stay and talk to me. It is for you we have come.' 'Welcome that, indeed,' said the girl, 'if it were possible. I can do nothing for you.' 'Will you come away with me?' asked Fróech. 'Indeed, I will not,' she replied, 'for I am the daughter of a king and queen. You are not so poor that you cannot get me from my people, and it will be my choice to go with you, for it is you I have loved. Take this thumb ring as a token; my father gave it to me, but I will say that I have lost it.' They parted after that.

'I fear,' Ailill said to Medb, 'that our daughter will run off with Fróech.' 'There would be profit in giving her to him,' replied Medb, 'for he would return with his cattle to help us on the raid.' Fróech found them in the house of council. 'Is it a secret?' he asked. 'There is room for you,' said Ailill. 'Will you give me your daughter?' Fróech asked. 'I will,' said Ailill, 'if you pay the stated bride price.' 'It will be paid,' said Fróech. 'Three score of dark grey horses,' said Ailill, 'with gold bridle bits, and twelve milch cows such that a drink of milk might be had from each, and a white calf with red ears for each cow, and your bringing your entire number and your musicians to help us take the cattle from Cúailnge.' 'I swear by my shield and my sword and my apparel, I would not give such a bride price for Medb herself,' said Fróech, and he strode out of the house.

After that, Ailill and Medb conversed. 'A multitude of the kings of Ériu will besiege us if he takes the girl,' said Ailill. 'It would be best to set upon him and kill him now, before he can bring about our destruction.' 'Pitiful that,' replied Medb, 'and we will be dishonoured.' 'We will not be dishonoured, for I will arrange it so,' said Ailill.

Ailill and Medb returned to the royal house. 'Let us go out,' he said, 'to see the hounds hunt, until noon comes and they grow tired.' Ailill and Medb went out to bathe in the river. 'I am told,' Ailill said to Fróech, 'that you are good in the water. Come into this pool, that we may see you swim.' 'What sort of pool is this?' Fróech asked. 'We know of nothing dangerous in it,' said Ailill, 'and it is our custom to bathe here.' Fróech took off his clothes, then, and went into the water, leaving his belt behind. Ailill opened Fróech's wallet, then, and the thumb ring was in it, and he recognized it. 'Come here, Medb!' he said; Medb came, and he said to her 'Do you recognize this?' 'I do,' she replied. Ailill threw the ring into the river; Fróech perceived this, and he saw a salmon leap for the ring and catch it in its mouth. Fróech leapt after the salmon and caught it by the gills; he made for land and hid the fish in a secret place on the river bank.

After that, Fróech made to leave the water. 'Do not come out,' said Ailill, 'until you have brought me a branch from yonder rowan on the river bank. I find its berries beautiful.' Fróech went back, then, and brought the branch through the water on his shoulders. Findabair said afterwards that, whatever beautiful thing she saw, she thought it more beautiful to look at Fróech across the dark water, his body very white, his hair very beautiful, his face very shapely, his eyes very blue, he a gentle youth without fault or blemish, his face narrow below and broad above, he straight without blemish, the branch with the red berries between his throat and his white face. Findabair used to say that she had never seen anything to match a half or a third of his beauty.

Fróech brought the branches from the water to them, then. 'These berries are choice and delicious. Bring us more.' Fróech went back into the water, and in the centre of the pool a monster seized him. 'A sword for me!' he cried, but not a man there dared give him one for fear of Ailill and Medb. Findabair, however, threw off her clothes and leapt into the water with a sword. Her father cast a five-pointed spear at her so that it went through her two tresses. Fróech caught the spear, the monster at his side, and sent it back in a kind of play of weaponry, so that it went through Ailill's scarlet mantle and through his shirt. The youths rose about Ailill then. Findabair came out of the water, but she left the sword in Fróech's hand, and he struck off the monster's head and brought it with him to land. Thus is named Dublind Froích in the river Brei in the land of the Connachta.

Ailill and Medb went back into the fort, then. 'A great evil have we done,' said Medb. 'We regret what we have done against the man,' said Ailill. 'The girl, however, will die tomorrow night, and not for the crime of taking the sword to him. Have a bath prepared for the man, a broth of fresh bacon and the flesh of a heifer chopped up with an adze and an axe and added into the bath.' All this was done.

Fróech's hornplayers preceded him into the court, then, and such was their playing that thirty of Ailill's dearest ones died of yearning. Fróech entered the fort, then, and went into the bath. A company of women rose about him to rub him and to wash his hair; after that, he was taken from the tub, and a bed was prepared for him to lie down. But the people heard weeping outside Crúachu, and they saw three fifties of women wearing scarlet mantles and bright green headdresses and silver animal bracelets on their wrists. Messengers were sent to find out why the women were weeping, and one woman said 'Fróech son of Idath is the favourite youth of the king of the Síde of Ériu.' At that, Fróech heard the weeping, and he said to his people 'Bear me outside. The weeping of my mother this, and of the women of Bóand.' Fróech was borne outside, then, and the women gathered about him and took him off into the síd of Crúachu. On the evening of the following day, the people saw him return, accompanied by fifty women and completely healed, without fault or blemish. Of equal age and form and beauty and fairness and comeliness and grace the women about him, so that there was no telling one from the other; and they had the look of the women of the Síde. Men all but suffocated about them. The women departed at the entrance to the courtyard, but in leaving they so poured forth their lament that the people in the courtyard were laid prostrate. Thus it is that the musicians of Ériu possess the weeping of the women of the Síde.

Fróech entered the fort after that; the hosts rose to meet him, and they welcomed him as if he had come from another world. Ailill and Medb rose also, and they expressed regret for what they had done to him, and peace was made. That night, a feast was held. Fróech called a lad of his people to him and said 'Go out to where I entered the pool. I left a salmon there; take it to Findabair and leave it with her, and have her cook it well. The thumb ring is inside the salmon, and I expect that it may be demanded of her tonight.'

After that, everyone grew intoxicated, and the singers and musicians entertained them. 'Bring all my treasures to me!' said Ailill, and these were brought before him. 'Wonderful! Wonderful!' said everyone. 'Call Findabair to me,' said Ailill; Findabair came, with fifty girls about her. 'Daughter,' said Ailill, 'the thumb ring I gave you last year, do you still have it? Give it to me that the warriors may see it – you will get it back.' 'I do not know what has happened to it,' said Findabair. 'Find out, then!' said Ailill. 'Otherwise, your soul must leave your body.' 'It is not worth that,' said the youths, 'not with all the treasures that are here already.' 'There is no treasure I would not give for the girl,' said Fróech, 'for she brought the sword that saved my life.' 'You have no treasure that can save her if she does not restore the thumb ring,' replied Ailill. 'I have no power to restore it,' said Findabair. 'Do with me as you like.' 'I swear by the god my people swear by, you will die unless you restore it,' said Ailill. 'That is why I demand it of you – I know you cannot produce it. That ring will not come from where it has been put until the dead come to life.' 'Then neither wealth nor wishing will restore it. But since your need is urgent, let me go that I may bring it,' said Findabair. Ailill replied 'You will not go – let one of your people go for it.' Findabair sent her maid to look for the ring, and she said to Ailill 'I swear by the god my people swear by, if the ring is found, I will not remain under your protection so long as there is someone else to undertake it.' 'If the ring is found,' said Ailill, 'I would not refuse you that even if you went to the stableboy.'

The maid brought a platter into the royal house, then, and the salmon was on it; Findabair had cooked it well, and the gold thumb ring lay upon it. Ailill and Medb looked at the ring; Fróech said 'Give it here that I may see it', and he looked into his wallet. 'I believe I was observed when I took off my belt,' he said to Ailill. 'By the truth of your sovereignty, tell us what you did with the ring.' 'That will not be concealed from you,' said Ailill. 'Mine the thumb ring that was in your wallet, and I knew that Findabair had given it to you. That is why I threw it into the dark water. By the truth of your honour and your soul, Fróech, tell how you managed to bring it out.' 'That will not be concealed from you,' said Fróech. 'I found the thumb ring at the entrance to the courtyard my first day here; I knew it was a fair treasure, and so I put it carefully into my wallet. The day I went into the water I perceived the girl who had lost it looking for it, and I said to her "What reward will you give me for finding it?" She said that she would give me her love for a year. It happened that I did not have the ring with me, for I had left it behind in the house. We did not meet again until she put the sword in my hand in the river. After that, I saw you open my wallet and throw the thumb ring into the water, and I saw the salmon that leapt to catch the ring in its mouth. I caught the salmon, then, I took it to shore, and I gave it to Findabair. That is the salmon on the platter before you.'

There was great praise and wonder in the house over that story. 'I will not set my mind on any young warrior in Ériu but this one,' said Findabair. 'Promise yourself to him, then,' said Ailill and Medb, and they said to Fróech 'Come with your cattle to drive the cattle from Cúailnge. The night you return from the east with your cattle is the night you will spend with Findabair.' 'I will do that,' said Fróech. He and his people remained there that night, and the following day they prepared to go, and Fróech bade farewell to Ailill and Medb.

The company set out for their own land, then; it had happened, meanwhile, that Fróech's cattle were stolen. His mother came to him, saying 'Not prosperous your expedition – great sorrow has come of it, for your cattle and your three sons and your wife have been stolen and taken to the Alps. Three cows are in northern Albu with the Cruithnig.' 'What will I do?' Fróech asked his mother. 'You will not go in search of them,' she said, 'for you are not to give up your life for them. You will have my cattle, moreover.' 'Not at all,' said Fróech. 'I swore on my honour and my soul to go to Ailill and Medb with my cattle to drive the cattle from Cúailnge.' 'Their finding is not to be had,' said his mother, and with that she left him.

Fróech set out, then, with thrice nine men and a falcon

and a hound on a leash, and when he reached the land of the Ulaid, he met Conall Cernach at Benda Bairchi. He told Conall his problem, and Conall replied 'Unhappy that which lies before you. Great trouble lies before you, though it is there your mind would be.' 'Help me, then,' said Fróech. 'Come with me until we find them.' 'I will, indeed,' said Conall.

They set out across the sea, across northern England and the Channel to northern Lombardy, until they reached the Alps; they saw before them there a small woman herding sheep. 'Let the two of us go, Fróech, to speak with the woman,' said Conall, 'and let the warriors remain here.' They went to speak with her, then, and she said 'Whence do you come?' 'From the men of Ériu,' said Conall. 'Unhappy any men of Ériu who come to this land, indeed,' she said. 'My mother was of the people of Ériu.' 'Then help me out of kinship,' said Fróech. 'Tell us about our adventuring here – what sort of land have we come to?' 'A grim, frightful country with truculent warriors,' she replied. 'They seek to carry off cattle and women and booty on every side.' 'What have they brought back most recently?' asked Fróech. 'The cattle of Fróech son of Idath from the west of Ériu, along with his wife and his three sons. His wife is with the king; his cattle are before you,' the woman said. 'Give us your help,' said Conall. 'I have no power but what I know,' she replied. 'This is Fróech here,' said Conall, 'and they are his cattle that were taken.' 'Do you trust your wife?' asked the woman. 'We trusted her before she came, but perhaps we do not trust her now,' they said. 'Go to the woman who tends the cows and tell her your need. She is of the race of Ériu, of the Ulaid, in fact,' said the woman.

Fróech and Conall went to her and stopped her and identified themselves, and she welcomed them, saying 'What has brought you here?' 'Trouble has brought us,' said Conall.

'Ours the cattle, and the woman who is in the house.' 'Unhappy you,' she said, 'to have to face the woman's host, and most difficult of all the serpent that guards the courtyard.' 'I will not go to my wife,' said Fróech, 'for I do not trust her. I trust you. We know that you will not betray us since you are of the Ulaid.' 'How are you of the Ulaid?' she asked. 'This is Conall Cernach, the best warrior in Ulaid,' Fróech said. The woman threw her arms round Conall's neck. 'Now the destruction will take place,' she said, 'for Conall has come, and the destruction of the fort by him was foretold. Let me go, now – I will not be milking the cows, but I will leave the door open, for it is I who close it, and I will say that the calves have sucked. Go into the fort, provided that they are asleep. Most difficult the serpent that guards the fort – many people have been left to it.' 'All the same, we will go,' said Conall.

They set upon the courtyard. The serpent leapt into Conall Cernach's belt. They destroyed the fort at once; they freed the woman and the three sons, and they carried off the best treasures of the fort. Conall let the serpent out of his belt, and neither did the other any harm.

After that, they came to the land of the Cruithnig and bore off three cows from the cattle there. They went west past Dún Ollaich maicc Bríuin across the sea to Ard Úa nEchach. It is there that Conall's servant, Bicne son of Lóegure, died while driving the cows, so that there is an Indber mBicne at Bendchor. They drove the cows across, and the cows threw their horns, so that the place is called Trácht mBendchoir.

Fróech returned to his own land, then, with his wife and his three sons and his cattle, and he went with Ailill and Medb to drive the cattle from Cúailnge.

126

The Labour Pains of the Ulaid
&
The Twins of Macha

Introduction

Although 'The Labour Pains of the Ulaid' purports to be history, it has been erected upon a foundation of myth. Macha, like Rhiannon in the Welsh 'Pwyll Lord of Dyved', is a euhemerized horse goddess, another insular version of the continental deity Epona, whose name means 'great horse'. Like Rhiannon, Macha appears seemingly out of nowhere; like Rhiannon, she selects a mortal husband and brings him great prosperity; like Rhiannon, she is associated with great equine speed. Rhiannon, however, is more thoroughly euhemerized, for she merely rides a horse that is faster (like those of the three Reds in 'The Destruction of Da Derga's Hostel') than any other; Macha actually runs faster than any horse.

On the narrative level, this story answers the question 'How did Emuin Machae get its name?' According to this version, the word *emuin* means 'twins', so that the name means 'The Twins of Macha'; according to another tradition, however, the word means 'brooch' and the name 'The Brooch of Macha', because Macha measures out the confines of Emuin Machae with her brooch.

The story also explains why it was necessary for Cú Chulaind to stand alone against the Connachta during the initial stages of 'The Cattle Raid of Cúailnge'. To the storyteller, of course, the inaction of Conchubur and the Ulaid merely afforded additional opportunities to elaborate on Cú Chulaind's heroism; but some explanation had to be offered. Perhaps the idea of a general weakness originated in some kind of couvade ceremony.

Although 'The Labour Pains of the Ulaid' is grouped with the tales of the Ulster Cycle, the name Crunniuc does not appear elsewhere; and the king and his people are not named at all. It may be that the story's association with the Ulster Cycle is not early – in any case, it has not been well integrated.

The Labour Pains of the Ulaid
&
The Twins of Macha

Crunniuc son of Agnoman of the Ulaid was a hospitaller with many lands. He lived in the wildernesses and the mountains, and his sons lived with him; his wife was dead. One day, when he was alone in his house, he saw a woman coming towards him, and she seemed beautiful to him. She settled in at once and went to her tasks, just as if she had always been there, and, when evening came, she set the household in order without being asked. That night, she slept with Crunniuc. She was with him a long time after that, and there was no prosperity that she did not bring him, no want of food or clothing or wealth.

Not long afterwards, the Ulaid held a fair, and they all went, men and women, sons and daughters. Crunniuc set out as well, with good clothes on him and a great bloom in his face. 'Take care to say nothing foolish,' she said to him. 'Not likely that,' he replied. The fair was held, and at the end of the day the king's chariot was brought on to the field, and his chariot and horses were victorious. The hosts said 'Nothing is as fast as those horses are'; Crunniuc said 'My wife is that fast.' He was taken to the king at once, and the news was taken to his wife. 'A great misfortune my having to go and free him now, when I am with child,' she said. 'Misfortune or no,' said the messenger, 'he will die if you do not come.'

She went to the fair, then, and her labour pains seized her. 'Help me,' she said to the hosts, 'for a mother bore every one of you. Wait until my children are born.' She failed to move them, however. 'Well then,' she continued, 'the evil you suffer will be greater, and it will afflict Ulaid for a long time.' 'What is your name?' asked the king. 'My name and that of my children will mark this fairground for ever – I am Macha daughter of Sainrith son of Imbath,' she said. She raced against the chariot, then, and, as the chariot reached the end of the field, she gave birth in front of it, and she bore a son and a daughter. That is why the place is called Emuin Machae. At her delivery, she screamed that any man who heard her would suffer the pains of birth for five days and four nights. All the Ulaid who were there were so afflicted, and their descendants suffered for nine generations afterwards. Five days and four nights, or five nights and four days – that was the extent of the labour pains of the Ulaid; and, for nine generations, the Ulaid were as weak as a woman in labour. Three classes of people, however, did not suffer this affliction: the women and the children of Cú Chulaind. This was the inheritance of Ulaid from the time of Crunniuc son of Agnoman son of Curir Ulad son of Fíatach son of Urmi until the time of Furcc son of Dallán son of Manech son of Lugaid.

The Birth of Cú Chulaind

Introduction

'The Birth of Cú Chulaind' exists in two quite different versions, one going back, in written form, to the (now lost) Book of Druimm Snechtai, the other being somewhat later; it is the earlier version that is presented here. Cú Chulaind, like Conare Már, has two fathers, but the story of his birth is clearly corrupt. In the original version, Lug must have come to Deichtine (perhaps as a bird) in the strange house and slept with her and left her pregnant; in this version, Deichtine's visit to the Bruig accomplishes nothing, and there is no connection between Lug and the tiny creature in the copper vessel.

Lug himself was one of the most important Irish deities. His continental counterpart, who was probably named Lugos, is identified by Caesar as the Celtic Mercury and the most important of the Celtic gods, and he gave his name to a number of European towns, including Lyon, Leiden and Liegnitz (Legnica). In Irish literature, Lug is the most prominent of the Túatha Dé Danand in 'The Second Battle of Mag Tured'; while it is thus appropriate that Cú Chulaind, the greatest Irish hero, should be his son, the tradition that makes him so may not be very old. The last section of the story represents a not very refined attempt to explain why Cú Chulaind was known as the son of Súaltaim when his real father was Lug.

Like the birth of the Welsh hero Pryderi, the birth of Cú Chulaind is contemporaneous with the birth of a horse; and each hero subsequently receives the animal as a gift. Cú Chulaind's birth, however, is marked by other portents: the appearance and guidance of the flock of birds, which clearly is from the otherworld, and the great snowfall. The event takes place, oddly, at Bruig na Bóinde (New Grange), a site associated with the mythological tales and not with those about the Ulaid, but it may have been chosen to underline the assertion that he is of divine origin. That Cú Chulaind is the son of Conchubur's sister suggests a system of matrilinear descent in Ireland.

Cú Chulaind is also like Pryderi in that the name by which he is best known is not the one he is given at birth. His original name, Sétantae, means 'one who has knowledge of roads and ways' and would have been suitable for a divinity whose influence was widespread.

The Birth of Cú Chulaind

One time, when Conchubur and the chieftains of Ulaid were at Emuin Machae, a flock of birds frequented the plain outside Emuin, and it grazed there until not so much as a root or a stalk or a blade of grass remained. The Ulaid were distressed to see the land so devastated, and thus, one day, they harnessed nine chariots and set out to drive the birds away, for it was their custom to hunt birds. Conchubur sat in his chariot together with his grown daughter Deichtine, for she was his charioteer; and the other champions of the

Ulaid sat in their chariots, Conall and Lóegure and everyone else, even Bricriu. Before them the birds flew, over Slíab Fúait, over Edmund, over Brega, and the Ulaid were enchanted by the birds' flight and by their singing. There were nine score birds in all, each score flying separately, and each pair of birds was linked by a silver chain.

Towards evening three birds broke away and made for Bruig na Bóinde. Then night came upon the Ulaid, and a great snow fell, so Conchubur told his people to unyoke their chariots, and he sent a party to seek shelter. Conall and Bricriu searched the area and found a single house, new; they went inside and were welcomed by the couple there, and then they returned to their people. Bricriu complained that it would not be worthwhile to go to a house that had neither food nor clothing and was narrow into the bargain. All the same, the Ulaid went; they took their chariots with them, but they did not take much inside. Suddenly, they discovered a storehouse door before them. Then it came time to eat, and the Ulaid grew merry with drink, and their disposition was good. The man of the house told them that his wife was in labour in the storehouse, so Deichtine went back to help, and soon a son was born. At the same time, a mare that was at the entrance to the house gave birth to two foals. The Ulaid gave the colts to the boy as a gift, and Deichtine nursed him.

When morning came, the Ulaid found themselves east of the Bruig — no house, no birds, only their horses and the boy with his colts. They returned to Emuin Machae, and the boy was nursed until he was a young lad, but then he fell ill and died. Tears were shed, and Deichtine was greatly saddened by the death of her foster-son. Finally, when she had left off sighing, she felt thirsty and requested drink from a copper vessel, and that was brought. Every time she put the vessel to her mouth, a tiny creature would leap from the liquid towards her lips; yet, when she took the vessel from her mouth, there was nothing to be seen. That night, she had a dream: a man spoke to her and said that he had brought her towards the Bruig, that it was his house she had entered, that she was pregnant by him and that it was a son that would be born. The man's name was Lug son of Eithliu; the boy's name was to be Sétantae, and it was for him that the colts were to be reared.

Thereafter, Deichtine indeed became pregnant. The Ulaid were troubled since they did not know the father, and they surmised that Conchubur had fathered the child while drunk, for Deichtine used to sleep next to him. Conchubur then betrothed his daughter to Súaltaim son of Roech. Deichtine was greatly embarrassed at having to go to Súaltaim's bed while being pregnant, so, when the time came, she lay down in the bed and crushed the child within her. Then she went to Súaltaim, and at once she became pregnant by him and bore him a son.

The Boyhood Deeds of Cú Chulaind

Introduction

'The Boyhood Deeds of Cú Chulaind' is not an independent
tale but rather a series of extracts from 'The Cattle Raid of
Cúailnge' (here presented in the earlier, less refined Lebor
na huidre version). Fergus and a number of other Ulaid
chieftains have transferred their allegiance to Connachta in
protest at Conchubur's treacherous slaying of the sons of
Uisliu; and now, with the Connachta about to attack Ulaid,
the exiles are describing to Ailill and Medb the boyhood
feats of the great hero of the north.

The first exploit recalls the opening episode of the Welsh
tale 'Peredur': a naive, callow youth leaves his unwilling
mother (he does not have a father, possibly because his real
father is understood to be either royal or divine) and goes
forth to find his proper companions (the boy troop of Emuin
Machae in the one case, the knights of King Arthur's court in
the other). Cú Chulaind's feats with his ball and hurley and
toy javelin and his complete dominance over the boy troop
are superhuman and at the same time pure play; Peredur,
though merely precocious, is yet more mature, for, as well as
outrunning deer, he dispatches enemy knights and even
kisses women.

The second extract explains how Cú Chulaind once saved
Conchubur in battle. Even at this early stage of the Ulster
Cycle, Conchubur's role has deteriorated; and already Cú
Chulaind, as his sister's son, appears as his natural heir.

The third extract explains how Sétantae came to be known as Cú Chulaind. Such stories are common in Irish saga, but this explanation is unusually convincing – why else would a young hero be called the 'Hound of Culand'? The mystery is rather in why the central character of the Ulster Cycle, a figure whose divine origin is manifest, should have been given a name so much more appropriate to a mortal hero, especially when his original name suits him so well. In the case of both Pryderi and Cú Chulaind, there are objections to the new name: Rhiannon asks whether her son's own name does not suit him better, while Cú Chulaind himself expresses a preference for his original name; but, in each case, the advice of a wise elder (the Chieftain of Dyved in the Welsh tale, Cathub in the Irish one) prevails.

The fourth extract seems modelled on the tradition that Achilles chose a short life in order to win great fame. The episode at the end, where Cú Chulaind is seized by his ríastarthae, or battle fury, and has to be cooled off in vats of water, is entirely typical of him, as is his shyness in the presence of bare-breasted women.

The antiquity of these extracts is open to doubt: the mythic element is slight, and there is considerable humour.

The Boyhood Deeds of Cú Chulaind

'In truth, he was reared by his mother and his father at Airgdech in Mag Muirthemni,' said Fergus. 'There he was told of the fame of the boys at Emuin Machae, for three fifties of boys play there. Conchubur enjoys his sovereignty thus:

one third of the day watching the boys play, one third playing fidchell and one third drinking until he falls asleep. Although we are in exile because of him, there is not in Ériu a greater warrior.

'Cú Chulaind entreated his mother, then, to let him go to the boys. "You are not to go," she replied, "until one of the champions of Ulaid can accompany you." "Too long to wait, that," Cú Chulaind answered. "Just tell me in which direction Emuin lies." "To the north, there, and the path is dangerous," said his mother. "Slíab Fúait lies between you and Emuin." "Even so, I will try it," said Cú Chulaind. He went forth, then, with his toy javelin and his toy shield and his hurley and his ball. He would throw his javelin on ahead and then catch it before it could strike the ground.

'When he reached Emuin, he went to the boys without first securing their protection – at that time, no one went to the playing field without a guarantee that the boys would protect him. Cú Chulaind was unaware of this. "The boy outrages us," said Follomon son of Conchubur, "and yet we know he is of the Ulaid." The boys warned Cú Chulaind off, but he defeated them. They threw their three fifties of javelins at him, but he stopped every one with his toy shield. They threw their three fifties of balls at him, but he caught them all against his chest. They threw their three fifties of hurleys at him, but he warded them off and took an armful on his back.

'Then his ríastarthae came upon him.[1] You would have thought that every hair was being driven into his head. You would have thought that a spark of fire was on every hair. He closed one eye until it was no wider than the eye of a needle; he opened the other until it was as big as a wooden bowl. He bared his teeth from jaw to ear, and he opened his mouth until the gullet was visible. The warrior's moon rose from his head.

'Cú Chulaind struck at the boys and overthrew fifty of
them before they could reach the doors of Emuin. Nine of
them ran over Conchubur and myself as we were playing
fidchell; Cú Chulaind sprang over the board after them, but
Conchubur took his arm and said "Not good your treatment
of the boy troop." "Fair play it is," answered Cú Chulaind.
"I came from my mother and my father to play with them,
and they were not nice to me." "What is your name?" asked
Conchubur. "Sétantae, the son of Súaltaim and of Deichtine,
your sister. I did not expect such a reception here." "Why
did you not secure the boys' protection?" asked Conchubur.
"I did not know that was necessary," replied Cú Chulaind.
"Accept my protection now, then," said Conchubur. "That I
will," answered Cú Chulaind.

'That same day Cú Chulaind turned upon the boys in the
house. "What is wrong with you now?" asked Conchubur. "I
wish that their protection be given over to me," Cú Chulaind answered. "Undertake to protect them, then," said
Conchubur. "That I will," replied Cú Chulaind.

'They returned to the playing field, then, and those boys
who had been struck down arose, and their foster-mothers
and foster-fathers helped them.'

*

'Another time, there was a falling out between the Ulaid
and Éogan son of Durthacht. The Ulaid went into battle
while Cú Chulaind was still asleep; they were defeated, but
Conchubur and Cúscraid Mend Machae and a great multitude survived, and their wailing woke him. He stretched so
that the two stones on either side of him broke – this in the
presence of Bricriu yonder – and then he arose. I met him
at the courtyard entrance, I being wounded. "Alas! God preserve your life, popa Fergus," he said. "Where is Conchubur?" "I do not know," I answered.

137

'He set off, then, into the dark night. He made for the battlefield, and there he found a man with half a head, and half of another man on his back. "Help me, Cú Chulaind," the man said, "for I have been wounded, and I have half my brother on my back. Carry him a while with me." "That I will not," replied Cú Chulaind. The man put his burden on Cú Chulaind's back; Cú Chulaind threw it off. They wrestled, and Cú Chulaind was thrown. He heard the Badb from among the corpses: "A bad warrior he who lies at the feet of a spectre." Cú Chulaind rose to attack the man, then; he struck his head off with his hurley and drove it before him across the plain.

' "Is popa Conchubur in this battlefield?" Cú Chulaind asked, and his question was answered. He went on until he found Conchubur in a ditch, with dirt piled up about him on every side. "Why did you come to the battlefield and the mortal terror that is here?" asked Conchubur. Cú Chulaind raised Conchubur up out of the ditch — six Ulaid champions could not have raised him more bravely. "Bear me to that house yonder," Conchubur said, "and light me a great fire there." Cú Chulaind lit the fire. "Good that," said Conchubur. "Now if I were to get a roasted pig to eat, I would live." Cú Chulaind went out and found a man over a cooking spit in the middle of the forest, one hand holding his weapons, the other cooking a boar. The man was terrifying; even so, Cú Chulaind attacked and took the man's head and the boar. Conchubur ate the pig, after which he said "Let us go to our own house." On the way they met Cúscraid son of Conchubur; he was badly wounded, so Cú Chulaind carried him on his back, and the three returned to Emuin Machae.'

*

'We knew that boy, indeed,' said Conall Cernach, 'and we were none the worse for knowing him. He was our foster-

ling. Not long after the deeds Fergus has just related he
performed another feat.

'When Culand the smith offered Conchubur his hospitality,
he said that a large host should not come, for the feast
would be the fruit not of lands and possessions but of his
tongs and his two hands. Conchubur went with fifty of his
oldest and most illustrious heroes in their chariots. First,
however, he visited the playing field, for it was his custom
when leaving or returning to seek the boys' blessing; and he
saw Cú Chulaind driving the ball past the three fifties of
boys and defeating them. When they drove at the hole, Cú
Chulaind filled the hole with his balls, and the boys could
not stop them; when the boys drove at the hole, he defended
it alone, and not a single ball went in. When they wrestled,
he overthrew the three fifties of boys by himself, but all of
them together could not overthrow him. When they played
at mutual stripping, he stripped them all so that they were
stark naked, while they could not take so much as the
brooch from his mantle.

"Conchubur thought all this wonderful. He asked if the
boy's deeds would be similarly distinguished when he became a man, and everyone said that they would be. He said
to Cú Chulaind, then, "Come with me to the feast, and you
will be a guest." "I have not had my fill of play yet," replied
the boy. "I will come after you."

'When everyone had arrived at the feast, Culand said to
Conchubur "Do you expect anyone else?" "I do not,"
answered Conchubur, forgetting that his fosterling was yet
to come. "I have a watchdog," said Culand, "with three
chains on him and three men on every chain. I will loose him
now to guard our cattle and our herds, and I will close the
courtyard."

'By that time, the boy was on his way to the feast, and
when the hound attacked him he was still at play. He would

throw his ball up and his hurley after it, so that the hurley struck the ball and so that each stroke was the same; he would also throw his javelin on ahead and catch it before it could strike the ground. The hound's attack did not distract the boy from his play; Conchubur and his people, however, were so confounded they could not move. They could not believe that, when the courtyard doors were opened, they would find the boy alive. But, when the hound attacked him, the boy threw away his ball and hurley and went at it with his bare hands: he put one hand on the hound's throat and the other on its back and struck it against a pillar until every limb fell apart.

'The Ulaid rose to rescue him, some to the courtyard and some to the door of the courtyard, and they took him in to Conchubur. Everyone was greatly alarmed that the son of the king's sister had nearly been killed. But Culand entered the house and said "Welcome, lad, for the sake of your mother's heart. As for myself, however, this was an evil feast. My life is lost, and my household are out on the plain, without our hound. It secured life and honour; it protected our goods and cattle and every creature between field and house. It was the man of the family." "No great matter that," replied the boy. "I will rear for you a whelp from the same litter, and, until it is grown and capable of action, I will be the hound that protects your cattle and yourself. I will protect all Mag Muirthemni, and neither herd nor flock will be taken without my knowledge." "Cú Chulaind will be your name henceforth," said Cathub. "I prefer my own name," said Cú Chulaind.

'The boy who did that when he was six would not surprise by doing heroic deeds when he was seventeen,' said Conall Cernach.

'There were other deeds as well,' said Fíachu son of Fer Febe. 'Cathub the druid was with his son, Conchubur son of Ness, and he was teaching one hundred men the druid's art, for that is the number he used to instruct. One pupil asked him what that day would be good for, and he said that a warrior who took arms that day would be famous among the men of Ériu and that stories of him would be told forever.

'When Cú Chulaind heard that, he went to Conchubur to ask for arms. "Who instructed you?" Conchubur asked. "My tutor, Cathub," Cú Chulaind replied. "Indeed, we know him," said Conchubur. He gave Cú Chulaind a spear and shield, but Cú Chulaind shook them in the centre of the house until none of the fifteen spare sets of weapons in Conchubur's household escaped being broken or taken away. He was given Conchubur's own weapons, then; these endured him, and he shook them and saluted Conchubur and said "Happy the race and the people whose king has such weapons."

'Cathub went to Conchubur, then, and said "Is the boy taking arms?" "He is," answered Conchubur. "Ill luck, then, for his mother's son," said Cathub, but Conchubur replied "Why? Did you not instruct him to take arms?" "Indeed, I did not," answered Cathub. Then Conchubur said to Cú Chulaind "Why did you lie to me, sprite?" "No lie, king of the Féni.[2] He was instructing his students this morning, and I heard him to the south of Emuin, and thus I came to you," answered Cú Chulaind. "A good day, then," said Cathub, "for he who takes arms today will be great and famous – and short-lived." "Wonderful news that," answered Cú Chulaind, "for, if I am famous, I will be happy even to live just one day."

'The next morning, another pupil asked the druids what that day would be good for. "Anyone who steps into a

chariot today," Cathub replied, "will be known to the Ériu
for ever." When Cú Chulaind heard that, he went to Conchubur and said "Popa Conchubur, a chariot for me!" Conchubur gave him a chariot, but when Cú Chulaind put his
hand between the two chariot poles, it broke. He broke
twelve chariots that way, so Conchubur's own chariot was
brought for him, and that endured.

'Cú Chulaind went off in the chariot, taking Conchubur's
charioteer along with him. The charioteer – Ibor was his
name – turned the chariot about, saying "Come out of the
chariot, now." But Cú Chulaind replied "The horses are
beautiful, and I am beautiful, lad. Take a turn round Emuin
with us, and I will reward you." After that, Cú Chulaind
made Ibor take him to say goodbye to the boys, "so that
the boys might bless me." He then entreated the charioteer
to return to the road, and when they arrived he said "Put
the whip to the horses, now." "In what direction?" asked
Ibor. "As far as the road leads," Cú Chulaind answered.

'They went on to Slíab Fúait, where they met Conall
Cernach. That day it was Conall's turn to protect the
province – every Ulaid warrior of worth took a turn at Slíab
Fúait, protecting those who came with poems, fighting
enemies and seeing that no one came to Emuin unannounced.
"May you prosper," said Conall, "and may you be victorious and triumphant." "Return to the fort, Conall, and
leave me here to watch in your place," said Cú Chulaind.
"Well enough that," said Conall, "for protecting those with
poetry, but you are not yet able to fight." "Perhaps it will
not come to that," said Cú Chulaind. "In any case, let us go
to look at the sandbar at Loch nEchtrae, for it is customary
for young warriors to rest there." "Very well," replied
Conall.

'They started out, but Cú Chulaind cast a stone from his
sling and broke Conall's chariot pole. "Why did you cast

142

that stone, little boy?" asked Conall. "To test my hand and the straightness of my cast," answered Cú Chulaind. "It is an Ulaid custom not to drive through danger – therefore return to Emuin, popa Conall, and leave me here to watch." "All right, then," said Conall, and he did not drive across the plain after that.

'Cú Chulaind drove off to Loch nEchtrae, then, but he found no one there. Ibor told him they should return to Emuin and drink, but Cú Chulaind replied "By no means. What mountain is that yonder?" "Slíab Monduirn," Ibor told him. "Let us travel until we reach it," Cú Chulaind said. They drove to Slíab Monduirn, and when they arrived Cú Chulaind asked "What is that white cairn yonder on the upper part of the mountain?" "Findcharn." "What is the plain yonder?" "Mag mBreg." Ibor then told him the name of every major fort between Temuir and Cenandas; moreover, he identified the meadows and fords, the dwellings and illustrious places, the forts and the great heights. He pointed out the fort of the three sons of Nechta Scéne: Foill and Fannall and Túachell. "Is it they who say that there are not more of the Ulaid alive than they have slain?" asked Cú Chulaind. "It is they," replied Ibor. "Let us go on, then, until we meet them," said Cú Chulaind. "Dangerous that, indeed," said the charioteer. "Not to avoid danger have we come," said Cú Chulaind.

'They went on, then, and unyoked the horses at Cómbor Manae and Abae to the south and above the fort. Cú Chulaind took the spancel that was round the pillar and threw it into the river and let the water carry it, for such an action was a breach of geiss to the sons of Nechta Scéne. The sons perceived what he had done and started out to meet him, but Cú Chulaind went to sleep against the pillar, first saying to Ibor "Do not wake me just for a few but only for a large crowd." Ibor was very frightened; he yoked the chariot and tugged at its skins and coverings, which Cú Chulaind was sleeping on, but he dared not wake the boy since Cú Chulaind had said he was to wake him only for a great crowd.

'The sons of Nechta Scéne arrived, then, and one of them asked "What is this?" "A little boy making an expedition in his chariot," replied Ibor. "Neither prosperous nor auspicious this first taking of arms," said the warrior. "Let him leave this land, and let his horses not graze here any more." "I have the reins in my hand," said Ibor. "You have no reason to incur the enmity of the Ulaid – besides, the boy is asleep." "Indeed, he is not a boy at all," said Cú Chulaind, "but a lad who has come in search of combat." "My pleasure," said Foill. "Let it be your pleasure, then, in the ford yonder," said Cú Chulaind.

' "You must take note of the man who comes to meet you," Ibor told Cú Chulaind. "Foill is his name, and if you do not reach him with the first thrust, you will not reach him at all." Cú Chulaind answered "I swear by the god my people swear by, he will not play that trick upon the Ulaid after my father Conchubur's broad-pointed spear has reached him. An enemy hand mine." Cú Chulaind cast his spear at Foill and broke his back and took his head and his weapons.

' "Take heed of the next man, now," said Ibor. "Fannall his name, and he treads upon the water as lightly as would a swan or a swallow." "I swear by the god my people swear by, he will not play that trick upon the Ulaid again. Indeed, you have seen how I tread the pool at Emuin." They met at the ford; Cú Chulaind slew Fannall and took his head and his weapons.

' "Take heed now of the last man," said Ibor. "Túachell his name, and no mistake, for arms will not fell him." "Here, then, the del chliss to confound him and make a sieve of him."[8] Cú Chulaind cast his spear at Túachell, and the latter's limbs collapsed; he went and struck Túachell's head

144

off and gave the head and the spoils to Ibor. They heard the wailing of the sons' mother, Nechta Scéne, behind them, but Cú Chulaind took the spoils and the three heads with him into the chariot, saying "I will not abandon my triumph until I reach Emuin Machae."

'They set off with their victory, and Cú Chulaind said to Ibor "You promised me a good drive, and we need that now because of the pursuit behind us." They drove on to Slíab Fúait, and, with Ibor whipping, they went so fast that the horses overtook the wind and birds in flight, so fast that Cú Chulaind was able to catch a cast from his sling before it could strike the ground. When they reached Slíab Fúait, they found a herd of deer before them. "What beasts are these that are so nimble?" asked Cú Chulaind. "Deer," replied the charioteer. "Would the Ulaid think it better to bring them back dead or alive?" asked Cú Chulaind. "Alive, for not everyone could do that, but all can bring them back dead. But you are not capable of bringing any back alive," said the charioteer. "Indeed, I am," replied Cú Chulaind. "Whip the horses and drive them into the bog." Ibor did that; the horses stuck fast in the bog, and Cú Chulaind leapt out and seized the nearest, finest deer. He lashed the horses out of the bog, then, and tamed the deer immediately and bound it between the chariot poles.

'After that, they saw a flock of swans before them. "Would the Ulaid think it better to bring these back dead or alive?" asked Cú Chulaind. "The bravest and most accomplished warriors bring them back alive," answered the charioteer. Cú Chulaind aimed a small stone at the birds and brought down eight of them; he took a large stone, then, and brought down twelve more, with a stunning blow. "Collect the birds, now," he said to the charioteer, "for if I go myself, the deer will spring upon you." "Indeed, it will not be easy for me to go," replied Ibor, "for the horses have become so wild I cannot go past them. I cannot go past the two iron wheels of the chariot because of their sharpness, and I cannot go past the deer because its horns have filled the space between the chariot poles." "Step out on its antlers, then," said Cú Chulaind, "for I swear by the god the Ulaid swear by, I will turn my head and fix the deer with my eye so that it will not turn its head to you or dare to move." They did that: Cú Chulaind held the reins fast, and Ibor collected the birds. Cú Chulaind then bound the birds with strings and cords from the chariot, so that as they drove to Emuin Machae the deer was behind the chariot, the three heads were in the chariot and the swans were flying overhead.

'When they arrived at Emuin, the watchman said "A man in a chariot is approaching, and he will shed the blood of every person here unless naked women are sent to meet him." Cú Chulaind turned the left side of his chariot towards Emuin, and that was a geiss to the fort; he said "I swear by the god the Ulaid swear by, unless a man is found to fight me, I will shed the blood of everyone in the fort." "Naked women to meet him!" shouted Conchubur. The women of Emuin went to meet Cú Chulaind gathered round Mugain, Conchubur's wife, and they bared their breasts before him. "These are the warriors who will meet you today!" said Mugain. Cú Chulaind hid his face, whereupon the warriors of Ulaid seized him and thrust him into a vat of cold water. This vat burst, but the second vat into which he was thrust boiled up with fist-sized bubbles, and the third vat he merely heated to a moderate warmth. When he left the third vat, the queen, Mugain, placed about him a blue mantle with a silver brooch and a hooded tunic. He sat at Conchubur's knee, then, and that was his bed ever after. The man who did this in his seventh year,' said Fíachu son of Fer Febe, 'no wonder should he prevail against odds or demolish an equal opponent now that he is seventeen.'

The Death of Aífe's Only Son

Introduction

'The Death of Aífe's Only Son' is an Irish Sohrab and
Rustum story, more international than Irish in feeling and
probably not very old. It is the title that is distinctively
Irish; one would expect 'The Death of Cú Chulaind's Only
Son', but this title may reflect an older, matrilinear system
of descent – just as the son of Deichtine is Conchubur's heir,
so the son of Aífe might be Cú Chulaind's. The home of Scáthach and Aífe, not given here, is presumably in the north of
Britain.

That Cú Chulaind has a son at all further suggests that
the tale is late, for he is only a boy when he goes away to
learn weaponry from the warrior-woman Scáthach, and at
the time of the cattle raid of Cúailnge he appears to be only
seventeen. Condlae, moreover, is simply a regenerated
version of his father: he demonstrates the same arrogance,
performs the same feats and is fully a match for Cú Chulaind in combat save for mastery of the gáe bolga, a kind of
spear thrust. The reference to Rome and the un-Celtic lack
of emotional restraint at the end of the tale also point to a
late formulation. Even the rhetorical sections – where Condere calls Condlae 'the stuff of blood' and warns him against
turning his 'jaws and spears' (turning the left side of one's
chariot towards an enemy signalled hostile intent), or where

147

Cú Chulaind describes Condlae's gore upon his skin as a 'mist of blood' and predicts that his spears will 'suck the fair javelin' – do not seem very old, though in some phrases they are quite corrupt.

'The Death of Aífe's Only Son' is the source, at some distance, for Yeats's play *On Baile's Strand*.

The Death of Aífe's Only Son

Cú Chulaind went to study weaponry with Scáthach nŪanaind daughter of Airdgeme so that he might master feats. Aífe daughter of Airdgeme went to him there, and when she left she was pregnant, and he told her that she would bear a son. 'You are to keep this golden thumb ring,' he said, 'until the boy can wear it. When that time comes, let him follow me to Ériu. Let him turn aside for no one, and let him identify himself to no one, and let him refuse to fight no one.'

After seven years the boy went to seek his father. The Ulaid were assembled at Trácht Éise, and they saw the boy out on the sea, in a bronze ship, with golden oars in his hands. He had a heap of stones in the boat, and he placed these in his slingshot and dealt stunning blows to the birds overhead, so that the creatures were knocked unconscious; afterwards he revived them and sent them back into the air. He performed the jaw feat with his hands until his upper jaw reached his eye. After that, he modulated his voice until he had laid the birds low a second time, and he revived them a second time as well.

'Woe, indeed,' said Conchubur, 'to the land to which yonder lad comes. If the great men from his island were to arrive, they would pound us to dust, inasmuch as a mere boy performs such feats. Let someone go to meet him, and let him not enter this country.' 'Who should go to meet him?' 'Who but Condere son of Echu,' answered Conchubur. 'Why should Condere go?' asked everyone. 'Not difficult that,' replied Conchubur, 'Whatever good sense and eloquence may be required, Condere will possess it.' 'I will go to meet him,' said Condere. Condere went, then, and he met the boy as the latter came ashore. 'Far enough that, little boy, until you tell us where you come from and who your family is.' 'I will not identify myself to any man,' said the boy, 'and I will not turn aside for any man.' 'You will not enter this country until you have identified yourself,' said Condere. 'I will continue the journey on which I have come,' said the boy.

The boy turned away, then, but Condere said 'Turn to me, my boy. You are capable of great deeds. You are the stuff of blood. The pride of the warriors of Ulaid is in you. Conchubur welcomes you. Your jaws and spears away from the left side of your chariot, lest the warriors of Ulaid rise against you. Conchubur invites you to come to us. An ear for you if you turn towards me. Come to Conchubur, the impetuous son of Ness; to Senchae, the victorious son of Ailill; to Cethernd of the red sword edge, the son of Findtan, with a fire that wounds battalions; to Amorgen the poet; to Cúscraid of the great hosts. I welcome you; Conall Cernach invites you to stories, songs and the laughter of war heroes. Blaí Briugu would be greatly distressed if you journeyed on past him, he being a hero; moreover, to shame so many is not right. I, Condere, arose to meet the boy who detains champions. I vowed that I would meet this boy, though he has neither beard nor manly hair, provided he is not disobedient to the Ulaid.'

'Good your coming,' said the boy, 'for now you will have your conversation. I have modulated my voice. I have left off casting unerringly from chariots. I have collected a beautiful flight of birds by shooting far-flying little spears at them, and moreover without the hero's salmon leap. I have vowed great feats of arms lest anyone lay siege against me. Go and ask the Ulaid whether they wish to come against me singly or in a host. Turn back, now, for, even if you had the strength of a hundred, you would not be worthy to detain me.'

'Let someone else come to talk to you, then,' said Condere. He returned to the Ulaid and repeated the conversation, and Conall Cernach said 'The Ulaid will not be shamed while I am alive.' He went to meet the boy, saying 'Delightful your games, little boy.' 'They will not be any the less so for you,' answered the boy. He placed a stone in his slingshot and delivered a stunning blow; the thunder and shock of it knocked Conall head over heels, and before he could rise, the boy had taken the strap from his shield. Conall returned to the Ulaid and said 'Someone else to meet him!'; but the rest of the host only smiled.

Cú Chulaind, however, was approaching the boy, playing, with the arm of Emer daughter of Forgall round his neck. 'Do not go down there!' she said. 'It is your son who is there. Do not slaughter your son, O impetuous, well-bred lad. Neither fair nor right it is to rise against your son of great and valorous deeds. Turn away from the skin-torment of the sapling of your tree; remember Scáthach's warning. If Condlae sustained the left board, there would be a fierce combat. Turn to me! Listen! My advice is good! Let it be Cú Chulaind who listens. I know what name he bears, if that is Condlae the only son of Aífe who is below.' But Cú Chulaind answered 'Silence, woman! It is not a woman's advice I seek regarding deeds of bright splendour. Such deeds are not performed with a woman's assistance. Let us be triumphant in feats. Sated the eyes of a great king. A mist of blood upon my skin the gore from the body of Condlae. Beautifully spears will suck the fair javelin. Whatever were down there, woman, I would go for the sake of the Ulaid.'

Cú Chulaind went down to the shore, then. 'Delightful your games, little boy,' he said, but Condlae answered 'Not delightful the game you play, for no two of you will come unless I identify myself.' 'Must I have a little boy in my presence? You will die unless you identify yourself.' 'Prove that,' said the boy. He rose towards Cú Chulaind, then, and the two of them struck at each other; the boy performed the hair-cutting feat with his sword and left Cú Chulaind bald. 'The mockery is at an end. Let us wrestle,' Cú Chulaind said. 'I would not reach your belt,' answered the boy. But he stood upon two pillars and threw Cú Chulaind down between the pillars three times; he moved neither of his feet, so that they went into the stone up to his ankles.

They went to wrestle in the water, then, and the boy ducked Cú Chulaind twice. After that, Cú Chulaind rose out of the water and deceived the boy with the gáe bolga, for Scáthach had never taught that weapon to anyone but Cú Chulaind.[1] He cast it at the boy through the water, and the boy's innards fell at his feet.

'That,' said the boy, 'is what Scáthach did not teach me. Alas that you have wounded me!' 'True that,' said Cú Chulaind, and he took the boy in his arms and carried him up from the shore and showed him to the Ulaid, saying 'Here is my son.' 'Alas, indeed,' they said. 'True enough,' said the boy, 'for, had I stayed among you five years, I would have slain men on all sides, and you would have possessed kingdoms as far distant as Rome. Now show me the great men who dwell here, that I may take my leave of them.' He put his arms round the neck of each man in turn, then, and bade his father farewell and died. Cries of grief were raised, and his grave and marker were made, and for three days not a calf of the cattle of the Ulaid was left alive after him.

The Wasting Sickness of Cú Chulaind
&
The Only Jealousy of Emer

Introduction

'The Wasting Sickness of Cú Chulaind & The Only Jealousy of Emer' is one of the more remarkable Irish tales: part myth, part history, part soap opera. Even the text is unusual, for it is a conflation of two different versions. After the first quarter of the tale, there appears an interpolation (omitted in this translation) detailing Cú Chulaind's advice to Lugaid Réoderg after the latter has been made king of Temuir; when the story proper resumes, Cú Chulaind is married to Emer instead of to Eithne Ingubai, and Lóeg is making a second trip to the otherworld with Lí Ban. The two versions have not been well integrated, and much evidence of confusion and duplication remains; but it is hard to say which tradition is older. Throughout the rest of the Ulster Cycle Cú Chulaind's wife is named Emer, just as Conchubur's is named Mugain and not Eithne Attencháithrech.

The story opens on a historical note, with a description of how the Ulaid celebrated Samuin, the annual end-of-the-year assembly; but the arrival of beautiful, red-gold-chained, otherworld birds on the lake at Mag Muirthemni and the appearance of the two women, one in green and one in crimson, who beat Cú Chulaind with horsewhips testify to the story's mythic origin. The central idea is also that of the first section of the Welsh 'Pwyll Lord of Dyved': the shadowy rulers of the otherworld have need of mortal strength; the pursuit of the hero by the otherworld beauty, moreover, is common to the second section of 'Pwyll'. Much of the tale is related in verse, and, while the poetry is neither particularly old nor particularly dense, it is clear and brilliant and affecting:

> At the doorway to the east,
> three trees of brilliant crystal,
> whence a gentle flock of birds calls
> to the children of the royal fort.

Near the end of the tale, the tone shifts towards the psychological – an unusual circumstance in these stories – as Fand and Emer fight over Cú Chulaind; the writing, which seems very literary at this point, is emotional but never sentimental. Even the poetry assumes a gnomic quality: Emer complains that 'what's new is bright ... what's familiar is stale', while Fand merely points out that 'every rule is good until broken'. Although Fand ultimately yields – after Cú Chulaind has been moved by Emer's plea – she admits that she still prefers Cú Chulaind to her own husband; Cú Chulaind, seeing her leave, wanders madly into the mountains of Ulaid, and it requires the spells of Conchubur's druids and Manandán's magic cloak to make him forget.

The story is the original source for Yeats's play *The Only Jealousy of Emer*.

The Wasting Sickness of Cú Chulaind
&
The Only Jealousy of Emer

Each year the Ulaid held an assembly: the three days before Samuin and the three days after Samuin and Samuin itself. They would gather at Mag Muirthemni, and during these seven days there would be nothing but meetings and games and amusements and entertainments and eating and feasting. That is why the thirds of Samuin are as they are today.

Thus, the Ulaid were assembled at Mag Muirthemni. Now the reason they met every Samuin was to give each warrior an opportunity to boast of his valour and exhibit his triumphs. The warriors put the tongues of those they had killed into their pouches – some threw in cattle tongues to augment the count – and then, at the assembly, each man spoke in turn and boasted of his triumphs. They spoke with their swords on their thighs, swords that turned against anyone who swore falsely.

Now there had come to this particular assembly every man but two: Conall Cernach and Fergus son of Roech. 'Let the assembly be convened,' said the Ulaid. Cú Chulaind, however, protested, saying 'Not until Conall and Fergus come', for Conall was his foster-brother and Fergus his foster-father. So Senchae said 'Let us play fidchell and have the poets recite and the acrobats perform.'

While they were at these amusements, a flock of birds settled on the lake, and no flock in Ériu was more beautiful. The women grew very excited over these birds and began to argue over who should have them. Eithne Attencháithrech, Conchubur's wife, said 'I desire a bird for each shoulder', but the other women replied 'We all want that too.' 'If anyone is to have them, I should,' said Eithne Ingubai, the wife of Cú Chulaind. 'What will we do?' asked the women. 'Not difficult,' said Lebarcham, the daughter of Óa and Adarc. 'I will go and ask Cú Chulaind.'

She went to Cú Chulaind, then, and said 'The women desire those birds from you.' But he seized his sword to ply against her, saying 'Have the sluts of Ulaid nothing better for us than to hunt their birds?' 'Indeed, you ought not to be angry with them,' answered Lebarcham, 'for you are the cause of their third blemish.' The women of Ulaid suffered three blemishes: every woman who loved Conall had a crooked neck; every woman who loved Cúscraid Mend Machae son of Conchubur stammered; and every woman who loved Cú Chulaind blinded one eye in his likeness. It was Cú Chulaind's gift, when he was angry, that he could withdraw one eye so far into his head that a heron could not reach it, whereas the other eye he could protrude until it was as large as a cauldron for a yearling calf.

'Yoke the chariot for us, Lóeg,' said Cú Chulaind. Lóeg did that, and Cú Chulaind sprang into the chariot, and he dealt the birds such a stunning blow with his sword that claws and wings floated on the water. Then he returned with the birds and distributed them so that each woman had a pair – each woman save Eithne Ingubai. When he came to his wife, he said 'Angry you are.' 'I am not,' she replied, 'for it is by me that the birds were distributed. You did right, for every one of those women loves you or gives you a share of her love, but I share my love with you alone.' 'Then do not be angry,' said Cú Chulaind. 'When birds come to Mag Muirthemni or the Bóand, you will have the most beautiful pair.'

Not long afterwards, they saw flying over the lake two birds coupled by a red-gold chain; these birds sang a little, and sleep fell upon the host. Cú Chulaind rose to go after them, but Eithne said 'If you listen to me, you will not go, for those birds possess some kind of power. Other birds can be caught for me.' 'Am I likely to be denied?' answered Cú Chulaind. 'Lóeg, put a stone in my sling.' Lóeg did so and Cú Chulaind cast at the birds, but he missed. 'Alas!' he said. He cast a second stone and missed with that also. 'Now I am doomed,' he said, 'for since the day I first took up arms I have never missed my target.' He threw his javelin, but it only pierced the wing of one bird. The creatures then flew along the water.

Cú Chulaind walked on until he sat down with his back against a stone; he was angry, but then sleep overcame him. While sleeping he saw two women approach: one wore a green cloak and the other a crimson cloak folded five times, and the one in green smiled at him and began to beat him with a horsewhip. The other woman then came and smiled also and struck him in the same fashion, and they beat him for such a long time that there was scarcely any life left in him. Then they left.

The Ulaid perceived the state he was in, and they attempted to rouse him. But Fergus said 'No! Do not disturb him – it is a vision.' Then Cú Chulaind awoke. 'Who did this to you?' asked the Ulaid, but he was unable to speak. He was taken to his sickbed in An Téte Brecc, and he remained there a year without speaking to anyone.

At the end of that year, just before Samuin, the Ulaid were gathered round Cú Chulaind in the house: Fergus by the wall, Conall Cernach by the bedrail, Lugaid Réoderg by the pillow and Eithne Ingubai at his feet; and, as they were thus, a man entered the house and sat at the foot of the bed. 'What brings you here?' asked Conall Cernach. 'Not

difficult that. If this man were healthy, he would guarantee
my safety here; and, since he is weak and wounded, his
guarantee is that much stronger. So I fear none of you, and
it is to speak to him that I have come.' 'Have no fear,' said
the Ulaid.

Then the man rose and recited these verses:

> Cú Chulaind, sick as you are,
> waiting will be no help.
> If they were yours, they would heal you,
> the daughters of Áed Abrat.
>
> Standing to the right of Labraid Lúathlám,
> in Mag Crúaich, Lí Ban said
> 'Fand has expressed her desire
> to lie down with Cú Chulaind:
>
> ' "A joyous day it would be
> were Cú Chúlaind to come to my land.
> He would have gold and silver
> and plenty of wine to drink.
>
> ' "Were he my friend now,
> Cú Chulaind son of Súaltaim,
> perhaps he could relate what he saw
> in his sleep, apart from the host.
>
> ' "There at Mag Muirthemni in the south
> no misfortune will befall you this Samuin.
> I will send Lí Ban to you,
> Cú Chulaind, sick as you are." '

'Who are you?' the Ulaid asked. 'I am Óengus son of Áed
Abrat,' said the man, and then he left, and the Ulaid knew
neither whence he had come nor where he had gone. But
Cú Chulaind sat up and spoke. 'About time,' the Ulaid said.
'Tell us what happened to you.' 'I had a vision last year, at
Samuin,' Cú Chulaind replied, and he related what he had

seen. 'What now, Conchubur?' he asked. 'You must return to that same stone,' answered Conchubur.

Cú Chulaind walked out then until he reached the stone, and there he saw the woman in the green cloak. 'Good this, Cú Chulaind,' she said. 'Not good for me your journey here last year,' he replied. 'Not to harm you did we come, but to seek your friendship. Indeed, I have come to speak to you of Fand, the daughter of Áed Abrat: Manandán son of Ler has left her, and she has now given her love to you. My name is Lí Ban, and I bear a message from my husband, Labraid Lúathlám ar Cladeb: he will send Fand to you in exchange for one day's fighting against Senach Síaborthe and Echu Íuil and Éogan Indber.' 'Indeed, I am not fit to fight men today,' answered Cú Chulaind. 'That is soon remedied: you will be healed, and your full strength will be restored.' 'Where is this place?' 'In Mag Mell. Now I must return,' said Lí Ban. 'Let Lóeg go with you to visit your land,' said Cú Chulaind. 'Let him come, then,' said Lí Ban.

Lí Ban and Lóeg then went to see Fand. When they arrived, Lí Ban seized Lóeg by the shoulder and said 'Do not leave this place today, Lóeg, save under a woman's protection.' 'Being protected by women has not exactly been my custom,' replied Lóeg. 'A pity it is not Cú Chulaind who is here now,' moaned Lí Ban. 'I too would rather he were here,' said Lóeg.

They went, then, to the side facing the island, where they saw a bronze boat crossing the lake and coming towards them. They entered the boat and crossed to the island; there, they found a doorway, and a man appeared. Lí Ban asked the man:

> Where is Labraid Lúathlám ar Cladeb,
> head of the troops of victory,
> victory above a steady chariot,
> he who reddens spear points with blood?

The man answered her, saying:

> Labraid is fierce and vigorous;
> he will not be slow, he will have many followers.
> An army is being mustered; if Mag Fidgai is crowded,
> there will be great slaughter.

They entered the house, then, and saw three fifties of couches and three fifties of women lying on them. These women all greeted Lóeg, saying 'Welcome, Lóeg, for the sake of the woman with whom you have come, and for the sake of the man from whom you have come, and for your own sake.' Lí Ban asked 'Well, Lóeg? Will you go to speak with Fand?' 'I will, provided I know where we are.' 'Not difficult that – we are in a chamber apart.' They went to speak with Fand, and she welcomed them in the same way. Fand was the daughter of Áed Abrat, that is, fire of eyelash, for the pupil is the fire of the eye. Fand is the tear that covers the eye, and she was so named for her purity and beauty, since there was not her like anywhere in the world.

As they stood there, they heard the sound of Labraid's chariot coming to the island, and Lí Ban said 'Labraid is angry today. Let us go and talk to him.' They went outside, and Lí Ban welcomed Labraid, saying:

> Welcome, Labraid Lúathlám ar Cladeb!
> Heir of troops,
> of swift spearmen,
> he smites shields,
> scatters spears,
> wounds bodies,
> slays free men,
> sees slaughter.
> More beautiful than women,
> he destroys hosts
> and scatters treasures.
> Assailant of a warrior band, welcome!

Labraid did not answer, so Lí Ban spoke on:

> Welcome, Labraid Lúathlám ar Cladeb Augra!
> Prompt to grant requests,
> generous to all,
> eager for combat.
> Battle-scarred his side,
> dependable his word,
> forceful his justice,
> amiable his rule,
> skilful his right hand,
> vengeful his deeds –
> he cuts down warriors.
> Welcome, Labraid!

As Labraid still remained silent, Lí Ban recited another poem:

> Welcome, Labraid Lúathlám ar Cladeb!
> More warlike than youths,
> prouder than chieftains,
> he destroys valiant adversaries,
> fights battalions,
> sieves young warriors,
> raises up the weak,
> lays low the strong.
> Welcome Labraid!

'What you say is not good, woman,' replied Labraid, and he recited this poem:

> I am neither proud nor arrogant, woman,
> nor is my bearing over-haughty.
> We go to a battle with fierce spears everywhere,
> plying in our right hands red swords
> against the ardent multitudes of Echu Iuil.
> There is no pride in me.
> I am neither proud nor arrogant, woman.

'Do not be angry, then,' said Lí Ban, 'for Cú Chulaind's charioteer, Lóeg, is here with the message that Cú Chulaind will bring a host.' Labraid greeted the charioteer, saying 'Welcome, Lóeg, for the sake of the woman with whom you have come and for the sake of everyone from whom you have come. Go home, now, and Lí Ban will follow you.'

Lóeg returned to Emuin, then, and related his adventure to Cú Chulaind and everyone else. Cú Chulaind sat up in bed and passed his hand over his face; then he spoke clearly to Lóeg, for the news the charioteer had brought had strengthened his spirits.

*

Cú Chulaind told Lóeg 'Go now to Emer and say to her that women of the Síde have come and destroyed me; tell her that I am mending and let her come and visit me.' But Lóeg recited this poem to strengthen Cú Chulaind:

> Great folly for a warrior
> to lie under the spell of a wasting sickness;
> it shows that spirits,
> the folk of Tenmag Trogagi,
> have bound you,
> and tortured you,
> and destroyed you,
> through the power of a wanton woman.
> Awake! Then the woman's mockery will shatter
> and your glorious valour will shine
> among champions and warriors;
> you will recover fully,
> and take to action
> and perform glorious deeds.
> When the call of Labraid sounds,
> O warlike man, rise that you might be great.

Lóeg went then to Emer and told her of Cú Chulaind's condition. 'Bad luck to you,' she said, 'for you visited the

Síde and brought back no cure for your lord. Shame on the Ulaid for not trying to heal him. If Conchubur were consumed, or Fergus overcome by sleep, or Conall Cernach laid low with wounds, Cú Chulaind would aid them.' And she recited this poem:

> Alas, son of Ríangabur,
> that you visited the Síde
> and returned with no cure
> for the son of Deichtine's spectre.

> Shame on the Ulaid, with their generosity
> among foster-fathers and foster-brothers,
> not to be searching the dark world
> to help their friend Cú Chulaind.

> If Fergus had sunk into sleep,
> and a single druid's art could heal,
> the son of Deichtine would not rest
> until that druid had made his examination.

> Or if it were Conall
> who was beset by wounds and injuries,
> the Hound would search the wide world
> until he found a doctor to heal him.

> If Lóegure Búadach were faced
> with an overwhelming danger,
> Cú would search the meadows of Ériu
> to cure the son of Connad son of Iliu.

> If it were Celtchair of the deceits
> to whom sleep and long wasting had come,
> Sétantae would be journeying
> night and day through the Síde.

> If it were Furbude of the fían
> who was laid low for a long time,
> Cú would search the hard earth
> until he found a cure.

Dead the hosts of Síd Truim,
dispersed their great deeds;
since the sleep of the Síde seized him,
their Hound outstrips hounds no more.

Alas! Your sickness touches me,
Hound of the smith of Conchubur;
my heart and mind are troubled —
I wonder if I might heal him.

Alas! Blood my heart,
wasting for the horseman of the plain
unless he should come here
from the assembly of Mag Muirthemni.

He comes not from Emuin —
a spectre has parted us.
My voice is weak and mute
because he is in an evil state.

A month and a season and a year
without sleeping together,
without hearing a man
of pleasing speech, son of Ríangabur.

After that Emer went to Emuin to visit Cú Chulaind; she
sat on his bed and said 'Shame on you, lying there for love
of a woman — long lying will make you sick.' Then she
recited this poem:

Rise, warrior of Ulaid!
Awake healthy and happy from sleep!
See the king of Emuin early in the morning —
do not indulge in excessive sleep.

See his shoulder full with crystal,
see his splendid drinking horns,
see his chariots traversing the valley,
see his ranks of fidchell pieces.

164

The Wasting Sickness of Cú Chulaind

See his vigorous champions,
see his tall and gentle women,
see his kings — a course of danger —
see his very great queens.

See the onset of brilliant winter,
see each wonder in turn;
see then that which you serve,
its coldness and distance and dimness.

Heavy sleep wastes, is not good;
weariness follows oppression.
Long sleep is a draught added to satiety;
weakness is next to death.

Throw off sleep, the peace that follows drink,
throw it off with great energy.
Many gentle words have loved you.
Rise, warrior of Ulaid!

Cú Chulaind rose, then, and passed his hand over his face
and threw off all weariness and sluggishness; he rose and
went to Airbe Rofir. There he saw Lí Ban approaching; she
spoke to him and invited him to the síd. 'Where does
Labraid dwell?' he asked. 'Not difficult that,' she answered:

Labraid dwells on a clear lake
frequented by troops of women.
If you decide to meet him,
you will not regret your visit.

His bold right hand cuts down hundreds —
she who tells you knows.
Like the beautiful colour
of a violet his cheek.

Conchend keen for battle trembles
before the slender red sword of Labraid;
Labraid crushes the spears of foolish hosts
and breaks the shields of armoured warriors.

165

In combat his skin is as bright as his eyes.
More honourable than the men of the Síde,
he does not betray friends in great need.
He has cut down many thousands.

Greater his fame than that of young warriors:
he has invaded the land of Echu Íuil.
Like threads of gold his hair,
and his breath reeks of wine.

Most wonderful of men, he initiates battles;
fierce he is at distant borders.
Boats and horses race
past the island where Labraid dwells.

A man of many deeds across the sea:
Labraid Lúathlám ar Cladeb.
No fighting disturbs his domain –
the sleep of a multitude prevails.

Bridles of red gold for his horses,
and nothing but this:
pillars of silver and crystal.
That is the house where he dwells.

But Cú Chulaind replied 'I will not go upon the invitation of a woman.' 'Then let Lóeg come and see everything,' said Lí Ban. Lóeg accompanied Lí Ban, then. They went to Mag Lúada and An Bile Búada, over Óenach nEmna and into Óenach Fidgai, and there they found Áed Abrat and his daughters. Fand greeted Lóeg, asking 'Why has Cú Chulaind himself not come?' 'He would not come upon a woman's invitation, nor until he learned if it was from you that the invitation came.' 'It was from me,' said Fand. 'Now return to him at once, for the battle is today.'

Lóeg returned to Cú Chulaind, then, and Cú Chulaind asked him 'How does it look, Lóeg?' Lóeg answered 'Time it is to go, for the battle will be today.' Then he recited this poem:

> I arrived to find splendid sport,
> a wonderful place, though all was customary.
> I came to a mound, to scores of companies,
> among which I found long-haired Labraid.
>
> I found him sitting
> in the mound, with thousands of weapons;
> beautiful yellow hair he had,
> tied back with a gold apple.
>
> He recognized me, then,
> by my five-folded crimson cloak.
> He said to me 'Will you come with me
> to the house of Failbe Find?'
>
> Two kings there are in the house:
> Failbe Find and Labraid;
> a great throng in the one house:
> three fifties of men for each king.
>
> Fifty beds on the right side
> and fifty on the floor;
> fifty beds on the left side
> and fifty on the dais.
>
> Bedposts of bronze,
> white gilded pillars;
> the candle before them
> a bright precious stone.
>
> At the doorway to the west,
> where the sun sets,
> a herd of grey horses, bright their manes,
> and a herd of chestnut horses.

At the doorway to the east,
three trees of brilliant crystal,
whence a gentle flock of birds calls
to the children of the royal fort.

A tree at the doorway to the court,
fair its harmony;
a tree of silver before the setting sun,
its brightness like that of gold.

Three score trees there
whose crowns are meetings that do not meet.
Each tree bears ripe fruit.
for three hundred men.

There is in the síd a well
with three fifties of brightly coloured mantles,
a pin of radiant gold
in the corner of each mantle.

A vat of intoxicating mead
was being distributed to the household.
It is there yet, its state unchanging –
it is always full.

There is too in the house a woman
who would be distinguished among the women of Ériu:
she appears with yellow hair
and great beauty and charm.

Fair and wondrous
her conversation with everyone,
and the hearts of all men break
with love and affection for her.

This woman said, then,
'Who is that lad I do not recognize?
Come here a while if it is you,
servant of the man of Muirthemne.'

The Wasting Sickness of Cú Chulaind

I went very slowly,
fearing for my honour.
She said to me 'Will he come to us,
the excellent only son of Deichtine?'

A pity that son did not go himself,
with everyone asking for him;
he could have seen for himself
the great house I visited.

If I possessed all of Ériu
and the kingship of yellow Brega,
I would give it all, no bad bargain,
to live in the place I visited.

'Good that,' said Cú Chulaind. 'Good, indeed, and good
that you should go, for everything in that land is good,' said
Lóeg. And he spoke on about the delights of the síd:

I saw a bright and noble land
where neither lie nor falsehood is spoken.
There lives a king who reddens troops:
Labraid Lúathlám ar Cladeb.

Passing across Mag Lúada,
I was shown An Bile Búada;
At Mag Denda I seized
a pair of two-headed snakes.

As we were together,
Lí Ban said to me
'A dear miracle it would be
if you were Cú Chulaind and not you.'

A troop of beautiful women – victory without restraint –
the daughters of Áed Abrat,
but the beauty of Fand – brilliant sound –
neither king nor queen can match.

I could enumerate, as I know them,
the descendants of sinless Adam,
and still the beauty of Fand
would find no equal.

I saw gleaming warriors
slashing with their weapons;
I saw coloured garments,
garb that was not ignoble.

I saw gentle women feasting;
I saw their daughters.
I saw noble youths
traversing the wooded ridge.

I saw musicians in the house,
playing for the women;
but for the speed with which I left,
I would have been rendered helpless.

I have seen the hill where stood
the beautiful Eithne Ingubai,
but the woman I speak of now
would deprive troops of their senses.

Cú Chulaind went to this land, then; he took his chariot,
and they reached the island. Labraid welcomed him, and
all the women welcomed him, and Fand gave him a special
welcome. 'What now?' asked Cú Chulaind. Labraid
answered 'Not difficult that – we will take a turn round the
assembled host.' They went out and found the host and
looked it over, and the enemy seemed innumerable. 'Go
now,' Cú Chulaind said to Labraid, so Labraid left, but Cú
Chulaind remained with the host. Two druidic ravens announced Cú Chulaind's presence; the host perceived this and
said 'No doubt the ravens are announcing the frenzied one
of Ériu.' And the host hunted them down until there was
for the birds no place in the land.

Early one morning, Echu Íuil went to wash his hands in a spring; Cú Chulaind spied the man's shoulder through an opening in his mantle and cast a spear through it. Thirty-three of the host were killed by Cú Chulaind. Finally, Senach Síaborthe attacked, and they fought a great battle before Cú Chulaind killed him. Labraid came, then, and routed the entire host; he asked Cú Chulaind to desist from the slaughter, but Lóeg said 'I fear that the man will turn his anger against us, for he has not yet had his fill of fighting. Have three vats of cold water brought, that his rage might be extinguished.' The first vat that Cú Chulaind entered boiled over, and the second became so hot that no one could endure it, but the third grew only moderately warm.

When the women saw Cú Chulaind, Fand recited this poem:

> Stately the chariot-warrior who travels the road,
> though he be young and beardless;
> fair the driver who crosses the plain,
> at evening, to Óenach Fidgai.
>
> The song he sings is not the music of the Síde:
> it is the stain of blood that is on him;
> the wheels of his chariot echo
> the bass song that he sings.
>
> May the horses under his smooth chariot
> stay for me a little, that I may look at them;
> as a team their like is not to be found —
> they are as swift as a wind of spring.
>
> Fifty gold apples play overhead,
> performing tricks on his breath;
> as a king his like is not to be found,
> not among gentle, not among fierce.

In each of his cheeks
a spot red as blood,
a green spot, a blue spot
and a spot of pale purple.

Seven lights in his eye –
he is not one to be left sightless.
It has the ornament of a noble eye:
a dark, blue-black eyelash.

A man known throughout Ériu
is already good; and this one has
hair of three different colours,
this young beardless lad.

A red sword that blood reddens
right up to its hilt of silver;
a shield with a boss of yellow gold
and a rim of white metal.

He steps over men in every battle;
valorous he enters the place of danger.
None of your fierce warriors
can match Cú Chulaind.

The warrior from Muirthemne,
Cú Chulaind, came here;
the daughters of Áed Abrat
they who brought him.

A long red drop of blood,
a fury rising to the treetops,
a proud high shout of victory,
a wailing that scatters spectres.

Lí Ban greeted him, then, with this poem:

> Welcome, Cú Chulaind,
> advancing boar,
> great chieftain of Mag Muirthemni.
> Great his spirit,

> honour of battle-victorious champions,
> heart of heroes,
> strong stone of wisdom,
> red in anger,
> ready for the fair play of enemies,
> one of the valorous warriors of Ulaid.
> Beautiful his brilliance,
> bright of eye to women.
> Welcome, Cú Chulaind!

'What have you done, Cú Chulaind?' Lí Ban asked. Cú Chulaind answered:

> I have cast my spear
> into the camp of Éogan Indber;
> I do not know, famous its path,
> whether my shot hit or missed.
>
> Whether better or worse for my strength,
> I have never yet in fair play
> cast ignorantly at a man in the mist —
> perhaps not a soul is left alive.
>
> A fair shining host with splendid horses
> pursued me from every direction:
> the people of Manandán son of Ler
> whom Éogan Indber summoned.
>
> Whichever way I turned
> when my full fury came upon me,
> it was one man against three thousand,
> and I sent them towards death.
>
> I heard Echu Íuil groan,
> a sound that came from the heart;
> if that truly was one man, and not an army,
> then my cast was well aimed.

Cú Chulaind slept with Fand, then, and he stayed with her for a month. When he bade her farewell, she said to him

173

'Where will we meet?' They decided upon Ibor Cind Tráchta. This was told to Emer, and she prepared knives with which to kill Fand. Fifty women accompanied Emer to the place of the meeting. Cú Chulaind and Lóeg were playing fidchell and did not notice the advancing women, but Fand noticed, and she said to Lóeg 'Look over at what I am seeing.' 'What is it?' asked Lóeg, and he looked.

Fand then said 'Lóeg, look behind you. Listening to you is a troop of clever, capable women, glittering sharp knives in their right hands and gold on their breasts. When warriors go to their battle chariots, a fair form will be seen: Emer daughter of Forgall in a new guise.'

'Have no fear,' replied Cú Chulaind, 'for she will not come at all. Step up into my powerful chariot, with its sunny seat, and I will protect you from every woman in the four quarters of Ériu, for though the daughter of Forgall may boast to her companions about her mighty deeds, she is not likely to challenge me.' He said to Emer, then, 'I avoid you, woman, as every man avoids the one he loves. I will not strike your hard spear, held with trembling hand; neither do you threaten me with your thin, feeble knife and weak, restrained anger, for the strength of women is insufficient to demand my full power.'

'Why, then, Cú Chulaind, have you dishonoured me before the women of the province and the women of Ériu and all people of rank?' asked Emer. 'It is under your protection I have come, under the great power of your guarantee; and though the pride of mighty conflicts makes you boastful, perhaps your attempt to leave me will fail, lad, however much you try.'

'Emer, why will you not permit me to meet this woman?' replied Cú Chulaind. 'She is pure and modest, fair and clever and worthy of a king. A handsome sight she is on the waves of the great-tided sea, with her shapeliness and beauty and

noble family, her embroidery and handiwork, her good sense
and prudence and steadfastness, her abundance of horses and
herds of cattle. Whatever you may promise, there is nothing
under heaven her husband could desire that she would not
do. Neither will you find a handsome, combat-scarred,
battle-victorious champion to equal me.'

'Perhaps this woman you have chosen is no better than
I,' answered Emer. 'But what's red is beautiful, what's new
is bright, what's tall is fair, what's familiar is stale. The
unknown is honoured, the known is neglected – until all is
known. Lad, we lived together in harmony once, and we
could do so again if only I still pleased you.'

Cú Chulaind grew melancholy at this, and he said 'By my
word, you do please me, and you will as long as you live.'
'Leave me, then,' said Fand. 'Better to leave me,' said Emer.
'No, I should be left,' said Fand, 'for it is I who was threatened just now.' And she began to cry and grieve, for being
abandoned was shameful to her; she went to her house, and
the great love she bore Cú Chulaind troubled her, and she
recited this poem:

> I will continue my journey
> though I prefer my great adventure here;
> whoever might come, great his fame,
> I would prefer to remain with Cú Chulaind.
>
> I would prefer to remain here –
> that I grant willingly –
> than to go, it may surprise you to learn,
> to the sun-house of Áed Abrat.
>
> Emer, the man is yours,
> and may you enjoy him, good woman.
> What my hand cannot obtain
> I must still desire.

175

Many a man has sought me,
both openly and in secret;
yet I never went to meet them,
for I was upright.

Wretched she who gives her love
if he takes no notice of her;
better to put such thoughts aside
unless she is loved as she loves.

Fifty women came here,
Emer of the yellow hair,
to fall upon Fand — a bad idea —
and kill her in her misery.

But I have three fifties of women,
beautiful and unmarried, at home
with me in my fort —
they would not desert me.

When Manandán learned that Fand was in danger from the
women of Ulaid and that she was being forsaken by Cú
Chulaind, he came west after her and stood before her, and
no one but Fand could see him. When she perceived him,
Fand felt deep regret and sadness, and she recited this
poem:

See the warlike son of Ler
on the plains of Eogan Indber:
Manandán, lord of the world —
once I held him dear.

Then, I would have wept,
but my proud spirit does not love now —
love is a vain thing
that goes about heedlessly and foolishly.

When Manandán and I lived
in the sun-house at Dún Indber,
we both thought it likely
we would never separate.

176

The Wasting Sickness of Cú Chulaind

When fair Manandán married me,
I was a proper wife:
he never won from me
the odd game of fidchell.

When fair Manandán married me,
I was a proper wife:
a bracelet of gold he gave me,
the price of making me blush.

Outside on the heath I had
fifty beautiful women;
I gave him fifty men
in addition to the fifty women.

Two hundred, and no mistake,
the people of our house:
one hundred strong, healthy men,
one hundred fair, thriving women.

Across the ocean I see
(and he who does not is no fool)
the horseman of the foaming sea,
he who does not follow the long ships.

Your going past us now
none but the Síde might perceive;
your keen sight magnifies the tiniest host,
though it be far distant.

That keen sight would be useful to me,
for the senses of women are foolish:
the one whom I loved so completely
has put me in danger here.

Farewell to you, dear Cú!
I leave you with head held high.
I wish that I were not going —
every rule is good until broken.

Time for me to set out, now —
there is someone who finds that difficult.
My distress is great,
O Lóeg, O son of Ríangabur.

I will go with my own husband, now,
for he will not deny me.
Lest you say I left in secret,
look now, if you wish.

Fand set out after Manandán, then, and he greeted her and said 'Well, woman, are you waiting for Cú Chulaind or will you go with me?' 'By my word, there is a man I would prefer as husband. But it is with you I will go; I will not wait for Cú Chulaind, for he has betrayed me. Another thing, good person, you have no other worthy queen, but Cú Chulaind does.'

When Cú Chulaind perceived that Fand was leaving with Manandán, he asked Lóeg 'What is this?' 'Not difficult that — Fand is going away with Manandán son of Ler, for she did not please you.' At that, Cú Chulaind made three high leaps and three southerly leaps, towards Lúachair; he was a long time in the mountains without food or water, sleeping each night on Slige Midlúachra.

Emer went to Conchubur in Emuin and told him of Cú Chulaind's state, and Conchubur ordered the poets and artisans and druids of Ulaid to find Cú Chulaind and secure him and bring him back. Cú Chulaind tried to kill the artisans, but the druids sang spells over him until his hands and feet were bound and he came to his senses. He asked for a drink; the druids brought a drink of forgetfulness, and, when he drank that, he forgot Fand and everything he had done. Since Emer was no better off, they brought her a drink that she might forget her jealousy. Moreover, Manandán shook his cloak between Cú Chulaind and Fand, that they might never meet again.

The Tale of Macc Da Thó's Pig

Introduction

Although 'The Tale of Macc Da Thó's Pig', with its feasting
and fighting, may seem the quintessential Ulster Cycle story,
its antiquity is open to doubt. Every other important figure
of the Ulster Cycle – Aillill, Medb and Cet of the Connachta;
Conchubur, Fergus, Lóegure, Conall Cernach and all the
Ulaid warriors – is present; but Cú Chulaind is not only
absent, he is not even mentioned. One could argue that Cú
Chulaind is a late addition to the traditions of the Ulaid and
that this story predates his arrival.

There are, however, other puzzling elements. The pig of
the title is so large that forty oxen can be laid across it; such
a beast could be mythic in origin, but it could also be satiric.
In 'The Cattle Raid of Cúailnge', Ulaid and Connachta go
to war over a mythic beast, the finest bull in Ireland; in this
tale, the two provinces fall out over a dog. Macc Da Thó
promises the dog to both Ulaid and Connachta, then feigns
innocence when they show up to collect on the same day.
During the bragging contest for the right to carve the pig,
the Ulaid warriors – the heroes of any ordinary Ulster Cycle
story – not only are shamed but are made to look ridicu-
lous: Lóegure has been speared and chased from the border,
Óengus's father has had his left hand cut off, Éogan has had
an eye put out, and so on. And Fer Loga's demand that the

179

nubile women of Ulaid sing 'Fer Loga Is My Darling' to him every night is so comical its inclusion cannot possibly be inadvertent. Some of the rhetorical verse is old and obscure; but it is hard to resist the conclusion that 'The Tale of Macc Da Thó's Pig' is at later story, a parody of the Ulster Cycle in general and of 'The Cattle Raid of Cúailnge' in particular.

The Story of Macc Da Thó's Pig

There was once a famous king of Lagin named Macc Da Thó, and he possessed a hound. This dog, whose name was Ailbe, protected all of Lagin, so that its fame grew throughout Ériu. Messengers from Ailill and Medb came to ask for Ailbe; at the same time, however, arrived messengers from Conchubur and the Ulaid, and with the same request.

A welcome was given to all, and they were shown into Macc Da Thó's hostel. This was one of the five hostels in Ériu at that time, this and Da Derga's hostel in the territory of Cúalu and Forgall Manach's and Macc Da Réo's in Bréifne and Da Choca's in western Mide. Seven doors had Macc Da Thó's hostel, and seven entrances and seven hearths and seven cauldrons. Each cauldron contained beef and salted pork, and as each man passed by he thrust the flesh-fork into the cauldron, and what he brought up is what he ate; if he brought up nothing on the first try, he got no second chance.

Before being taken to the cauldrons, however, the messengers were first shown to Macc Da Thó's couch, in order that their requests might be granted. 'It is to ask for the hound that we have come,' said the messengers from Connachta (that is, from Ailill and Medb). 'You will receive one hundred and sixty milch cows immediately, and a chariot, and the two best horses in Connachta, and as much again at the end of the year.' 'It is to ask for the hound that we have come from Conchubur,' said the messengers from Ulaid, 'since he is no worse a friend for giving jewellery and cattle and everything else from the north, and since a great friendship will result.'

These messages so confounded Macc Da Thó that he went three days without food or drink, and at night he tossed and turned. His wife said 'You are a long time fasting. You have food, but you eat nothing – what is wrong?' When he did not reply, she went on:

'Sleeplessness has come   to Macc Da Thó's house.
He has need of advice   but he speaks to no one.

'He turns away to the wall,   a warrior in fierce combat.
His clever wife observes   that her husband cannot sleep.'

'Crumthand Níad Náir says   "Tell no secret to a woman.
A woman's secret is not kept;   jewels are not given to slaves." '

'You may speak to a woman   if no disaster ensues –
my mind may comprehend   what yours does not.'

'Evil the day they came for   the hound of Macc Da Thó.
Many a good man will die;   the battle will be indescribable.

'If Conchubur is refused,   there will be trouble for certain:
his hosts will not leave   any land or cattle with me.

'If Ailill is disappointed,   Ériu will be devastated.
Cet will carry us off;   we will be reduced to ashes.'

'I have advice for you,   and the result will not be bad:
give the dog to both sides –   let them fight over it.'

'The advice you offer   renews my spirit.
God sent Ailbe;   the dog's origin is unknown.'

After that, Macc Da Thó rose and was jubilant, saying
'Joy to us and to our guests.' The messengers stayed three
days and three nights. He took them aside then – first the
messengers of Connachta, to whom he said 'Great my perplexity and doubt, but I have decided to give the hound to
Ailill and Medb. Let them bring a large, magnificent host to
fetch it, and they will have food and drink and presents,
and the dog will be theirs.' The Connachta thanked him.
Macc Da Thó went then to the messengers of Ulaid and
said 'Free of doubt at last, I have awarded the hound to
Conchubur. Let the chieftains of Ulaid come for Ailbe with
a proud host; they will receive presents and be welcome.'

Now the people from Connachta and Ulaid proposed to
come on the same day, and neither province forgot to show
up, either. The two provinces arrived at the door of Macc
Da Thó's hostel. He himself came to greet them and make
them welcome, saying 'We were not expecting you, warriors! Nevertheless, I welcome you! Come into the courtyard!' They all trooped in, the Connachta to one side of
the hostel, the Ulaid to the other. The hostel was not small,
with seven entrances and fifty paces between each pair of
doorways. Still, the faces round the feast inside were not
friendly, for many had done injury to others there.

Macc Da Thó's pig was slaughtered for the feast. This
pig had been nourished by sixty milch cows for seven
years, and it was brought in to the feast with forty oxen laid
across it. Macc Da Thó himself presided over the feast,
saying 'Welcome! This may not be worthy of you, but there
are pigs and oxen in Lagin, and whatever is wanting today
will be slaughtered for you tomorrow.' 'The pig looks good,'
said Conchubur. 'It does, indeed,' said Ailill, 'but how should
it be divided, Conchubur?' 'How else,' said Bricriu son of

Carbad from his couch overhead, 'where the heroes of Ériu are assembled but by combat? You have all flattened each other's noses before.' 'Let that be done,' said Ailill. 'Fine,' said Conchubur, 'for we have youths who have strolled about the border.' 'The worth of your young men will be tested tonight, Conchubur,' said Senláech of the Araid, from Crúachu Con Alad in the west. 'Often enough I have left them sitting in the muddy water of Lúachair Dedad; often enough they have left fat oxen with me.' 'The ox you left with us was fatter,' said Muinremur son of Gerrgend, 'for it was your own brother, Crúaichniu son of Rúadluim from Crúachu Con Alad.' 'Crúaichniu was worth no more,' replied Lugaid son of Cú Ruí, 'than Inloth Már son of Fergus son of Léti, whom Echbél son of Dedad left dead at Temuir Lúachra.' 'What do you say,' boasted Celtchair son of Uthechar, 'to my having killed Congachnes son of Dedad and taken his head?'

At length one man triumphed over all Ériu: Cet son of Mágu from Connachta. He hung his weapons over those of everyone else; then he took knife in hand and sat down to the pig, saying 'Find among the men of Ériu one to match me in feats – otherwise I will carve the pig.' Inasmuch as his equal had not been found, the Ulaid fell silent. 'Just look at that, Lóegure,' said Conchubur at length. Lóegure spoke then: 'It is not right that Cet should carve the pig before our very eyes.' Cet answered 'One moment, Lóegure, that I might speak with you. You Ulaid have a custom: every one of you who takes arms makes Connachta his object. You came to the border, then, and I met you; you abandoned your horses and chariot and charioteer and escaped with my spear through you. Is that how you propose to take the pig?' Lóegure sat down.

A tall fair warrior arose from his couch and said 'It is not right that Cet should carve the pig before our very eyes.' 'Who is this?' asked Cet. 'Óengus son of Lám Gabuid,' said the Ulaid, 'and a better warrior than you.' 'Why is his father called Lám Gabuid?' 'Why indeed?' the Ulaid asked. 'I know why,' said Cet. 'Once I came east. There was screaming. People came, Lám Gabuid too, and he cast his great spear at me, but I threw it back so that it cut off his hand and left it on the ground. What could bring his son to challenge me?' Óengus sat down.

'On with the contest, or I will carve the pig,' said Cet. 'It is not right that Cet should carve the pig,' said another tall, fair Ulaid warrior. 'Who is this?' asked Cet. 'Éogan son of Durthacht, the king of Fernmag.' 'I have seen him before,' said Cet. 'Where have you seen me?' asked Éogan. 'At the entrance to your house, when I was stealing your cattle. Everyone in your land screamed, and that brought you. You cast a spear at me that stuck in my shield; I cast the same spear back at you so that it went through your head and put out one eye. That is why you are one-eyed before the men of Ériu.' Éogan sat down.

'On with the contest, Ulaid,' said Cet. 'You will not carve the pig yet,' said Muinremur son of Gerrgend. 'Is this Muinremur?' asked Cet. 'I have finally cleaned my spears, Muinremur. It is not six days since I took three warriors' heads about the head of your first-born son from your land.' Muinremur sat down.

'On with the contest!' said Cet. 'You will have that!' said Mend son of Salchad. 'Who is this?' asked Cet. 'Mend son of Salchad,' said everyone. 'What next!' said Cet. 'Now sons of herdsmen with nicknames are challenging me. I am the priest who baptized your father with that name, for I struck his heel with my sword so that he took but one foot away. What could bring the son of a one-footed man to challenge me?' Mend sat down.

'On with the contest!' said Cet. 'You will have that!' said a large, grey, very ugly Ulaid warrior. 'Who is this?' asked

Cet. 'Celtchair son of Uthechar,' said everyone. 'Just one moment, Celtchair, unless you want to crush me immediately. I arrived at the entrance to your house once; there was screaming and everyone came to the door and you with them. You cast your spear at me, but I cast another spear at you so that it pierced your thighs and your testicles. Since then you have fathered no sons or daughters. What could bring you to challenge me?' Celtchair sat down.

'On with the contest!' said Cet. 'You will have that!' said Cúscraid Mend Machae son of Conchubur. 'Who is this?' asked Cet. 'Cúscraid,' said everyone, 'and he has the look of a king.' 'No thanks to you, Cet,' said the lad. 'Right that is,' answered Cet. 'You came to Connachta for your first feat of arms, and we met at the border. You abandoned one third of your retinue and left with a spear through your neck, so that today you have not a proper word in your head — the spear injured the cords in your throat. Since then you have been called Cúscraid Mend.' Cet thus brought shame upon the entire province of Ulaid.

Knife in hand, then, Cet was exulting over the pig when Conall Cernach entered the hostel; he leapt into the middle of the hall, and the Ulaid gave him a great welcome. Conchubur took the helmet from Conall's head and brandished it, and Conall said 'We will be happy to obtain our share of the pig. Who is carving?' 'That has been granted to the man with the knife: Cet son of Mágu,' answered Conchubur. 'Is it true, Cet, that you are carving?' asked Conall.

Cet answered 'Welcome, Conall, heart of stone, angry ardour of the lynx, glitter of ice, red strength of anger in the breast of a champion. Full of wounds, victorious in battle, you are my equal, son of Findchóem.'

Conall replied 'Welcome, Cet son of Mágu, dwelling-place of a hero, heart of ice, plumage of a swan, strong chariot-fighter, warlike sea, fierce beautiful bull, Cet son of Mágu.'

Conall continued 'All will be clear from our encounter and our separation, a famous tale told by the men of goads and witnessed by the men of awls. Noble warriors will meet in an angry combat of lions, two chariot-fighters will match angry deeds, men will step over men in this hall tonight.'

'Now move away from the pig,' said Conall. 'What could bring you to it?' asked Cet. 'Cet, it is right that you should challenge me,' replied Conall. 'I will meet you in single combat. I swear by what my people swear by: since I first took spear in hand, there has not been a single day when I have not killed a Connachta warrior, not a single night when I have not destroyed with fire, and I have never slept without a Connachta head under my knee.' 'You are a better warrior than I, it is true,' said Cet. 'If Anlúan were here, he would give you another kind of contest. It is our misfortune that he is not in the house.' 'Oh, but he is,' said Conall, and taking Anlúan's head from his wallet he threw it at Cet's breast so that a mouthful of blood splattered over the lips. Cet left the pig, then, and Conall sat down to it, saying 'On with the contest!' The Connachta could not find a warrior to equal him; even so, the Ulaid formed a protective shelter with their shields, for some ill-mannered guests had begun to shoot at him from the corners.

Conall then began to carve the pig. He took the end of the belly in his mouth until he had made a division, and he sucked on the belly (a burden for nine men) until not a particle was left. He did leave the foretrotters to the Connachta, however. They thought their share small; they rose, the Ulaid rose, and everyone hit someone. Blows fell upon ears until the heap on the floor reached the centre of the house and the streams of gore reached the entrances. The hosts broke through the doors, then, and a good drinking bout broke out in the courtyard, with everyone striking his neighbour. Fergus pulled up a great oak by the roots; meanwhile, the battle broke out of the courtyard and towards the outer doors.

At last, Macc Da Thó came out with the dog in hand and unleashed it to see which side it would choose. Ailbe chose the Ulaid and precipitated the slaughter of the Connachta, for they were routed. At Mag nAilbi the hound bit the chariot pole of Ailill and Medb, and there the charioteer Fer Loga struck the dog so that its body fell away and its head remained on the pole. The place is thus called Mag nAilbi.

The rout swept south past Belach Mugna, over Áth Mid bine in Maistiu, past Cill Dara, past Ráith Imgain, into Fid nGaible at Áth Macc Lugnai, past Druimm Dá Mage and over Drochet Coirpri. At Áth Chind Chon in Bile the dog's head fell from the chariot pole. As the hosts swept west over Mide, Fer Loga, Ailill's charioteer, hid himself in the heather; when the Ulaid came past, he leapt into a chariot and seized Conchubur by the head from behind. 'Beware, Conchubur!' he said. 'Whatever you want!' said Conchubur. 'Not much my wish,' answered Fer Loga: 'Take me with you to Emuin Machae, and every evening send the women of Ulaid and their nubile daughters to sing in chorus "Fer Loga Is My Darling".' The Ulaid granted that, since for Conchubur's sake they dared not refuse. A year later Fer Loga returned west across Áth Lúain, taking with him two of Conchubur's horses and golden bridles for both.

The Intoxication of the Ulaid

Introduction

One of the wildest and most comical of the Ulaid stories, 'The Intoxication of the Ulaid' reveals both a mythic and a historical subtext. The text itself, however, is a problem. The story survives incomplete in both of our early manuscripts, and while the Lebor na huidre account takes up about where the Book of Leinster account leaves off, the juncture is only approximate. Moreover, the two versions are quite disparate: names change (Triscatail becomes Triscoth; Róimít turns into Réordae), roles change (the gadfly part played by Bricriu is taken up by Dubthach Dóeltenga), important plot elements (such as the iron house) disappear altogether. The Lebor na huidre version is generally less psychological and less refined, and, while it has its own merits, it is frustrating not to know how the Book of Leinster story would have been resolved.

The mythic subtext harbours the remains of a ritual killing story. 'The Intoxication of the Ulaid' takes place at Samuin, which as the end of the old year and the beginning of the new one would have been an appropriate time for a new king to replace an old one; moreover, there are traditions that make Cú Chulaind and Cú Ruí rivals, and in 'The Death of Cú Ruí', Cú Chulaind kills Cú Ruí for the sake of his wife, Bláthnait (another example of the regeneration motif found so often in these stories). The idea appears also in 'The Destruction of Da Derga's Hostel' (which takes place at Samuin and wherein invaders attempt to burn and perhaps drown Conare) and in 'The Destruction of Dind Rig' (wherein Labraid burns Cobthach in an iron house).

The historical subtext treats the theme of tribal warfare that obtains in all three stories. It may well be that, in an older recension, 'The Intoxication of the Ulaid' described an attack by the Ulaid upon Temuir, which would have been a much more logical target. Subsequently, however, the story was grafted on to a mythological fragment involving Cú Chulaind and Cú Ruí, and since the 'historical' Cú Ruí had been localized in the south-west, it became necessary to reconcile that tradition with the one about the attack on Temuir. The result: Temuir Lúachra (Temuir of the Rushes), located, conveniently, in south-west Ireland.

In any case, the storytellers have turned the improbability of the Ulaid's careering across Ériu into a splendidly comic tale. What might have been a heroic foray is reduced to a drunken stagger; Cú Chulaind's inability to navigate from Dún Dá Bend to Dún Delga except by way of Temuir Lúachra (like going from London to Canterbury by way of Edinburgh) is a humorous reflection upon his original name, Sétantae, which means 'one who knows the way'; and the exchanges between Cromm Deróil and Cromm Darail are more characteristic of comedians than of druids.

The Intoxication of the Ulaid

When the sons of Mil Espáne reached Ériu, their wisdom circumvented the Túatha Dé Danand. Ériu was left to the division of Amorgen Glúnmár son of Mil, for he was a king's poet and a king's judge; Amorgen divided Ériu into two parts, giving the part under the ground to the Túatha Dé Danand and the other part to the sons of Mil Espáne, his own people.

The Túatha Dé Danand went into the hills – the region of the Síde – then, and they submitted to the Síde under the ground. But they left behind, in each province of Ériu, five of their number to incite the sons of Mil to battle and combat and strife and slaughter. They were particularly careful to leave five men in the province of Ulaid: Brea son of Belgan in Drommanna Breg, Redg Rotbél in Slemna Mage Ítha, Tindell son of Boclachtnae in Slíab Edlicon, Grici in Crúachu Aí and Gulban Glass in Bend Gulbain Guirt maicc Ungairb. These men aroused discontent among the Ulaid over the province's division into three parts, and they did this when the province was at its best – at the time of Conchubur son of Fachtnae Fáthach. The two who shared the province with Conchubur were his own fosterlings: Cú Chulaind son of Súaltaim and Findtan son of Níall Níamglonnach at Dún Dá Bend. This is the division that was imposed upon the province: from Cnocc Úachtair Forcha, which is now called Uisnech Mide, to the very centre of Tráig Baile was Cú Chulaind's share, while Conchubur's third extended from Tráig Baile to Tráig Tola and Findtan's from Tráig Tola to Rind Semni and Latharnai.

The province was thus divided into thirds for a year, or until Conchubur held the feis of Samuin at Emuin Machae. One hundred vats of every kind of drink were provided, and Conchubur's officers said that the excellence of the feast was such that all the chieftains of Ulaid would not be too many to attend. And this is the plan that Conchubur devised: to send Lebarcham to Cú Chulaind at Dún Delga and Findchad Fer Bend Uma son of Fróeglethan to Findtan son of Níall Níamglonnach at Dún Dá Bend.

Lebarcham arrived at Dún Delga and told Cú Chulaind to go and speak with his dear foster-father at Emuin Machae. At that time, Cú Chulaind was giving a great feast for the people of his own territory, and he said that he would not go but would attend to his own people. But Emer Foltchaín, the daughter of Forgall Manach and one of the six best women in Ériu, said that he should not stay but should rather go to speak with his foster-father Conchubur.

Cú Chulaind ordered his horses harnessed, then, and his chariot yoked. 'The horses are harnessed, and the chariot is yoked,' said Lóeg. 'Do not delay, or an evil hour may blot your valour. Step into the chariot when you please.' Cú Chulaind seized his war gear and leapt into the chariot; he took the straightest roads and the shortest ways to Emuin Machae, and there Senchae son of Ailill came to greet him, saying 'Always welcome your arrival, O chief of prosperity of the host of Ulaid, salmon of valorous weaponry of the Goídil, dear, many-hosted, crimson-fisted son of Deichtine.'

'The welcome of a man asking a present that,' said Cú Chulaind. 'It is, indeed,' said Senchae son of Ailill. 'Name the present,' said Cú Chulaind. 'I will provided that I have a proper guarantee,' answered Senchae. 'Then name your guarantors, in return for a counter-present for me,' said Cú

Chulaind. 'The two Conalls and Lóegure,' said Senchae, 'that is, Conall Ánglonnach son of Íriel Glúnmár and Conall Cernach son of Amorgen and Lóegure Londbúadach.' These guarantors sufficed to secure the present, in return for a counter-present for Cú Chulaind.

'What guarantors do you ask for your counter-present?' Senchae then asked. 'Three young, noble, valorous lads,' said Cú Chulaind. 'Cormac Cond Longes son of Conchubur, Mess Ded son of Amorgen and Echu Cendgarb son of Celtchair.' 'This is my request, then,' said Senchae, 'that you give the third of Ulaid that is in your possession to Conchubur for a year.' 'If the province were the better for being in his possession,' said Cú Chulaind, 'that would not be difficult, for he is a well-spring of authority; there is no refuting or contradicting him, and he descends from the kings of Ériu and Albu. But if the province is not better, then we will have a skirmish of little boys, and he will be returned to his own third.'

After that, Findtan son of Níall Níamglonnach arrived. The most excellent druid Cathub took charge and greeted him, saying 'Welcome your arrival, fair, noble youth, chief warrior of the great province of Ulaid. Against you neither reavers nor raiders nor foreign plunderers strive, man who guards the borders of the province.'

'The welcome of a man asking a present that,' said Findtan. 'It is, indeed,' said Cathub. 'Name it, that you may have it,' said Findtan. 'I will provided that I have a proper guarantee,' replied Cathub. 'Then name your guarantors, in return for a counter-present for me,' said Findtan. 'Celtchair son of Uthechar, Uma son of Remanfissech from Fedan Chúailnge and Errge Echbél from Brí Errgi,' said Cathub, and these guarantors sufficed. 'What guarantors do you ask for your counter-present?' asked Cathub. 'The three sons of Uisliu of great deeds,' said Findtan, 'the three torches of valour of Europe: Noísiu and Aindle and Arddán.' These guarantors were ratified by both parties.

After that, they went to An Téte Brecc, the house where Conchubur was. 'Conchubur is now king of Ulaid,' Cathub said, 'for Findtan has yielded his third.' 'So has Cú Chulaind,' said Senchae. 'In that case,' said Cú Chulaind, 'let Conchubur come to drink and make merry with me, for that is my counter-request.' 'What guarantees and assurances do I have when that is permitted to be said?' asked Findtan. Everyone's guarantors came forth savagely, then, and the fighting was so fierce that nine were wounded and nine bleeding and nine at the point of death between one side and the other. But Senchae son of Ailill rose and shook his peacemaking branch, and the Ulaid fell silent. 'Why such quarrelling?' he asked. 'Conchubur will not be king of Ulaid for a year yet.' 'We will do as you wish,' said Cú Chulaind, 'provided that you do not intervene at the end of the year.' 'That I will not,' said Senchae. Cú Chulaind held him to that promise. They remained three days and three nights, drinking up Conchubur's feast until they had finished it; then they returned to their own houses and strongholds and fine dwellings.

Anyone who arrived at the end of the following year would have found Conchubur's province a well-spring of justice and abundance, without a single dwelling waste, empty or desolate, from Rind Semni and Latharnai to Cnocc Úachtair Forcha to Dub and Drobaís, and without a single son usurping the place of his father and grandfather – everyone served his proper lord. At this time, then, fair words passed between Cú Chulaind and Emer. 'It seems to me,' said Emer, 'that Conchubur is now high king of Ériu.' 'No harm if he is,' replied Cú Chulaind. 'You must prepare a king's feast for him, then, for he will be king always,' Emer said. 'That will be done,' said Cú Chulaind.

The feast was prepared, and there were one hundred vats of every kind of drink. At the same time, though, Findtan son of Níall Níamglonnach decided to prepare a feast, with one hundred vats of every kind of drink. Work on both feasts began on the same day, and work on both concluded the same day. Both men harnessed their horses and yoked their chariots the same day, but Cú Chulaind was the first to arrive at Emuin. He was just unyoking his horses when Findtan arrived, so that he entered Emuin before Findtan; thus, he was already inviting Conchubur to his feast when Findtan entered. 'What guarantees and assurances do I have when that is permitted to be said?' Findtan asked. 'We are here,' said the sons of Uisliu, and they rose. 'I myself,' said Cú Chulaind, 'am not without guarantees.'

With that, the Ulaid rose savagely to take arms, and, since Senchae did not dare to intervene, they began to fight. Conchubur could do no more than leave the royal house to them, and he was followed out by a son of his whose name was Furbude and whom Cú Chulaind had fostered. Conchubur drew this lad aside and said 'Son, you have the power to make peace among the Ulaid.' 'How?' asked the lad. 'By weeping and lamenting before your foster-father, Cú Chulaind,' Conchubur answered, 'for never has he been in strife or combat that he did not think of you.'

Furbude returned, then, and he wept and lamented before Cú Chulaind until the latter asked him what was wrong. Furbude replied 'Just when the province is a well-spring of abundance, you are destroying it for the sake of a single night.' 'I have given my word,' said Cú Chulaind, 'and it will not be contravened.' 'I have sworn my oath,' said Findtan, 'and I will not leave until the Ulaid come with me tonight.' 'I have an excellent solution for you, if I be permitted to speak,' said Senchae son of Ailill. 'The first half of the night with Findtan, the second half with Cú Chulaind —

that will alleviate the lad's sorrow.' 'I will permit that,' said Cú Chulaind. 'I also will accept it,' said Findtan.

The Ulaid rose about Conchubur, then, and he sent messengers out to invite the people of the province to Findtan's feast. Conchubur himself went, in the company of the Cráebrúad, to Dún Dá Bend and the house of Findtan son of Níall Níamglonnach. All the Ulaid assembled at the feast, so that there was not a man from the smallest hamlet who did not attend. Each king came with his queen, each lord with his lady, each musician with his proper mate, each hospitaller with his female companion; but they were attended to as well as if only a small company had arrived. Lovely, well-built, finely appointed sleeping chambers were prepared. Beautiful, lofty balconies were strewn with rushes and fresh rushes, and there were long houses for the hosts, broad, capacious cooking houses, and a broad-entranced, multicoloured hostel, wide and high and handsome, with four corners and four doors, where the chieftains of Ulaid, men and women, might assemble and drink and make merry. Choice portions of food and drink were served them, so that sustenance for one hundred men reached every nine guests. Conchubur ordered the drinking house by deeds and divisions and families, by grades and arts, and by gentle manners, all towards the fair holding of the feast. Servers came to serve, cupbearers to pour, doorkeepers to guard the doors. Musicians came to play and sing and amuse. Poems and tales and encomia were recited, and jewels and gems and treasures were distributed.

It was then that Cú Chulaind said to Lóeg son of Ríangabur: 'Go outside, good Lóeg, and examine the stars, and determine if midnight has arrived, for you have often waited and watched for me at the boundaries of distant lands.' Lóeg went out, then, and he watched and waited until it was midnight; then he returned to the house and said

'Midnight now, O Cú of the feats.' When Cú Chulaind heard that, he told Conchubur, for he was sitting in the hero's seat beside the king. Conchubur rose with a bright, shining buffalo horn, and the Ulaid fell silent when they saw their king standing. They were so quiet, a needle falling from the ridge pole to the floor could have been heard. It was geiss for the Ulaid to speak before their king did, but it was also geiss for the king to speak before his druids did. Thus, the most excellent druid Cathub said 'What is it, Conchubur, noble high king of Ulaid?' 'Cú Chulaind here thinks it time to go to his feast,' Conchubur replied. 'Does he wish to earn the collective blessing of the Ulaid by leaving the young and the weak and the women behind?' asked Cathub. 'I do,' said Cú Chulaind, 'provided that our champions and warriors and fighters and singers and poets and musicians come with us.'

The Ulaid rose as one, then, and they went out on to the hard-turfed green. 'Good friend Lóeg,' said Cú Chulaind, 'set a leisurely pace for the chariot.' Lóeg possessed the three virtues of charioteering: turning round, backing up straight and leaping over chasms. 'Good friend Lóeg,' Cú Chulaind then said, 'put the goad of battle to the horses', whereupon Cú Chulaind's horses broke into a warlike white leap. The horses of the Ulaid followed their example, and this is the road they took: on to the green of Dún Dá Bend, past Cathir Osrin, Lí Thúaga and Dún Rígáin to Ollarba in Mag Machae, past Slíab Fúait and Áth na Forare to Port Nóth Con Culaind, past Mag Muirthemni and Crích Saithni, across Dubad, across the rush of the Bóand and into Mag mBreg and Mide, into Senmag Léna in Mucceda, into Cláethar Cell, across the Brosnas of Bladma, with Berna Mera ingine Trega (today called Bernán Ele) on their left and Slíab nEblinni ingine Gúare on their right, across Findsruth (today called Aband Úa Cathbad), into Machare Már na

Muman, through Lár Martini and the territory of the Smertani, with the bright crags of Loch Gair on the right, across the rush of the Máig and into Clíu Máil maicc Úgaine, into Crích na Dési Bice, into the land of Cú Ruí son of Dáre. Every hill over which they travelled they levelled, so that flat glens were left behind; in every wood through which they passed the iron wheels of their chariots sliced through the roots of the great oaks, so that level plains were left behind; in every stream and ford and estuary they crossed, their horses' knees splashed the water out, so that for a great distance and for a long time afterwards the streams and fords and estuaries were left bare-stoned and bone dry.

At that time, Conchubur, king of Ulaid, said 'Never before have we taken this route from Dún Dá Bend to Dún Delga.' 'Indeed not,' said Bricriu. 'But a whisper is clearer to us than a shout is to anyone else: in fact, we seem not to be within the borders of Ulaid at all.' 'We give our word,' said Senchae son of Ailill, 'that we are not.' 'We give our word, as well,' said Conall. At that, the Ulaid charioteers tightened the bits in the mouths of their horses, from first chariot to last, and Conchubur said 'Who will find out for us what territory we are in?' 'Who but Cú Chulaind,' said Bricriu, 'for he has boasted that there is no district in which he has not slaughtered one hundred men.' 'I am responsible, Bricriu,' Cú Chulaind said, 'and I will go.'

Cú Chulaind thus went down to Druimm Collchailli, which is called Áne Chlíach, and he said 'Tell me, friend Lóeg, do you know what territory we are in?' 'Indeed, I do not,' said Lóeg. 'Well, I do,' replied Cú Chulaind. 'Cend Abrat and Slíab Caín to the south, there, and Slíab nEblinni to the north-east. The large, bright pond yonder is Lind Luimnig. Druimm Collchailli is where we are now — it is called Áne

Chlíach and lies in Crích na Dési Bice. To the south of us
is the host, in Clíu Máil maicc Úgaine, in the territory of
Cú Ruí son of Dáre son of Dedad.'

While Cú Chulaind and Lóeg were talking, a tremendous,
heavy snow fell upon the Ulaid, and it was as high as the
shoulders of the men and the shafts of their chariots. Extra
work was performed by the Ulaid charioteers in erecting
stone columns to shelter their horses from the snow, and
these 'Stables for the Horses of the Ulaid' survive still. And
they prove the story.

After that, Cú Chulaind and Lóeg returned to the Ulaid.
'Well,' said Senchae son of Ailill, 'what territory are we in?'
'We are in Crích na Dési Bice, the land of Cú Ruí son of
Dáre, in Clíu Máil maicc Úgaine,' replied Cú Chulaind. 'Woe
to us, then,' said Bricriu, 'and woe to the Ulaid.' 'Not so,
Bricriu,' said Cú Chulaind, 'for I will show the Ulaid how
we can retrace our way and arrive in front of our enemies
before dawn.' 'Woe to the Ulaid,' said Celtchair son of
Uthechar, 'that ever was born the sister's son who gives
such advice.' 'We have never before known you to offer the
Ulaid a plan of weakness and cowardice, Cú Chulaind,' said
Fergnae son of Findchóem, a royal hospitaller. 'Alas that a
person who gives such advice should escape without our
making him a place of points and edges of weapons,' said
Lugaid Lámderg son of Léti king of the Dál nArade. 'What
would you prefer, then?' asked Cú Chulaind, and Celtchair
answered 'This, that we spend a day and a night in this
territory, for to leave it would signify defeat, and we have
not left so much as a fox's track in land or desert or
wilderness.' 'Then tell us, Cú Chulaind,' said Conchubur,
'where we ought to encamp for a day and a night.' 'Óenach
Senclochar is here, and this rough winter season is not fair-
time,' said Cú Chulaind. 'And Temuir Lúachra lies on the
slope of Irlúachair, and there there are buildings and dwell-

ings.' 'It would be right to go to Temuir Lúachra, then,' said Senchae.

So they went straight on to Temuir Lúachra, and Cú Chulaind showed them the way. But if Temuir Lúachra was uninhabited before or after, it was not uninhabited that night. No surprise this, for a son had been born to Ailill and Medb and given the name Mane Mó Epirt and sent out to be fostered by Cú Ruí son of Dáre; and that night Ailill and Medb and the chieftains of Connachta had come to drink to the end of the boy's first month. They had all gathered there, and so had Echu son of Luchtae with his province and Cú Ruí son of Dáre with the Cland Dedad. Despite the presence of so many, the woman-warrior Medb, the daughter of Echu Feidlech high king of Ériu, was still cautious, and so there were two watchmen, two druids, guarding her. Their names were Cromm Deróil and Cromm Darail, two foster-sons of the most excellent druid Cathub.

It happened that these two druids were on the wall of Temuir Lúachra that night, looking and watching and waiting and guarding on all sides, when Cromm Deróil said 'Have you seen what I just saw?' 'What is that?' asked Cromm Darail. 'I seemed to see a red-armoured company and the thundering of a host on the slopes of Irlúachair from the east,' said Cromm Deróil. 'I would not think a mouthful of blood and gore too much for the person who said that,' said Cromm Darail. 'No host or multitude that, but the great oaks we passed yesterday.' 'If that is so, then why the great royal chariots under them?' asked Cromm Deróil. 'Not chariots they, but the royal strongholds we passed,' answered Cromm Darail. 'If that is so, then why are there beautiful, pure white shields in them?' asked Cromm Deróil. 'Not shields at all those, but the stone columns at the entrances to the royal strongholds,' answered Cromm Darail. 'If those are columns, then why all the red-pointed

spears over the great dark breasts of the mighty host?'
asked Cromm Deróil. 'Not spearpoints at all those, but the
deer and wild beasts of the land with their horns and
antlers overhead,' answered Cromm Darail. 'If those are
deer and wild beasts, then why do the horses' hooves blacken
the air overhead with the clods they send up?' asked Cromm
Deróil. 'Not horses they, but the herds and flocks and cattle
that have been let out of their stalls and pens – it is in their
pastures that birds and other winged creatures alight in the
snow,' answered Cromm Darail.

'My word, if those are birds and winged creatures, it is not
a single flock,' Cromm Deróil said, and he recited this poem:

> If that is a flock, with the colour of a flock,
> they are not one kind of bird.
> A multicoloured cloak with a golden brooch
> seems to hang round the neck of each bird.
>
> If these are flocks from a rugged glen,
> their tips are very black:
> not scarce their bitter spears
> with the warlike points.
>
> They seem to me not flurries of snow
> but small men, in truth,
> arriving in a multitude
> with their straight spears,
> a man behind each hard crimson shield.
> That is a huge flock.

'And do not contradict me, either,' said Cromm Deróil, 'for
it is I who am telling the truth. Why did they bend under
the branches of the oaks of Irlúachair on their journey west
if they were not men?' Cromm Deróil reproved Cromm
Darail thus, and he recited this poem:

The Intoxication of the Ulaid

Cromm Darail, what do I see
through the mist?
Whose blood is presaged
after the slaughter?

Not right for you to contend with me
on every point.
You are saying, hunchback, they are
slow bushes.

If they are bushes they will remain
in silence.
They will not rise unless there is need
for them to go.

If they were a grove of alder trees
over the wood of a cairn,
they would not follow a deceptive path,
they being dead.

Since they are not dead, fierce their slaughter,
rough their colour.
They traverse plains and wood hedges
for they are alive.

If they were trees on hilltops,
they would be without deeds of combat;
those mantles would not move
if they were speckled.

Since they are not trees, ugly their clamour,
without any lie;
men of triumphs these men of alder shields,
red their weapons.

Since they ride dark horses,
they form a row of hosts;
if they are rocks, they row swiftly,
red if they are stones.

201

Why is there a gleam on each point –
a contest dark and certain.
Men go past the tips –
why do they bend over?

Cú Ruí, the son of handsome Dáre, overheard the contention between the two druids outside on the wall of
Temuir Lúachra, and he said 'Not in harmony those druids
outside.' Meanwhile, the sun rose over the earth's orb,
whereupon Cromm Deróil said 'Now the host is evident.'
The sun rose over the slopes of Irlúachair, and Cromm Deróil
recited this poem:

I see many-hilled Lúachair,
the bright-fronted sun shining against its flanks;
they are youths who travel from afar,
between the brown moor and the trees.

If that is a flock of ravens yonder in the east,
if it is a flock of fat landrails,
if it is a flock of noisy starlings,
if it is a flock of herons or barnacle geese,

if it is a flock of shrill barnacle geese,
if it is a flock of shrill swans,
they are still far from heaven,
they are still close to the earth.

Cú Ruí, son of dear Dáre,
man who traverses the streams of the ocean,
tell us, since you know best,
what crosses the ancient mountain.

Cú Ruí answered with this poem:

The two watchmen, the two druids,
great their perplexity.
What their eyes see terrifies them;
their resistance wavers.

If those are curly-horned cattle,
if they are hard-skinned rocks,
if it is a sparse, dark green wood,
if it is the roar of waves of Muir Miss,

if they are cattle, with the colour of cattle,
they are not one kind of cow;
there is a fierce man with a bloody spear
on the back of each cow.

There is a sword for each cow
and a shield on the left side;
hard standard against hard standard
above the cows that I see.

They had not been there long, the two druids, before a destructive white leap broke from the first troop across the glen. The men advanced with such ferocity that there was not a shield on its peg or a sword or spear on its rack that did not fall down. Every thatched house in Temuir Lúachra had its thatching fall away in flakes the size of tablecloths. It was as if the ocean had washed over the walls and across the corners of the earth towards them. Faces fell and teeth chattered within Temuir Lúachra. The two druids grew dizzy and swooned and fainted; Cromm Darail fell outside the wall, and Cromm Deróil fell inside. Even so, it was Cromm Deróil who rose and cast his eye over the first troop to reach the green. This troop descended upon the green and sat there as one man, and the heat of the great valorous warriors was such that the snow softened and melted for thirty feet on every side.

Cromm Deróil then went inside to Medb and Ailill and Cú Ruí and Echu son of Luchtae, and Medb asked 'Whence has this loud clamour come: down from the air, or across the sea from the west, or from the east across Ériu?' 'Indeed, across Ériu from the east, across the slopes of Irlúachair the march of this barbarous host,' said Cromm Deróil.

'I do not know if they are Ériu or foreigners. If they are Ériu and not foreigners, then they are Ulaid.' 'Would Cú Ruí not recognize the Ulaid by their description?' asked Medb. 'He has often accompanied them on raids and hostings and expeditions.' 'I would recognize them if they were described for me,' said Cú Ruí. 'Indeed, I can describe the first troop that descended upon the green,' said Cromm Deróil. 'Do so, then,' said Medb.

'Outside and to the east of the fort,' said Cromm Deróil, 'I saw a great regal band, and each man was the equal of a king. Three men stood before the band; the middle man was a tall, regal, broad-eyed warrior, his face like the moon in its fifteenth day. His forked beard was fair and narrow; his hair was short and reddish yellow and bound at the back. A fringed, scarlet cloak round him; a brooch inlaid with gold fastening the mantle over his white shoulders; a tunic of kingly satin next to his white skin. A dark crimson shield with bosses of yellow gold he had, and a sword with an inlaid gold hilt. A spear with a glittering blade in his white, illustrious right hand, and a smaller forked spear with it. On his right a true warrior with a face as bright as snow; on his left, a small, dark-browed man, but very resplendent. A very bright, fair man was performing the sword-edge feat overhead, his very sharp, ivory-hilted sword naked in one hand and his great warrior's sword in the other. These swords he juggled up and down so that they cast shadows against the hair and cheeks of the tall warrior in the middle, but, before the swords could strike the ground, he caught them by their points and edges.'

'Regal the description,' said Medb. 'Regal the people described,' said Cú Ruí. 'Who are they, then?' asked Ailill. 'Not difficult that,' said Cú Ruí. 'The tall warrior in the middle is Conchubur son of Fachtnae Fáthach, the worthy, rightful king of Ulaid, descendant of the kings of Ériu and Albu.

The man on his right, with face as white as snow, is Findtan son of Níall Níamglonnach, ruler of one third of Ulaid; the small, dark-browed man on Conchubur's left is Cú Chulaind son of Súaltaim. Ferchertnae son of Coirpre son of Iliu is the very bright, fair man performing weapon feats overhead. Chief poet of the chief poets of the Ulaid he is, and rearguard when Conchubur invades the territory of his enemies. Whoever wishes to speak with the king must speak with this man first.'

'Outside and to the east of the fort,' said Cromm Deróil, 'I saw a swift, handsome trio, all fitted out like champions. Two of them were youthful; the third lad, however, had a forked, dark-shining beard. These three came so swiftly and so lightly that they did not remove the dew from the grass; no one in the great host sees them, and yet they see the entire host.'

'Gentle and light and peaceable the description,' said Medb. 'Gentle and peaceable the people described,' said Cú Ruí. 'Who are they?' asked Ailill. 'Not difficult that,' said Cú Ruí. 'Three noble youths of the Túatha Dé Danand they: Delbáeth son of Eithliu and Óengus Óc son of the Dagdae and Cermait Milbél. They arrived at dawn today to stir up strife and contention, and they have mingled with the host, and it is true that the host cannot see them but that they can see the host.'

'Outside and to the east of the fort,' said Cromm Deróil, 'I saw a valorous warriorlike band led by a distinguished trio. One was dark and furious, and one was fair and truly handsome; but the third was strong and stout and mighty, with short, reddish yellow hair that shone like the crown of a birch tree at the end of autumn or like a brooch of pale gold. He had a forked, dark brown beard the length of a warrior's hand, and his face was like the shining foxglove or a fresh ember. The three bore dark red warrior's shields, great multipointed spears, and heavy, powerful swords, and their apparel was fair and glittering.'

'Warlike and heroic that description, indeed,' said Medb. 'Warlike and heroic the people described,' said Cú Ruí. 'Who are they, then?' asked Ailill. 'Not difficult that,' said Cú Ruí. 'The three chief warriors of Ulaid they are, the two Conalls and Lóegure: Conall Ánglonnach son of Íriel Glúnmár and Conall Cernach son of Amorgen and Lóegure from Ráith Immel.'

'Outside and to the east of the fort,' said Cromm Deróil, 'I saw a frightful, unfamiliar trio standing before their band. Three linen tunics were next to their skin; three woolly, dun grey mantles covered the tunics; three iron stakes fastened the mantles at the breast. Their hair was dark and· bristling, and they carried gleaming dun shields with hard, bronze bosses, spears with broad, flat heads, and swords with gold hilts. Like the cry of a strange hound on the scent the snorting and bellowing each of these men makes when he catches the sound of an enemy in the fort.'

'Savage and heroic that description,' said Medb. 'Savage and heroic the people described,' said Cú Ruí. 'Who are they, then?' asked Ailill. 'Not difficult that,' said Cú Ruí. 'The three battle-stays of Ulaid they: Uma son of Remanfissech of Fedan Chúailnge, Errge Echbél of Brí Errgi and Celtchair Már son of Uthechar of Ráith Celtchair at Dún Dá Lethglas.'

'Outside and to the east of the fort,' said Cromm Deróil, 'I saw a large-eyed, broad-thighed, broad-shouldered, huge, tall man with a splendid tawny cloak about him. Seven smooth black hoods about him, each upper one shorter, each lower one longer. There were nine men on either side of him, and in his hand a dreadful iron club, one end violent, the other mild. This is his game and his feat: he lays the violent end across the heads of the nine men so that they die in an instant; then he lays the gentle end across them so that they are brought back to life in an instant.'

'Wondrous that description,' said Medb. 'Many guises has the one described,' said Cú Ruí. 'Who is it, then?' asked Ailill. 'Not difficult that,' said Cú Ruí. 'That is the Dagdae Már, son of Eithliu, the good god of the Túatha Dé Danand. He has mingled with the host this morning to stir up trouble and strife, but no one of the host has seen him.'

'Outside and to the east of the fort,' said Cromm Deróil, 'I saw a stout, broad-faced man, brawny and black-browed, broad-countenanced and white-toothed, with neither garment nor apparel nor weapon nor blade but only a well-kneaded dark leather apron that reached to his armpits. Each of his limbs was as stout as a large man. The entire Cland Dedad could not lift the stone pillar outside, but he raised it and performed the apple feat with it, from one finger to the other. Then he put it down as if it were a wisp of thistle, all fluff and lightness.'

'Sturdy, stout and strong that description,' said Medb. 'Mighty the one described,' said Cú Ruí. 'Who is it, then?' asked Ailill. 'Not difficult that,' said Cú Ruí. 'Triscatail Trénfer he, the strongman of Conchubur's house. He has slain three nines with no more than an angry look.'

'Outside and to the east of the fort,' said Cromm Deróil, 'I saw a young lad, almost a child, bound and fettered. Three chains round each leg and a chain round each arm; three chains round his neck, and seven men holding each chain, seventy-seven men in all. He turned strongly and powerfully and overthrew the seventy-seven men, dealing with them as lightly and swiftly as he would have dealt with puffballs. When he perceived the smell of his enemies, when he struck the head of a man against a projecting clod or against a rock of stone, then that man would say "It is not for valour or glory that this trick is performed, but by reason of the food and drink in the fort." The lad blushed and fell silent and went about with them a while until the same wave of savagery overcame him.'

'Destructive and intractable that description, indeed,' said Medb. 'Destructive and intractable the one described,' said Cú Ruí. 'Who is it, then?' asked Ailill. 'Not difficult that,' said Cú Ruí. 'He is the son of the three champions of whom I spoke a short while ago: Uma son of Reman-fissech, Errge Echbél and Celtchair son of Uthechar. That many of the host are needed to guard him and to restrain his valour when he goes to the land of his enemies. Úanchend Arritech he, and he is only eleven years old, and never has he consumed a portion of food that he did not offer to everyone in the house.'

'Outside and to the east of the fort,' said Cromm Deróil, 'I saw a rabbly sort of band. One man among them was balding, with short, black hair, bulging, great eyes – one bright – in his head, and a smooth, blue, Ethiopian face. A dappled cloak wrapped round him, a brazen pin in the cloak at his breast and a long bronze crook in his hand. A sweet little bell he had, too. He plied his horsewhip upon the host and brought joy and merriment to the high king and to the entire host.'

'Comic and risible that description,' said Medb. 'Comic the one described,' said Cú Ruí. 'Who is it?' asked Ailill. 'Not difficult that,' said Cú Ruí. 'Rómit Rígóinmit, Con-chubur's fool. No want or sorrow that has ever afflicted the Ulaid has not departed when they saw Rómit Rígóinmit.'

'Outside and to the east of the fort,' said Cromm Deróil, 'I saw a bright, just-greying man in a hooded chariot over very tall horses. He had a huge, multicoloured cloak with golden threads about him, and a gold bracelet on each arm, and a gold ring on each finger, and weapons with gold ornamentation. Nine chariots preceded him, nine followed and nine were on either side.'

'Regal and dignified that description,' said Medb. 'Regal and dignified the one described,' said Cú Ruí. 'Who is it, then?' Ailill asked. 'Not difficult that,' Cú Ruí said. 'Blaí Briugu son of Fiachnae from Temuir na hArdda, and he needs nine chariots about him everywhere he goes, and of the entire host he listens to their speech alone. Seldom do they talk to anyone but him.'

'Outside and to the east of the fort,' said Cromm Deróil, 'I saw a vast, kingly troop, with one man standing before it. Bristling dark hair he had. A gentle blush in one cheek, a furious red blush in the other – a kind, civil answer on the one hand, an angry answer on the other. On his shoulders an open-mouthed leopard; in his hands a white-fronted shield, a bright-hilted sword and a great warrior's spear the height of his shoulder. When its ardour came upon the spear, he gave the butt a blow against the palm of his hand, and a bushel full of fiery sparks broke out along the point and the blade. Before him was a cauldron of dark blood, a dreadful pool of night made through druidry from the blood of dogs and cats and druids, and the head of the spear was submerged in the poisonous liquid whenever its ardour came upon it.'

'Poisonous that description, indeed,' said Medb. 'Poisonous the one described,' said Cú Ruí. 'Who is it, then?' asked Ailill. 'Not difficult that,' said Cú Ruí. 'Dubthach Dóeltenga, a man who has never earned the thanks of anyone. When the Ulaid go out together, he goes out alone. He has the death-dealing Lúin of Celtchair on loan, and the cauldron of very red blood is before him since otherwise the spear would burn its shaft or the man carrying it, and it is prophesying battle.'

'Outside and to the east of the fort,' said Cromm Deróil,

'I saw another band, with a sleek, ancient, hoary-white man standing before it. He had a bright cloak about him with fringes of pure white silver, a handsome pure white tunic next to his skin, a glittering white sword under his cloak and a bronze branch the height of his shoulder. As sweet as music was his voice; very loud and slow was his speech.'

'Judicial and wise that description, indeed,' said Medb. 'Judicial and wise the one described,' said Cú Ruí. 'Who is it, then?' asked Ailill. 'Not difficult that,' said Cú Ruí. 'Senchae Már son of Ailill son of Máelchlód from Carnmag Ulad, a good speaker among mortal men and a peacemaker among the Ulaid. A man of the world from sun to sun, a man who can make peace with three fair words.'

'Outside and to the east of the fort,' said Cromm Deróil, 'I saw an ardent, very handsome band. A youthful lad with curly yellow hair stood before it, and the judgement that the man before him could not give he gave.'

'Wise and clever that description,' said Medb. 'Wise and clever the one described,' said Cú Ruí. 'Who is it, then?' asked Ailill. 'Not difficult that,' said Cú Ruí. 'Caín Caínbrethach son of Senchae son of Ailill he, and the judgement that his father cannot give he gives.'

'Outside and to the east of the fort,' said Cromm Deróil, 'I saw a dreadful foreign trio with short bristling shaggy hair and foreign, dun-coloured clothing; they carried short brazen spears in their right hands and iron clubs in their left. None of them spoke to each other, and none of the host spoke to them.'

'Foreign and servile that description,' said Medb. 'Foreign and servile those described,' said Cú Ruí. 'Who are they, then?' asked Ailill. 'Not difficult that,' said Cú Ruí. 'They are the three doorkeepers of Conchubur's royal house: Nem and Dall and Dorcha.'

That was the description of the first troop to reach the green. The great druid had no more descriptions for Cú Ruí to interpret. 'The Ulaid are yonder, then,' said Medb. 'They are, indeed,' replied Cú Ruí. 'Was this predicted or prophesied that you know of?' asked Medb. 'I do not know that it was,' answered Cú Ruí. 'Is there anyone in the fort who might know?' Medb asked. 'There is the ancient of Cland Dedad,' said Cú Ruí, 'that is, Gabalglinde son of Dedad, who is blind and who has been attended in the fort for thirty years.' 'Let someone go to ask him was this prophesied and what provision was made for it,' said Medb. 'Who should go?' asked Cú Ruí. 'Let Cromm Deróil and Fóenglinde son of Dedad go,' Medb replied.

These two went out to the house where Gabalglinde was attended. 'Who is it?' he asked. 'Cromm Deróil and Fóenglinde son of Dedad,' they replied, 'to ask you if there is a prophecy or a prediction concerning the coming of the Ulaid, and whether any provision has been made.' 'There have long been prophecies and predictions, and there is a provision, and it is this: an iron house with two wooden houses about it, and a house of earth underneath with a very sturdy iron stone on top. All the dead wood and fuel and tinder are to be packed into the house of earth until it is quite full, for it was prophesied to us that the chieftains of Ulaid would gather one night in the iron house. There are about the feet of the bed seven chains of fresh iron for binding and making fast; fasten them about the seven pillars on the green outside.'

Cromm Deróil and Fóenglinde son of Dedad returned to Ailill and Medb and the chieftains of the province, then, and told them what provision had been made for the Ulaid. 'Let one of my people and one of yours go to meet them, Cú Ruí,' said Medb. 'Who should go?' asked Cú Ruí. 'The same pair,' said Medb, 'that the Ulaid might be welcomed by me and the chieftains of the province of Connachta and by you and the chieftains of the province of Mumu.' 'I will be able to tell by the man who receives the welcome whether they have come for peace or war,' said Cú Ruí. 'If it is Dubthach Dóeltenga who answers, they have come to fight; but if it is Senchae son of Ailill, then they have come in peace.'

Cromm Deróil and Fóenglinde son of Dedad went to greet the Ulaid on the green. 'Welcome, welcome, most noble and valorous high king of Ulaid, from Medb and Ailill and the chieftains of the province of Connachta,' said Cromm Deróil. 'Welcome, welcome, most valorous high king of Ulaid,' said Fóenglinde son of Dedad, 'from Cú Ruí son of Dáre and the chieftains of the two provinces of Mumu that are in the fort yonder.' 'We accept your welcome, as does the king,' said Senchae son of Ailill. 'It is not to fight or do evil that the Ulaid have come but on an intoxicated spree from Dún Dá Bend Clíu Máil maicc Úgaine; and we considered it dishonourable to leave the territory without spending a night in it.'

The messengers then returned to Medb and Ailill and Cú Ruí and Echu and the chieftains of the three provinces and related these words. Poets and musicians and entertainers were sent to the Ulaid until a house could be prepared for their entertainment and amusement. Messengers were also sent to the Ulaid, to ask their best warrior to choose a house. At this, a contention arose among the Ulaid: one hundred champions, all equally valorous, rose as one for their weapons, but Senchae son of Ailill pacified them, saying 'Let Cú Chulaind go, since it is for the sake of his house that you came, and accept his protection until he returns.' Cú Chulaind rose, then, and the Ulaid rose as one behind him. He examined the largest house in the place, and that was the iron house, about which the two wooden houses were.

After that, attendants came to look after the Ulaid; a huge

bonfire was kindled, and their portions of food and drink were served. As night approached, the servants and attendants slipped away one by one, and, when the last servant left, he locked the door after him. The seven chains of fresh iron were wrapped round the house and fastened about the seven pillars on the green outside. Three fifties of smiths with their bellows were brought to fan the flames; three circles were made round the house, and the fire was kindled from above and below until its heat reached the iron house from below. At that, the host outside the house sent up a shout, and the Ulaid fell silent. Bricriu said 'Ulaid, what is this great heat that burns our feet? A whisper is clearer to me than a shout is to anyone else: it seems to me that we are being burned from above and below and that the house is locked.' 'This is how we will find out,' said Triscatail Trénfer, and he rose and kicked at the iron door, but it neither creaked nor groaned nor yielded. 'Not good the feast you have prepared for the Ulaid, Cú Chulaind,' said Bricriu, 'for you have led us into the lair of the enemy.' 'Not so, Bricriu,' said Cú Chulaind, 'for I will perform a feat with my Crúadin that will enable the Ulaid to leave.'[1] Cú Chulaind thrust his sword up to the hilt into the iron house and the two wooden houses. 'There is an iron house here,' he said, 'between two houses of wood.' 'The worst of all tricks that,' said Bricriu.

*

... should visit them, my club will slay them.' 'Let me go,' said Triscoth, 'for anyone that I gaze upon with my wrathful look will die.' 'Let me go,' said Réordae Drúth. 'Let me,' said Nía Natrebuin Chró. 'Let me,' said Dóeltenga. 'One of us will go,' said Dub and Rodub. Everyone rose against his fellow, then, but Senchae said 'Do not quarrel over this. The man the Ulaid choose should go, even if he is not the best warrior here.' 'Which of us is that?' asked the Ulaid.

'Cú Chulaind should go, even though he is not the best warrior here,' said Senchae.

They rose and went to the courtyard, then, and Cú Chulaind led them. 'Is this sprite the best warrior of the Ulaid?' Findtan asked. With that, Cú Chulaind leapt up to the top of the courtyard, and he leapt valorously upon the front bridge so that the weapons in the fort all fell from their racks. The Ulaid were then taken into a house of oak with a vaulted roof and a door of yew three feet thick and two iron hooks and an iron bolt. This house was strewn with quilts and coverlets. Cromm Deróil brought their weapons and bade them sit down, and Cú Chulaind's weapons hung overhead.

'Heat water so that they may wash,' said Ailill, and food and beer were brought to the Ulaid until they were intoxicated. Cromm Deróil visited them once more to see if there was anything else they might like. And when they were intoxicated, Senchae called for attention, and they all listened. 'Give now your blessing to the sovereign to whom you have come, for he has been munificent. No hand in a poor field here. He has provided an abundance of food and beer – no need to complain about the preparations.' 'That is true,' said Dóeltenga. 'I swear by what my people swear by, there will return to your land only what the birds might carry away in their claws – the men of Ériu and Albu will inhabit your land and take your women and goods and break the heads of your children against stones.'

During the cattle raid of Cúailnge, Fergus said this about Dóeltenga:

> Away with Dubthach Dóeltenga,
> drag him behind the host.
> Never has he done any good;
> he has slain young women.

He has done a hideous, shameful deed:
the slaying of Fíachu son of Conchubur.
Neither is he any the more illustrious
for the slaying of Mane son of Fedilmid.

He does not contest the kingship of Ulaid,
this son of Lugaid son of Casrubae.
Those people whom he cannot kill
he incites against each other.

'No lie that,' said Dubthach Dóeltenga. 'But note the strength of the house and how the door is closed. Do you not see that, though you might want to leave, you cannot? Shame on me if, outside, there is not some dispute about attacking us. Let him whom the Ulaid consider their best warrior obtain news for us.'

With that, Cú Chulaind rose and did the hero's salmon leap upwards, so that he went from the ridge pole of the house to the ridge pole of another house; and he saw the host gathered below, forming a solid front for the attack. Ailill placed his back against the door to protect those inside, and his seven sons joined hands in the doorway; but the host broke into the middle of the courtyard.

Cú Chulaind returned to his people, then, and he kicked at the door so that his leg went through it up to the knee. 'If that blow had been delivered against a woman,' said Dubthach, 'she would be in bed.' Cú Chulaind kicked again, and the door frame fell into the hearth. 'Advice!' said Senchae. 'That is here,' answered Cú Chulaind. 'You will have whatever is fit from youths in combat. Your enemies approach.' 'What is your advice?' asked Senchae. 'Put your backs against the wall, and have your weapons before you, and charge one man to speak with them,' said Cú Chulaind. 'If that which comes is heavier to raise, then throw the house from you.' 'Who should speak with them?' asked

Senchae. 'I will, for any of them whom I stare at will die,' said Triscoth.

Outside, their enemies were holding a council. 'Who should speak with them and be the first to go inside?' asked a youth. 'I will go,' said Lopán. Lopán went inside, then, taking nine men with him, and he said 'A warrior's deed, warriors.' 'Man against man – that is a warrior's deed,' said Triscoth. 'True enough. Triscoth as spokesman for the Ulaid? No other worthy spokesman?' said Lopán. But Triscoth looked balefully at him, and the soles of Lopán's feet turned deathly white.

After that, Fer Calliu came into the house with nine men. 'A warrior's deed, warriors!' he said. 'Man against man – that is a warrior's deed,' said Triscoth, and he looked balefully at Fer Calliu until the soles of the latter's feet turned deathly white.

After that, Míanach Anaidgned entered the house with nine men. 'Those on the floor seem pale to us,' he said. Triscoth looked at him, but Míanach said 'Look at me and see if I die.' Triscoth seized him, then, and hurled him against the three nines that had entered the house, and not one of those men left alive.

After that, the host gathered about the house to take it from the Ulaid, and the Ulaid overturned the house so that it fell upon three hundred of the host. The fighting broke out, then, and it lasted until the middle of the following day; and the Ulaid were routed, for they were few in number. Ailill watched this from his dwelling in the fort, and he said 'The tales of the Ulaid were tales to be told until today. I was told that there were no youths in Ériu to equal them, but today I see in them nothing but shame. It is an old proverb that no battle is fought without a king; a battle fought round me, however, would not long endure. But I may not fight them, for that would violate my honour.'

With that, Cú Chulaind bounded through the troop and attacked them three times. Furbude Fer Bend son of Conchubur also assailed them, but his enemies would not strike at him because of his great beauty. 'Why do you not attack him?' said one man. 'Not pleasing the little games of this magnificent fellow. I swear by what my people swear by, if he had a head of gold, I would still slay the man who slew my brother.' But Furbude cast his spear at the man and killed him. Thereafter, the Erainn were routed, so that only three of them escaped; the Ulaid plundered the fort, but they spared Ailill and his seven sons, none of whom had fought. Since that time, Temuir Lúachra has not been inhabited.

Crumthand Níad Náir, of the Erainn, escaped. To the west, at the Lemuin, he encountered the female satirist Riches, who was his foster-mother. 'Was my son left?' she asked. 'He was,' Crumthand replied. 'Come with me, and I will avenge him,' she said. 'How will you do that?' Crumthand asked. 'You will slay Cú Chulaind in return,' Riches said. 'How will I do that?' Crumthand asked. 'Not difficult that,' she said. 'If you can use your two hands you will need nothing else, for you will find him all ready for you.'

Riches went out after the host, then, and she found Cú Chulaind up ahead at a ford in Crích Úaithne. She took her clothes off in front of Cú Chulaind, and he turned his face to the ground that he might not see her nakedness. 'Attack now, Crumthand,' she said. 'There is a man coming at you,' said Lóeg. 'Indeed not,' said Cú Chulaind, 'for, while the woman is in that state, I may not rise.' Lóeg took a stone from the chariot and hurled it at Riches so that it broke her back and slew her. Cú Chulaind rose, then, and met Crumthand; they fought, and Cú Chulaind took his head and his gear.

Cú Chulaind and Lóeg followed the host, then, until they

reached Cú Chulaind's fort, and they slept there. Cú Chulaind entertained the Ulaid for forty nights with one feast; after that, they departed and left their blessing with him. Ailill, moreover, came north to Ulaid to visit. He was given the width of his face in gold and silver and seven cumals for each of his sons; then he returned to his own land, in peace and harmony with the Ulaid. Thereafter, Conchubur's kingship was unimpaired for as long as he lived.

Bricriu's Feast

Introduction

'Bricriu's Feast', perhaps the most characteristic Ulster Cycle story, has just about everything: a mythic subtext, a heroic competition, visits to and from the otherworld, elements of humour and parody and a rambling, patchwork structure. The mythic subtext comprises the beheading sequence known to English literature from *Sir Gawain and the Green Knight*; but there, even though the tale is of later date, the regeneration theme is clearer because the ritual slaying takes place at New Year (the English equivalent of Samuin) and because the earth-goddess figure (the Green Knight's wife) is present. Irish tradition frequently presents otherworld judges as large, ugly churls in rough, drab clothing; one might also compare Cú Ruí's appearance with that of Arawn at the outset of 'Pwyll Lord of Dyved'. As for the Green Knight's colour, which has led some to identify him as a vegetation figure, grey and green are not always clearly distinguished in Irish – the word *glass*, for example, might signify either colour.

The actual text, or theme, of 'Bricriu's Feast' is much simpler: the contest among Lóegure Búadach, Conall Cernach and Cú Chulaind for the champion's portion – that is, for the biggest and best serving at feasts and for the privilege of sitting at Conchubur's right. The competition

takes the folktale form wherein each of three brothers attempts a feat (Cú Chulaind, of course, is the youngest).

Bricriu, whose sobriquet Nemthenga means 'poison
tongue', is a mischief-maker, an Irish Lóki; yet he seldom
perpetrates any permanent or serious damage (such as the
death of Baldur). 'Bricriu's Feast' is, in fact, comic as well
as heroic. Although Bricriu threatens to turn the Ulaid
against one another, to set father against son and mother
against daughter, it is not until he threatens to set the
breasts of each Ulaid women beating against each other
that the chieftains agree to attend his feast. The risibility
of Fedelm, Lendabair and Emer racing each other to the
drinking house, their suspicions raised as high as their skirts,
cannot have escaped the storyteller; neither can the
spectacle of Bricriu's beautiful house left lopsided, nor that
of Bricriu himself thrown down on to the garbage heap and
reappearing at the door so filthy with dirt and mud that the
Ulaid do not recognize him.

The structure of 'Bricriu's Feast' leaves something to be
desired. Doubtless the storyteller has stretched his material
(and his host's hospitality), and perhaps he has tried to
reconcile conflicting traditions; still, the resultant repetitions and duplications must have sounded better in a chieftain's banquet hall than they look in print, and it is also
fair to presume some degree of deterioration in both transmission and transcription.

'Bricriu's Feast' is the ultimate source for Yeats's play
The Green Helmet.

Bricriu's Feast

Bricriu Nemthenga prepared a great feast for Conchubur
son of Ness and all of Ulaid. He spent an entire year
preparing this feast: he had an ornamented mansion built
for the guests, and he had it erected at Dún Rudrige. Bricriu's
house was built in the likeness of the Cráebrúad at Emuin
Machae, but his house surpassed the Cráebrúad as to materials and workmanship, beauty and decoration, pillars and
façades, carvings and lintels, radiance and beauty, comeliness
and excellence — in short, it surpassed every house of that
time. It was constructed on the plan of the Tech Midchúarta:
there were nine apartments between the hearth and the
wall, and each façade was thirty feet high and made of
bronze, and there was gold ornamentation everywhere. A
royal apartment for Conchubur was erected at the front of
the royal house, high above the other couches, and it was
ornamented with carbuncle and other precious things; it
shone with the radiance of gold and silver and carbuncle
and every colour, so that it was as bright by night as by
day. Round this apartment were built twelve apartments,
for the twelve warriors of Ulaid. The workmanship of this
house was as good as the materials used to build it: a team
of oxen was required to draw each pillar, and seven of
the strongest men of Ulaid to fix each pillar; and thirty
of the chief seers of Ériu came to place and arrange everything.

Bricriu also had built, for himself, a bower, and it was as

high as Conchubur's apartment and those of his warriors. This bower was decorated with marvellous embroideries and hangings, and glass windows were set in on every side. And one of these windows was set over Bricriu's couch, in order that he might see what was going on, for he knew that the Ulaid would not allow him inside the house.

When all was ready – the great house, and the bower, and their provisioning with plaids and coverlets and quilts and pillows and food and drink – and when nothing was wanting as to furnishings and materials for the feast, Bricriu went off to Emuin Machae to see Conchubur and the chieftains of Ulaid. The Ulaid were holding a fair at Emuin that day; Bricriu was welcomed and placed at Conchubur's shoulder, and he said to Conchubur and to the chieftains 'Come and enjoy my feast with me.' 'I am willing if the Ulaid are,' Conchubur answered, but Fergus son of Roech and the other chieftains said 'We will not go. If we go to his feast, he will incite us against each other, and our dead will outnumber our living.' 'I will do worse than that if you do not come,' said Bricriu. 'What will you do?' asked Conchubur. 'I will incite the kings and the chiefs and the warriors and the young warriors,' said Bricriu, 'so that you will all kill one other unless you come to drink at my feast.' 'We will not go to avoid that,' said Conchubur. 'Then I will set son against father and incite them to kill each other,' said Bricriu. 'If that is not enough, I will set daughter against mother. And if that is not enough, I will incite the two breasts of every Ulaid woman to beat against each other and become foul and putrid.' 'In that case, it would be better to go,' said Fergus. 'Let a few chieftains form a council, if that seems right,' said Senchae son of Ailill, and Conchubur agreed, saying 'Evil will come of our not adopting some plan.'

The chieftains formed a council, then, and, as they discussed the matter, Senchae gave the following advice: 'Since you must go with Bricriu, require him to give hostages, and, as soon as he has set out the feast, send eight swordsmen to escort him from the house.' Furbude son of Conchubur took that decision to Bricriu, and Bricriu replied 'I will be happy to abide by that.' Thus the Ulaid set out from Emuin Machae, each band with its king, each troop with its leader, each host with its chieftain – a marvellously handsome procession it was, with the warriors and the men of might making for the royal house.

Bricriu, meanwhile, began to think how he might incite the Ulaid once he had given them their hostages; and when he had given the matter considerable thought, he went to Lóegure Búadach son of Connad son of Iliu. 'Well met, Lóegure Búadach,' he said, 'mighty blow of Brega, seething blow of Mide, bearer of red flame, victor over the youth of Ulaid! Why should you not always have the champion's portion at Emuin?' 'Indeed, it is mine if I want it,' said Lóegure. 'I will make you king over all the warriors of Ériu if you follow my advice,' said Bricriu. 'Then I will follow it,' said Lóegure. 'Once the champion's portion is yours at my house,' Bricriu continued, 'it will be yours at Emuin for ever. And the champion's portion at my house will be worth contesting, for it is not the portion of a fool. I have a cauldron that would hold three of the warriors of Ulaid, and it has been filled with undiluted wine. I have a seven-year-old boar that since it was a piglet has eaten nothing but gruel and meal and fresh milk in spring, curds and sweet milk in summer, nuts and wheat in autumn and meat and broth in winter. I have a lordly cow that is also seven years old, and, since it was a calf, it has eaten nothing but heather and twigs and fresh milk and herbs and meadow grass and corn. I have one hundred wheat cakes cooked in honey; twenty-five bushels of wheat were brought for these cakes, so that each bushel made just four cakes. That is what the champion's portion is like at my house. Since you are the best warrior in Ulaid, it is yours by right, and I intend that you should have it. Once the feast has been set out, at the end of the day, have your charioteer rise, and the champion's portion will be given to him.' 'Indeed, it will,' said Lóegure, 'or blood will flow.' Bricriu laughed at that and was content.

When he had finished with Lóegure Búadach, Bricriu went to the host of Conall Cernach. 'Well met, Conall,' he began, 'for you are a warrior of combats and victories – already you have earned great triumphs over the youths of Ulaid. When the Ulaid venture out to the borders of enemy lands, you are three days and three nights ahead of them in crossing fords; and, when they return, you protect their rear – no enemy slips past them or through them or round them. Is there any reason why you should not have the champion's portion at Emuin Machae for ever?' If Bricriu was treacherous in dealing with Lóegure, he was twice as deceitful when he spoke with Conall. And after he had induced Conall to agree with him, he went to the host of Cú Chulaind. 'Well met, Cú Chulaind,' he began, 'battle victor of Brega, bright flag of the Life, darling of Emuin, sweetheart of the women and the young girls. Today, Cú Chulaind is no nickname, for you are the great boaster of Ulaid. You defend us from great onslaughts and attacks, you seek the rights of everyone in Ulaid, and where everyone else attempts, you succeed. All Ériu acknowledges your bravery and valour and high deeds. Why, then, should you leave the champion's portion to anyone else in Ulaid when there is not a man in Ériu capable of meeting you in combat?' 'Indeed! I swear by what my people swear by,' said Cú Chulaind, 'the man who comes to fight me will be a man without a head!' After that, Bricriu left the three heroes and mingled with the hosts as if he had done no mischief at all.

The Ulaid arrived at Bricriu's house, and each man settled into his apartment in the royal dwelling, king and prince and chieftain and young lord and young warrior. On one side of the house, the heroes of Ulaid gathered round Conchubur, while, on the other side, the women of Ulaid assembled round Conchubur's wife, Mugain daughter of Echu Feidlech. The heroes who gathered round Conchubur in the front of the house included Fergus son of Roech, Celtchair son of Uthechar, Éogan son of Durthacht, the king's two sons Fíachu and Fíachach, Fergnae son of Findchóem, Fergus son of Léti, Cúscraid Mend Machae son of Conchubur, Senchae son of Ailill, Fíachu's three sons Rus and Dáre and Imchad, Muinremur son of Gerrgend, Errge Echbél, Amorgen son of Ecet, Mend son of Salchad, Dubthach Dóeltenga, Feradach Find Fechtnach, Fedilmid Chilair Chétach, Furbude Fer Bend, Rochad son of Fathemon, Lóegure Búadach, Conall Cernach, Cú Chulaind, Connad son of Mornae, Erc son of Fedilmid, Illand son of Fergus, Findtan son of Níall, Cethernd son of Findtan, Fachtna son of Senchad, Condlae Sáeb, Ailill Miltenga, Bricriu himself and the choicest warriors of Ulaid, together with the youths and the entertainers.

The musicians and the players performed while the feast was being set out, and when everything was in place, Bricriu was ordered to leave the house, as a consequence of the hostages he had given. The hostages rose, naked swords in hand, to expel Bricriu from the house, and so he left, with his household, and repaired to the bower. But, as he was about to leave the royal house, he said to the gathering 'Yonder you see the champion's portion, and it is no portion from the house of a fool; therefore, let it be given to the best warrior in Ulaid.' With that, he left.

Thereupon, the servers rose to do their work, and there rose also the charioteer of Lóegure Búadach, Sedlang son of Ríangabur, and he said to the distributors 'Bring that champion's portion over here, to Lóegure Búadach, for he is the most deserving of it in Ulaid.' Id son of Ríangabur, Conall Cernach's charioteer, rose and said the same about Conall. And Lóeg son of Ríangabur, Cú Chulaind's charioteer, said to the distributors 'Bring the champion's portion to Cú Chulaind – no shame for the Ulaid to give it to him, for he is the most accomplished warrior here.' 'Not true that,' said Lóegure Búadach and Conall Cernach, and, at that, the three heroes rose out into the middle of the house with their spears and swords and shields; and they so slashed at each other that half the house was a fire of swords and glittering spear edges, while the other half was a pure-white bird flock of shield enamel. A great alarm went up in the royal house, and the valiant warriors of Ulaid trembled; Conchubur and Fergus son of Roech were furious at seeing the unfair and unconscionable attack of two against one, Lóegure and Conall attacking Cú Chulaind. Not a man of the Ulaid dared separate them, however, until Senchae said to Conchubur 'Part the men', for Senchae was the earthly god among the Ulaid in the time of Conchubur.

Conchubur and Fergus stepped between the combatants, then, and the men at once dropped their hands to their sides. 'Let my will prevail,' said Senchae. 'We agree,' said the men. 'It is my will,' said Senchae, 'that the champion's portion be divided among the host tonight and that tomorrow the dispute be submitted to Ailill son of Mágu, since it is bad luck for the Ulaid to settle an argument without a judgement from Crúachu.' The food and drink were shared out, then, and everyone formed a circle round the fire, and the assembly grew drunken and merry.

Bricriu, meanwhile, was in his bower with his queen, and he could see from his couch how matters stood in the royal house. He pondered how he might incite the women as he had incited the men, and, just as he finished his meditation, Fedelm Noíchride and her fifty women emerged from the royal house after some heavy drinking. Bricriu perceived her going past and said 'Well met tonight, wife of Lóegure Búadach! Fedelm Noíchride is not just a nickname, not considering your form and your intelligence and your lineage. Conchubur, a provincial king of Ériu, is your father, Lóegure Búadach is your husband, and it would hardly be to your honour if any woman of Ulaid were to precede you into the Tech Midchúarta – rather, the women of all Ulaid should follow upon your heel. If you enter the house first tonight, you will always be first among the women of Ulaid.' Thereupon Fedelm went out to the third ridge from the house.

After that, Lendabair, the daughter of Éogan son of Durthacht and the wife of Conall Cernach, came out. Bricriu accosted her and said 'Well met, Lendabair! No nickname yours, for you are the centre of attention and the sweetheart of the men of all the world, and that by reason of your beauty and your fame. As your husband outdoes the men of the world in weaponry and in appearance, so you outdo the women of Ulaid.' As deceitful as he had been in talking to Fedelm, he was twice as deceitful in dealing with Lendabair.

After that, Emer came out with her fifty women, and Bricriu greeted her, saying 'Your health, Emer, daughter of Forgall Manach and wife of the best man in Ériu. Emer Foltchaín is no nickname, either, for the kings and princes of Ériu glitter round you. As the sun outshines the stars of the sky, so you outshine the women of the entire world, and that by reason of your shape and form and lineage, your youth and beauty and fame and your intelligence and discernment and eloquence.' Although he had been very deceitful in dealing with the other two women, Bricriu was thrice as deceitful in dealing with Emer.

All three companies of women then went out to the same spot, the third ridge from the house, and no wife knew that the other two had been incited by Bricriu. And all three women set out for the house. At the first ridge, the procession was steady and stately and measured – one foot was scarcely lifted above the other. At the second ridge, however, the steps became shorter and quicker. By the third ridge, the women were striving to keep up with each other, and they all raised their skirts to their hips, for Bricriu had told each woman that she who entered the house first would be queen over the entire province. The tumult that arose from their striving was like the tumult from the arrival of fifty chariots; it so shook the house that the warriors inside sprang for their weapons and tried to kill each other. But Senchae said 'Wait! This is not the arrival of enemies – rather, Bricriu has incited the women outside to strife. I swear by what my people swear by, if he is not expelled from the house, the dead will outnumber the living.' At that, the doorkeepers closed the door. Emer daughter of Forgall Manach reached the door first, by reason of her speed, and she put her back against the door and entreated the doorkeepers to open it before the other women arrived. Thereupon the men inside rose, each meaning to open the door for his own wife so that she might be the first to enter. 'An evil night,' said Conchubur, and he struck the silver sceptre in his hand against the bronze pillar of his couch, and the host sat down. Senchae said 'Wait! Not a war of weapons this, but a war of words.'

With that, each woman drew back from the door, under the protection of her husband, and there began a war of words among the women of Ulaid. Upon hearing the praises of their wives, Lóegure and Conall sprang up into the warrior's moon; each of them broke off a pole as tall as himself from the house, and that way Fedelm and Lendabair were able to enter. Cú Chulaind, however, lifted the side of the house opposite his apartment so high that the stars were visible beneath the wall; Emer was thus able to enter with her fifty women and the fifty women of each of the other two wives. He then set the house back down; seven feet of panelling sank into the ground, and the fort shook so much that Bricriu's bower fell, and Bricriu and his wife were thrown on to the garbage heap in the courtyard, among the dogs.

'Alas! Enemies are attacking the fort,' said Bricriu, and he rose quickly and looked at his house, and it seemed to have been destroyed, for one side had fallen down. He beat on the door, then, and the Ulaid let him in, for he was so besmirched that they did not recognize him until he began to speak. He stood in the middle of the house and said 'Unlucky this feast that I have prepared for you, men of Ulaid. My house is dearer to me than all my possessions, and there is a geiss against your eating or sleeping until you leave it just as you found it when you arrived.'

Thereupon all the warriors of Ulaid rose and tried to restore the house, but they could not even raise it high enough for the wind to pass underneath. This was a problem for the Ulaid. Senchae said 'I can only advise you to ask the man who made the house lopsided to set it straight.' The Ulaid then asked Cú Chulaind to put the house to rights, and Bricriu said 'King of the warriors of Ériu, if you cannot restore the house, no one in the world can.' All the Ulaid entreated Cú Chulaind to help them, and he rose up so that the feasters would not have to go without food and drink. He attempted to straighten the house, and he failed. Then his ríastarthae came over him: a drop of blood appeared at the tip of each hair, and he drew his hair into his head, so that, from above, his jet black locks appeared to have been cropped with scissors; he turned like a mill wheel, and he stretched himself out until a warrior's foot could fit between each pair of ribs. His power and energy returned to him, and he lifted the house and reset it so that it was as straight as it had been before.

After that, they had a pleasant time enjoying the feast. On one side of the illustrious Conchubur, the glorious high king of Ulaid, gathered the kings and chiefs, and on the other side were the queens: Mugain Attencháithrech daughter of Echu Feidlech and wife of Conchubur son of Ness, Fedelm Noíchride daughter of Conchubur (nine forms she displayed, and each was lovelier than the last), Fedelm Foltchaín (Conchubur's other daughter and the wife of Lóegure Búadach), Findbec daughter of Echu and wife of Cethernd son of Findtan, Brig Brethach wife of Celtchair son of Uthechar, Findige daughter of Echu and wife of Éogan son of Durthacht, Findchóem daughter of Cathub and wife of Amorgen Íarngiunnach, Derborcaill wife of Lugaid Réoderg son of the three Finds of Emuin, Emer Foltchaín daughter of Forgall Manach and wife of Cú Chulaind son of Súaltaim, Lendabair daughter of Éogan son of Durthacht and wife of Conall Cernach, and Níam daughter of Celtchair son of Uthechar and wife of Cormac Cond Longes son of Conchubur. There was no counting the number of beautiful women at that feast.

And yet the women began once again to squabble over their men and themselves, with the result that the three heroes all but resumed their combat. Senchae son of Ailill rose and shook his staff, and the men of Ulaid fell silent. He spoke words to chasten the women, but Emer continued to praise her husband. Thereupon Conall Cernach said

'Woman, if your words are true, let that lad of feats come here, that I might oppose him.' 'Not at all,' said Cú Chulaind, 'for I am tired and broken to pieces. Today, I will eat and sleep, but I will not undertake combat.' All this was in fact true, by reason of Cú Chulaind's encounter that day with the Líath Machae by the shore of Lind Léith near Slíab Fúait. The horse had come towards him from the lake, Cú Chulaind had put his arms round its neck, and the two of them had circled all Ériu until at last night fell and the horse was broken. (Cú Chulaind found the Dub Sainglend in the same way, at Loch Duib Sainglend.) Cú Chulaind went on: 'Today the Líath Machae and I have sought out the great hostels of Ériu: Brega, Mide, Muresc, Muirthemne, Macha, Mag Medba, Currech, Cletech, Cernae, Lía, Líne, Locharna, Fea, Femen, Fergna, Urros, Domnand, Ros Roigne, Anni Éo. Better every feat of sleeping, dearer food than anything else. I swear by the god my people swear by, if I had my fill of food and sleep, there would be no trick or feat that any man could meet me at.'

It happened, thus, that the dispute over the champion's portion arose again. Conchubur and the chieftains of Ulaid intervened to pronounce judgement, and Conchubur said 'Go now to the man who will undertake to decide this matter, Cú Ruí son of Dáre.' 'I will agree to that,' said Cú Chulaind. 'So will I,' said Lóegure. 'Let us go, then,' said Conall Cernach. 'Let horses be brought and yoked to Conall's chariot,' said Cú Chulaind. 'Alas!' said Conall. 'Indeed,' replied Cú Chulaind, 'for everyone knows well the clumsiness of your horses and the slowness of your gait and bearing and the great ponderousness with which your chariot moves; each wheel digs a ditch, so that everywhere you leave a track that is visible to the Ulaid for a year.' 'Do you hear that, Lóegure?' Conall asked. 'Indeed — but it is not I who have been disgraced and embarrassed. I am quick to

cross fords – many fords – and I breast storms of many
spears in front of the youths of Ulaid. I will not grant the
superiority of kings until I have practised my chariot feats
before kings and heroes in single chariots, over difficult
and treacherous terrain, in wooded places and along enemy
borders, in order that no single-charioted hero might dare
to meet me.'

With that, they yoked Lóegure's chariot, and he sprang
into it; he drove across Mag Dá Gabul and Berrnaid na
Forare and Áth Carpait Fergussa and Áth na Mórrígna to
Cáerthend Clúana Dá Dam and into Clithar Fidbude, into
Commur Cetharsliged, past Dún Delga, across Mag Slicech
and west towards Slíab Breg. There, a great mist fell, thick
and dark and impenetrable, so that he could not see his way.
'Let us stay here until the fog lifts,' he said to his charioteer,
and he leapt down from the chariot. His charioteer was
putting the horses out in a nearby meadow when he saw a
giant man coming towards him, not a handsome fellow,
either, but broad-shouldered, fat-mouthed, puffy-eyed, short-
toothed, horribly wrinkled, beetle-browed, horrible and
angry, strong, violent, ruthless, arrogant, destructive, snorting, big-sinewed, strong-forearmed, brave, rough and rustic.
Cropped black hair he had, and a dun garment on him, and
his rump swelled out under his tunic; there were filthy old
shoes on his feet, and on his back he carried a great, heavy
club, the size of a mill shaft. 'Whose horses are these, boy?'
he asked, looking fierce. 'The horses of Lóegure Búadach
these,' answered the lad. 'True,' said the giant, 'and it is a
good man whose horses these are.' As he said this, he took
his club and gave the lad a blow from head to toe. At
that, Lóegure came and said 'Why did you strike my
charioteer?' 'As punishment for trespassing in my meadow,'
replied the giant. 'I will meet you myself,' said Lóegure,
and they fought until Lóegure fled back to Emuin, leav-

Ing his horses and his charioteer and his weapons behind.

Not long afterwards, Conall Cernach took the same route and arrived at the same plain where the druidic mist had fallen upon Lóegure. The same thick, dark, heavy clouds confronted Conall, so that he could see neither the sky nor the ground. He leapt down, then, and his charioteer turned the horses out into the same meadow, and soon they saw the giant coming towards them. The giant asked the lad who his master was, and the lad answered 'Conall Cernach.' 'A good man he,' said the giant, and he raised his club and gave the lad a blow from head to toe. The lad cried out, and Conall came running; Conall and the giant wrestled, but the latter had the stronger holds, so Conall fled, just as Lóegure had done, leaving behind his horses and his charioteer and his weapons.

After that, Cú Chulaind took the same route and arrived at the plain where the dark mist fell, just as before; he leapt down, Lóeg turned the horses out into the meadow. Soon Lóeg saw the giant coming towards him and asking him who his master was, and he answered 'Cú Chulaind.' 'A good man he,' said the giant, and he struck Lóeg with his club. Lóeg cried out, and Cú Chulaind came and wrestled with the giant; they pounded away at each other until the giant was worsted and forfeited his horses and chariot. Cú Chulaind took these, and his opponent's weapons, and bore them back to Emuin Machae in great triumph, presenting them as evidence of his victory.

'Yours is the champion's portion,' Bricriu then said to Cú Chulaind, 'for it is clear that no one else's deeds deserve comparison with yours.' But Lóegure and Conall said 'Not true, Bricriu. We know that it was one of his friends from the Síde who came to play tricks on us and do us out of the champion's portion. We will not acknowledge his superiority on that account.' Conchubur and Fergus and the Ulaid failed to resolve the dispute, so they decided to seek out either Cú Ruí son of Dáre or Ailill and Medb at Crúachu. The Ulaid assembled in council to discuss the pride and haughtiness of the three champions, and their decision was that the three should go to the house of Ailill son of Mágu and Medb in Crúachu for a judgement as to the champion's portion and the dispute of the women.

Handsome and graceful and effortless the procession of the Ulaid to Crúachu; Cú Chulaind, however, lagged behind the hosts, for he was entertaining the women of Ulaid with his feats of nine apples and nine javelins and nine knives, no one feat interfering with either of the others. His charioteer, Lóeg son of Ríangabur, went to where he was performing these feats and said 'Pitiful wretch, your valour and your weaponry have disappeared, and the champion's portion has gone with it, for the Ulaid have long since reached Crúachu.' 'I had not noticed that, Lóeg. Yoke up the chariot, then,' said Cú Chulaind. By that time, the rest of the Ulaid had already reached Mag mBreg, but, after being scolded by his charioteer, Cú Chulaind travelled with such speed that the Líath Machae and the Dub Sainglend drew his chariot from Dún Rudrige across the length of Conchubur's province, across Slíab Fúait and Mag mBreg, and reached Crúachu before either Lóegure or Conall.

By reason of the speed and noise with which Conchubur and the warriors and chieftains of Ulaid reached Crúachu, the latter was badly shaken; weapons fell from their racks on the walls, and the host in the stronghold trembled like rushes in a river. Thereupon Medb said 'Since the day I took possession of Crúachu, I have never heard thunder from a clear sky.' Findabair, the daughter of Ailill and Medb, went up to the balcony over the outer door of the fort, and she said 'I see a chariot on the plain, dear mother.' 'Describe it,' said Medb, 'its form and appearance and equipment, the shape of its men, the colour of its horses and the manner of its arrival.' 'I see a chariot with two horses,' said Findabair, 'and they are furious, dapple grey, identical in form and colour and excellence and triumph and speed and leaping, sharp-eared, high-headed, high-spirited, wild, sinuous, narrow-nostrilled, flowing-maned, broad-chested, spotted all over, narrow-girthed, broad-backed, aggressive and with curly manes and tails. The chariot is of spruce and wicker, with black, smooth-turning wheels and beautifully woven reins; it has hard, blade-straight poles, a glistening new body, a curved yoke of pure silver, and pure yellow braided reins. The man has long, braided, yellow hair with three colours on it: dark brown at the base, blood red in the middle and golden yellow at the tip. Three circlets on his head, each in its proper place next to the others. A fair scarlet tunic round him and embroidered with gold and silver; a speckled shield with a border of white gold in his hand; a barbed, five-pointed spike in his red-flaming fist. A flock of wild birds above the frame of his chariot.'

'We recognize that man by his description,' said Medb. 'I swear by what my people swear by, if it is in anger and rage that Lóegure Búadach comes to us, his sharp blade will cut us to the ground like leeks; a nice slaughter he will bring upon the host here at Crúachu unless his strength and ardour and fury are heeded and his anger is diminished.'

'I see another chariot on the plain, dear mother,' said Findabair, 'and it looks no worse.' 'Describe it,' said Medb. 'I see one of a pair of horses,' Findabair said, 'white-faced, copper-coloured, hardy, swift, fiery, bounding, broad-hooved, broad-chested, taking strong victorious strides across fords and estuaries and difficulties and winding roads and plains and glens, frenzied after a drunken victory like a bird in flight; my noble eye cannot describe the step by which it careers on its jealous course. The other horse is red, with a firmly braided mane, a broad back and forehead and a narrow girth; it is fierce, intense, strong and vicious, coursing over wide plains and rough and heavy terrain; it finds no difficulty in wooded land. The chariot is of spruce and wicker with wheels of white bronze, poles of pure silver, a noble, creaking frame, a haughty, curved yoke and reins with pure yellow fringes. The man has long, braided, beautiful hair; his face is half red and half white and bright and glistening all over. His cloak is blue and dark crimson. In one hand, a dark shield with a yellow boss and an edge of serrated bronze; in the other, which burns red, a red-burning spear. A flock of wild birds above the frame of his dusky chariot.'

'We recognize that man by his description,' said Medb. 'I swear by what my people swear by, we will be sliced up the way speckled fish are sliced by iron flails against bright red stones – those are the small pieces Conall Cernach will cut us into if he is raging.'

'I see yet another chariot on the plain,' said Findabair. 'Describe it,' said Medb. 'One horse,' said Findabair, 'is grey, broad-thighed, fierce, swift, flying, ferocious, war-leaping, long-maned, noisy and thundering, curly-maned, high-headed, broad-chested; there shine the huge clods of earth that it cuts up with its very hard hooves. Its victorious stride overtakes flocks of birds; a dreadful flash its breath, a ball of flaming red fire, and the jaws of its bridle-bitted head shine. The other horse is jet black, hard-headed, compact, narrow-hooved, narrow-chested, strong, swift, arrogant, braided-maned, broad-backed, strong-thighed, high-spirited, fleet, fierce, long-striding, stout-blow-dealing, long-maned, long-tailed, swift at running after fighting, driving round paths and runs, scattering wastes, traversing glens and plains. The chariot is of spruce and wicker with iron wheels of rust yellow, poles of white gold, a bright, arching body of copper, and a curved yoke of pure gold and two braided reins of pure yellow. The sad, dark man in the chariot is the most beautiful man in Ériu. He wears a beautiful scarlet tunic, and over his white breast the opening is fastened by a brooch ornamented with gold, and his chest heaves violently. Eight dragon-red gems in his two eyes. His bright-shining, blood-red cheeks emit vapours and missiles of flame. Above his chariot he performs the hero's salmon leap, a feat for nine men.'

'A drop before the storm that,' said Medb. 'We recognize that man by his description. I swear by what my people swear by, if it is in anger that Cú Chulaind comes to us, we will be ground into the earth and gravel the way a mill stone grinds very hard malt – even with the men of the entire province gathered round us in our defence – unless his anger and fury are diminished.'

Medb then went to the outer door of the courtyard, and she took with her three fifties of women and three vats of cold water with which to cool the ardour of the three heroes who were advancing before the host. The heroes were offered one house each or one house for the three of them. 'A house for each of us,' Cú Chulaind said, so magnificent bedding was brought into the houses, and the heroes were given their choice of the three fifties of girls, but Findabair was taken by Cú Chulaind into his own house.

The rest of the Ulaid arrived later; Ailill and Medb and their entire household went to greet the visitors, and Senchae son of Ailill replied 'We are content.' The Ulaid entered the fort, then, and the royal house was given over to them. There were façades of bronze and partitions of red yew, and three strips of bronze in the vault of the roof. The house itself was of oak and was covered with shingles, and there was glass for each of the twelve windows. The apartments of Ailill and Medb were in the centre of the house and had

silver façades and strips of bronze; Ailill's façade had in it
a silver wand that extended to the rafters of the house, and
he used this to chastise the household. The warriors of
Ulaid went round the house, from one door to the next,
and the musicians played while everything was being prepared. The house was so large that there was room for all
the Ulaid to gather round Conchubur; Conchubur himself,
however, and Fergus son of Roech and nine other Ulaid
warriors gathered round Ailill's couch. A great feast was
set out, and the visitors stayed three days and three
nights.

Thereafter, Ailill inquired of Conchubur and the Ulaid why
they had come, and Senchae explained the problem that had
brought them: the rivalry of the three heroes for the champion's portion, the contention of the women over being first
in to the feast, and how they would not suffer being judged
by anyone but Ailill. Ailill fell silent at hearing that, and he
was not happy. 'It would not be proper for me to give a
judgement here,' he said, 'unless I were to do it out of
hatred.' 'But no one is better qualified than you,' said Senchae. 'I would need time to ponder the matter,' said Ailill.
'I expect three days and three nights would be enough.' 'No
loss of friendship for that much time,' said Senchae.

Being satisfied, the Ulaid said farewell and took their leave
of Ailill and Medb; they cursed Bricriu, for he had brought
about the contention, and they returned to their own land,
leaving behind Lóegure and Conall and Cú Chulaind to be
judged by Ailill. That night, as the three heroes were being
given their food, three cats, three druidic beasts, were loosed
from the cave of Crúachu. Lóegure and Conall left their
food to the beasts and fled to the rafters of the house, and
they remained there all night. Cú Chulaind did not budge
when the beasts approached him; when one beast stretched
its neck out to eat, Cú Chulaind dealt it a blow on the head,

but his sword glided off as if the creature were made of stone. The cat settled itself, then, and Cú Chulaind neither ate nor slept until morning. At dawn, the cats left, and the heroes were found where they had spent the night. 'Does this contest not suffice for judgement?' Ailill said. 'Not at all,' replied Lóegure and Conall, 'for it is not beasts that we fight but men.'

Ailill went to his chamber, then, and put his back against the wall, and he was troubled in his mind. The problem that had been brought to him was so perplexing that for three days and three nights he neither ate nor slept; finally, Medb said to him 'You are a weakling. If you are a judge, then judge.' 'It is difficult to judge them,' replied Ailill, 'and wretched he who must.' 'It is not difficult at all,' said Medb, 'for Lóegure and Conall are as different as bronze and white gold, and Conall and Cú Chulaind are as different as white gold and red gold.'

Medb thought over her advice after that, whereupon she summoned Lóegure Búadach to her and said 'Welcome, Lóegure! You deserve the champion's portion, and so we make you king over the warriors of Ériu from this time forth, and we give you the champion's portion and this bronze cup, with a bird of white gold at the bottom, to bear before all as a token of our judgement. Let no one see it until you appear in Conchubur's Cráebrúad at the end of the day, and then, when the champion's portion is set out, display your cup to the chiefs of Ulaid. The champion's portion will be yours, and no other Ulaid warrior will challenge you for it, for your cup will be a token of recognition to the Ulaid.' Then the cup, filled with undiluted wine, was given to Lóegure, and there, in the centre of the royal house, he drained it at a swallow. 'Now yours is the feast of a champion,' said Medb, 'and may you enjoy it one-hundred-fold for one hundred years before the youths of all Ulaid.'

Lóegure bade farewell, then, and Conall was called to the centre of the royal house in the same way. 'Welcome, Conall,' Medb said. 'You deserve the champion's portion', and she went on as she had with Lóegure, except that she gave him a cup of white gold with a golden bird at the bottom. It was filled with undiluted wine and given to Conall, and he drained it at a swallow, and Medb wished him the champion's portion of all Ulaid for one hundred years.

Conall bade farewell, then, and Cú Chulaind was summoned; a messenger went to him and said 'Come and speak with the king and queen.' At the time, Cú Chulaind was playing fidchell with Lóeg. 'You mock me,' he said to the messenger. 'Try your lies on another fool', and he threw a fidchell piece at the man so that it entered his brain; the messenger returned to Ailill and Medb and fell dead between them. 'Alas! Cú Chulaind will slaughter us if he is aroused,' said Medb. She rose, then, and went to Cú Chulaind and put her arms round his neck. 'Try another lie,' he said. 'Glorious lad of Ulaid, flame of the warriors of Ériu, we tell you no lies,' Medb replied. 'Were the choice of the warriors of Ériu to come, it is to you we would grant precedence, for the men of Ériu acknowledge your superiority, and that by reason of your youth and beauty, your courage and valour, your fame and renown.'

Cú Chulaind rose, then, and accompanied Medb to the royal house, and Ailill welcomed him warmly. He was given a cup of red gold with a bird of precious stone at the bottom, and it was filled with excellent wine; moreover, he was given the equivalent of two dragon's eyes. 'Now yours is the feast of a champion,' said Medb, 'and may you enjoy it one-hundred-fold for one hundred years before the youths of all Ulaid.' Ailill and Medb added 'It is our judgement, moreover, that just as no Ulaid youth is your equal, so no Ulaid woman is the equal of your wife, and it is our pleasure that Emer always be the first woman of Ulaid to enter the drinking house.' Cú Chulaind drained the cup at one swallow, bade farewell to king and queen and household, and followed Lóegure and Conall.

'My plan now,' Medb said to Ailill, 'is to keep the three heroes with us tonight, in order to test them further.' 'Do as you like,' replied Ailill. The heroes were detained, then; their horses were unyoked, and they were taken to Crúachu. They were given a choice of food for their horses: Lóegure and Conall chose two-year-old oats, but Cú Chulaind asked for barley. The heroes slept at Crúachu that night, and the women were apportioned among them: Findabair and her fifty women were taken to Cú Chulaind's house, Sadb Sulbair (the other daughter of Ailill and Medb) and her fifty women were taken to Conall, and Conchend daughter of Cet son of Mágu and her fifty women were taken to Lóegure.

The next morning, the heroes rose early and went to the house where the lads were performing the wheel feat. Lóegure took the wheel and threw it halfway up the wall of the house; the lads laughed and smiled in mockery, but it seemed to Lóegure that they had raised a shout of victory. Conall then lifted the wheel from the floor and threw it up to the ridge pole of the royal house; the lads raised a shout of mockery, but Conall thought it a shout of applause and triumph. Cú Chulaind, however, caught the wheel in mid-air and threw it so high that it knocked the ridge pole from the house and sank into the ground outside the length of a man's arm; the lads raised a shout of praise and victory, but Cú Chulaind thought it a laugh of scorn and ridicule. After that, he went to the women and took their needles from them, and he threw the three fifties of needles into the air one after another; each needle went into the eye of the next, so that they all formed a chain. Afterwards, he returned each needle to its owner, and the lads praised him for that.

The three heroes then bade farewell to the king and the queen and the rest of the household. 'Go to the house of my foster-father and foster-mother, Ercol and Garmuin,' said Medb, 'and be their guests tonight.' The three left after the horse-racing at the fair of Crúachu, where Cú Chulaind was victorious three times; they arrived at the house of Ercol and Garmuin and were welcomed. 'Why have you come?' Ercol asked. 'That you might judge us,' they replied. 'Go to the house of Samera, for it is he who will judge you,' Ercol said.

They left and were directed to Samera, and he welcomed them. Moreover, his daughter Búan fell in love with Cú Chulaind. They told Samera that they had come to him for judgement, and he sent them out, one by one, to the spectres of the air. Lóegure went first, but he left his weapons and his clothing and fled. Conall went out in the same fashion, but he left his spears and his sword behind. Cú Chulaind went the third night. The spectres screeched at him and attacked; they shattered his spear and broke his shield and tore his clothing, and they bound and subdued him. 'Shame, Cú Chulaind,' said Lóeg, 'hapless weakling, one-eyed stripling, where are your skill and valour when spectres can destroy you?' At that, Cú Chulaind's ríastarthae overcame him, and he turned against the spectres; he tore them apart and crushed them, so that the air was full of their blood. Then he took their military cloaks and their weapons and returned triumphant to the house of Samera. Samera welcomed him and said 'It is my judgement that the champion's portion should go to Cú Chulaind, that his wife should enter before all the women of Ulaid, and that his weapons should hang above the weapons of all others save those of Conchubur.'

After that, the three heroes returned to the house of Ercol, and he welcomed them, and they slept there that night. Ercol then announced that they would face himself and his horse. Lóegure and his horse went first: Ercol's gelding killed Lóegure's horse, and Ercol likewise prevailed over Lóegure, who fled, taking the road over Ess Rúaid to Emuin and reporting there that Ercol had killed his two companions. Conall fled in the same way after his horse had been killed by Ercol's gelding; en route to Emuin he crossed Snám Rathaind, and there his lad, Rathand, drowned in the river, and that is why the place is called Snám Rathaind.

The Líath Machae, however, killed Ercol's gelding, while Cú Chulaind overcame Ercol and bound him behind his chariot and drove off to Emuin Machae. Búan daughter of Samera followed the three chariots; she recognized the track of Cú Chulaind's chariot, for it left no narrow trail and moreover dug up walls and extended itself to leap over chasms. The girl made a fearful spring after the chariot; she struck her head against a rock and died, and thereafter the place was called Úaig Búana.[1] In time, Conall and Cú Chulaind reached Emuin Machae, and they found the Ulaid in mourning, for, according to the report that Lóegure had brought back, the two of them had been killed. They related their news and adventures to Conchubur and the chieftains of Ulaid, and everyone reproached Lóegure for the false report he had brought back.

The youths left off their talk and their chatter, then, for their feast was set out, and that night it was Cú Chulaind's father himself, Súaltaim son of Roech, who served them. Their food was brought to them, and the distributors began to distribute, but first they set the champion's portion aside. 'Why not give the champion's portion to one of the other heroes?' asked Dubthach Dóeltenga. 'After all, the three

yonder would not have returned from Crúachu without some
token showing that the champion's portion should be
awarded to one of them.' At that, Lóegure Búadach rose
and brandished his bronze cup with the silver bird at the
bottom and said 'Mine the champion's portion – therefore,
let no one challenge me for it.' 'Not yours at all,' said
Conall Cernach, 'for our tokens are not alike: you have
brought a cup of bronze, but I have brought a cup of white
gold. It is clear from the difference between them that the
champion's portion is mine.' 'It belongs to neither of you,'
said Cú Chulaind, and he rose and said 'You have brought
no token that merits the champion's portion. The king and
queen of Crúachu were reluctant to arouse further hostility
among us; nevertheless, you received from them only what
you deserved. The champion's portion is mine, for it is I
who have brought the most distinguished token.'

Cú Chulaind then brandished his cup of red gold with
its bird of precious stone at the bottom, and he showed
his equivalent of two dragon's eyes so that all the chieftains
gathered round Conchubur could see. 'If there is any justice,
it is I who should receive the champion's portion,' he
concluded. 'We award it to you,' said Conchubur and
Fergus and the other chieftains, 'for the champion's portion
is yours, by the judgement of Ailill and Medb.' 'I swear by
what my people swear by,' said Lóegure, 'that cup that
you have brought was bought with jewels and treasures.
You purchased your cup from Ailill and Medb so that you
might not be disgraced and so that the champion's portion
might not be given to anyone else.' 'I swear by the god my
people swear by,' said Conall Cernach, 'the judgement you
have brought back is no judgement, and the champion's
portion will not be yours.' At that, each of the three rose
up with naked swords; Conchubur and Fergus stepped between them, then, and they sheathed their swords at once

and sat down. 'Let my will prevail,' said Senchae. 'We agree to that,' they said. 'Then go to the ford of Bude son of Bain, and he will judge you,' said Senchae.

The three went to the house of Bude, then, and told him of the contention over which they had come and of their wish for a judgement. 'Was a judgement not given you by Ailill and Medb at Crúachu?' Bude asked. 'Indeed, it was, but yonder men did not accept it,' said Cú Chulaind. 'Indeed, we do not,' said Lóegure and Conall, 'for the judgement that was given is no judgement at all.' 'Not easy for anyone to judge those who will not accept the judgement of Ailill and Medb,' said Bude. 'But I have someone who will undertake to judge you — Úath son of Imoman, who lives by the lake. Go to him, and he will decide.' This Úath son of Imoman was a man of great power: he could change into any form he wished, and he could perform druidry and discharge claims of mutual obligation. He was the spectre after which Belach Muni in tSiriti was named, and he was called a spectre because of his ability to transform himself into any shape.

The heroes went to Úath's lake, then, and Bude accompanied them as a witness. They told Úath why they had come; he replied that he would undertake to judge them but that they would have to accept his judgement. They agreed to accept it, and he took their pledges. Then he said 'I will propose a bargain, and he who fulfils it with me is he who will bear off the champion's portion.' 'What sort of bargain?' they asked. 'I have an axe,' he replied. 'Let one of you take it in his hand and cut off my head today, and I will cut off his head tomorrow.'

Lóegure and Conall said that they would not undertake that bargain, for, though he might have the power to remain alive after being beheaded, they did not. Thus, they refused the bargain. (Other books say, however, that they accepted the proposal: Lóegure cut the man's head off the first day but avoided him thereafter, and Conall did the same.) Cú Chulaind, however, said that he would undertake the bargain so that the champion's portion might be his. Lóegure and Conall said that, if he fulfilled that bargain with Úath, they would not contest his right to the champion's portion, and he accepted their pledges. Then he pledged to fulfill the bargain. Úath stretched his neck out on a stone (after first casting spells in the edge of the blade), and Cú Chulaind took the axe and cut off his head. Úath rose, took his axe, put his head on his chest and returned to his lake.

The following day, Úath reappeared, and Cú Chulaind stretched his neck out on the stone. Three times Úath drew the axe down on Cú Chulaind's neck, and each time the blade was reversed. 'Rise, Cú Chulaind,' he said, then, 'for you are king of the warriors of Ériu, and the champion's portion is yours, without contest.' The three heroes returned to Emuin after that, but Lóegure and Conall did not accept the judgement that had been given to Cú Chulaind, and so the same strife arose regarding the champion's portion. It was the advice of the Ulaid that the three go to Cú Ruí for judgement, and they agreed to that.

The following morning, then, the three heroes went to Cú Ruí's stronghold; they unyoked their chariots at the entrance and went into the royal house and were welcomed by Bláthnait daughter of Mend, for she was Cú Ruí's wife. Cú Ruí himself was not there that night, but he had known that they were coming, and he had instructed his wife what to do with the heroes until he returned from Scythia. From the time that he took arms until his death, Cú Ruí never reddened his sword in Ériu, and the food of Ériu did not pass his lips once he had reached the age of seven, for Ériu could not contain his strength and valour and courage and pride and fame and supremacy. Bláthnait followed his instructions in washing and bathing the heroes, in serving them intoxicating drink and in providing them excellent beds; and the three men were greatly pleased. When it came time to go to bed, she said that one of them would have to watch over the stronghold each night until Cú Ruí returned and that Cú Ruí had said that the watch should be taken in order of age. Whatever part of the world Cú Ruí might be in, he sang a spell over his stronghold each night; it would then revolve as swiftly as a mill wheel turns, so that its entrance was never found after sunset.

Lóegure Búadach went to watch the first night, for he was the eldest of the three. Towards morning, he saw a giant approaching out of the ocean from the west, from as far away as the eye could see. This giant was huge and ugly and terrifying; it seemed to Lóegure that he was as tall as the sky and that the glimmer of the sea was visible between his legs. He came towards Lóegure, and his fists were full of stripped oak trunks; each would have been a burden for a team of oxen, and they had not been cut with repeated blows, either – each trunk had been severed with just one blow of a sword. The giant cast a trunk, but Lóegure let it go by; two or three more trunks were cast, but they did not even strike Lóegure's shield, much less Lóegure himself. Lóegure in turn cast his spear at the giant and also failed. After that, the giant stretched out his hand towards Lóegure; the hand was so large that it spanned the three ridges that had been between the combatants when they were casting at each other, and it seized Lóegure. For all Lóegure's size and excellence, he fitted in the giant's grip like a one-year-old child, and the giant ground him between his palms the way a fidchell piece would be ground by mill stones. When Lóegure was half dead, the giant dropped him over the stronghold wall and into the ditch at the entrance to the royal house. Since there was no entrance into the stronghold, Conall Cernach and Cú Chulaind and the people inside thought that Lóegure had leapt over the stronghold wall as a challenge to the other heroes.

At the end of the following day, Conall Cernach went out to watch, for he was older than Cú Chulaind, and everything that had happened to Lóegure the previous night happened to him also. The third night, Cú Chulaind went out to watch, and it was that night that the Three Greys of Sescend Úairbéoil and the Three Cowherds of Brega and the Three Sons of Dornmár Céoil gathered to destroy the stronghold. It was also that night that, according to prophecy, the monster in the lake nearby would devour everything in the stronghold, both man and beast. Cú Chulaind watched through the night, then, and many evil things happened. At midnight, he heard a loud noise approaching. 'Who goes there?' he shouted. 'If friends, let them halt; if enemies, let them flee.' At that, the enemies raised a great shout; Cú Chulaind sprang at them, then, and nine of them fell dead to the ground. He put their heads into his watch seat, but scarcely had he sat down to watch when another nine shouted at him. He killed three nines in all and made a single heap of their heads and goods.

Night was drawing to a close, and Cú Chulaind was sad and weary when he heard the lake rising up as if it were a heavy sea. Tired as he was, his ardour would not let him remain, so he went towards the great noise, and he saw the monster – it seemed to have risen thirty cubits above the lake. The monster leapt at the stronghold and opened its mouth so wide that one of the royal houses would have fitted in its gullet. At that, Cú Chulaind remembered his coursing feat, and, leaping into the air, he circled the beast as quickly as a winnowing sieve. Then he put one hand on the monster's neck and the other down its gullet; he tore out its heart and threw that on the ground, and the beast fell heavily from the air. Cú Chulaind then hacked away until he made mincemeat of the monster, and he took its head and put it with the pile of other heads.

Dawn was drawing on, and Cú Chulaind was wretched and broken when he saw the giant coming towards him from the western sea, just as Lóegure and Conall had seen. 'A bad night for you,' said the giant. 'A worse one for you, churl!' said Cú Chulaind. At that, the giant cast a tree trunk, but Cú Chulaind let it go by; two or three more casts were made, but they did not strike even Cú Chulaind's shield, much less Cú Chulaind himself. Cú Chulaind in turn cast his spear at the giant and also failed. The giant then stretched out his hand to take Cú Chulaind in his grasp as he had taken the other two men, but Cú Chulaind performed the hero's salmon leap and his coursing feat, with his sword overhead, so that he was as swift as a hare, and he hovered in a circle like a mill wheel. 'My life for yours!' said the giant. 'My requests, then,' said Cú Chulaind. 'You will have them even as you breathe them,' said the giant. 'Supremacy over the warriors of Ériu from this time on and the champion's portion without contest and precedence for my wife over the women of Ulaid for ever,' said Cú Chulaind. 'You will have that,' said the giant. With that, he vanished, and Cú Chulaind did not know where he had gone.

Cú Chulaind then thought about the leap that his comrades had made over the stronghold wall, which was high and broad, for he assumed that Lóegure and Conall must have leapt it. He attempted the leap twice and failed twice. 'A shame all the trouble I have taken over the champion's portion, to see it pass from me through failing to make the leap the others made,' he said, and he mused over this folly. He sprang back from the stronghold the length of a spearcast, and he sprang forward to where he had been standing, so that his forehead just touched the wall. He leapt straight up so that he could see everything that was happening inside, and he descended so that he sank into the ground up to his knees. And he did not remove the dew from the grass, even with the ardour of his feeling and the vigour of his disposition and the extent of his valour. With the fury and the ríastarthae that overcame him, he finally leapt the stronghold wall, so that he landed at the entrance to the royal house. He went inside and heaved a great sigh, and Bláthnait said 'Indeed, not a sigh of shame but a sigh after victory and triumph', for the daughter of the king of Inis Fer Falga knew of the trials Cú Chulaind had endured that night.

Not long after that, they saw Cú Ruí coming towards them in the house; he had the war gear of the three nines whom Cú Chulaind had killed, along with their heads and the head of the beast. After taking the heads from his chest and putting them in the centre of the house, he said 'The lad who has collected all these trophies in one night is fit to watch over the stronghold of a king. That which they dispute, the champion's portion, truly belongs to Cú Chulaind in preference to every youth of Ériu, for none could meet him in combat.' Cú Ruí thus awarded the champion's portion to Cú Chulaind, naming him the most valorous of the Goídil and giving his wife precedence over the other women of Ulaid in entering the drinking house. Moreover, he gave Cú Chulaind seven cumals' worth of gold and silver as a reward for the deeds he had done that night.

The three heroes bade farewell to Cú Ruí, then, and returned to Emuin Machae before the end of the day. When it came time for the servers to divide and distribute, they removed the champion's portion and its drink and set them aside. 'We are certain that you will not be contesting the champion's portion tonight,' said Dubthach Dóeltenga, 'for you will have received judgement from him to whom you went.' But Lóegure and Conall said that the champion's

portion had not been awarded to any of the three in preference to the others, and, as for the judgement of Cú Ruí
upon the three, they said that he had awarded nothing at
all to Cú Chulaind since they had reached Emuin Machae.
Cú Chulaind then said that he would not contest the
champion's portion, for the good of having it would be no
greater than the trouble involved. Thus, the champion's
portion was not awarded until after the warriors' bargain
at Emuin Machae.

Once, when the Ulaid were at Emuin Machae, tired after
the fair and the games, Conchubur and Fergus and the other
Ulaid chieftains returned from the playing field to sit in
Conchubur's Cráebrúad. Lóegure and Conall and Cú
Chulaind were not there that evening, but the best of the
other warriors of Ulaid were. As night drew on, they saw
a huge, ugly churl coming towards them in the house, and
it seemed to them that there was not in all Ulaid a warrior
half as tall. His appearance was frightful and terrifying: a
hide against his skin, and a dun cloak round him, and a
great bushy tree overhead where a winter shed for thirty
calves could fit. Each of his two yellow eyes was the size of
an ox-cauldron; each finger was as thick as a normal
man's wrist. The tree trunk in his left hand would have
been a burden for twenty yoked oxen; the axe in his right
hand, whence had gone three fifties of glowing metal pieces,
had a handle that would have been a burden for a team of
oxen, yet it was sharp enough to cut hairs against the
wind.

He came in this guise and stood beneath the forked beam
at one end of the fire. 'Do you find the house so narrow,'
said Dubthach Dóeltenga, 'that there is no place to stand
but under the forked beam? You may wish to contest the
position of house candlebearer, but you are more likely to
burn the house than to illuminate the company inside.

'Although that is my gift,' the churl replied, 'perhaps you will grant that, despite my height, the entire household may be lit without the house's being burnt. But that is not my primary gift, and I have others. That which I have come to seek I have not found in Ériu or the Alps or Europe or Africa or Asia or Greece or Scythia or Inis Orc or the Pillars of Hercules or Tor mBregoind or Inis Gaid. Nowhere have I found a man to keep my bargain. Since you Ulaid surpass the hosts of every land in anger and prowess and weaponry, in rank and pride and dignity, in honour and generosity and excellence, let one of you keep faith with me in the matter over which I have come.'

'It is not right,' said Fergus, 'to dishonour a province because of one man's failure to keep his word – perhaps death is no nearer to him than it is to you.' 'It is not I who shirk death,' replied the churl. 'Then let us hear your proposal,' said Fergus. 'Only if I am allowed fair play,' said the churl. 'It is right to allow him that,' said Senchae son of Ailill, 'for it would be no fair play if a great host broke faith with a completely unknown individual. Besides, it would seem to us that if you are to find the man you seek, you will find him here.' 'I exempt Conchubur, for he is the king, and I exempt Fergus, for he is of equal rank,' said the churl. 'Whoever else may dare, let him come that I may cut off his head tonight, he mine tomorrow.'

'After those two,' said Dubthach, 'there is certainly no warrior here worthy of that.' 'Indeed, there is,' said Muinremur son of Gerrgend, and he sprang into the centre of the house. Now, Muinremur had the strength of one hundred warriors, and each arm had the strength of one hundred. 'Bend down, churl,' he said, 'that I may cut off your head tonight – you may cut off mine tomorrow night.' 'I could make that bargain anywhere,' said the churl. 'Let us rather make the bargain I proposed: I will cut off your head tonight, and you will avenge that by cutting off my head tomorrow night.' 'I swear by what my people swear by,' said Dubthach Dóeltenga, 'such a death would not be pleasant if the man you killed tonight clung to you tomorrow. But you alone have the power to be killed one night and to avenge it the next.' 'Then whatever conditions you propose I will fulfil, surprising as you may find that,' said the churl, whereupon he made Muinremur pledge to keep his part of the bargain the following night.

With that, Muinremur took the churl's axe, whose two edges were seven feet apart. The churl stretched his neck out on the block, and Muinremur so swung the axe that it stuck in the block underneath; the head rolled to the foot of the forked beam, and the house was filled with blood. At once, the churl rose, gathered his head and his block and his axe and clutched them to his chest, and left the house, blood streaming from his neck and filling the Cráebrúad on every side. The household were horrorstruck by the wondrousness of the event they had witnessed. 'I swear by what my people swear by,' said Dubthach Dóeltenga, 'if that churl returns tomorrow after having been killed tonight, not a man in Ulaid will be left alive.'

The following night, the churl returned, but Muinremur avoided him. The churl complained, saying 'Indeed, it is not fair of Muinremur to break his part of the bargain.' Lóegure Búadach, however, was present that night, and, when the churl continued 'Who of the warriors who contest the champion's portion of Ulaid will fulfil this bargain with me tonight? Where is Lóegure Búadach?', Lóegure said 'Here I am!' The churl pledged Lóegure as he had pledged Muinremur, but Lóegure, like Muinremur, failed to appear the following night. The churl then pledged Conall Cernach, and he too failed to appear and keep his pledge.

When he arrived on the fourth night, the churl was seeth-

ing with rage. All the women of Ulaid had gathered there
that night to see the marvel that had come to the Cráebrúad,
and Cú Chulaind had come as well. The churl began to re-
proach them, then, saying 'Men of Ulaid, your skill and
courage are no more. Your warriors covet the champion's
portion, yet they are unable to contest it. Where is that
pitiful stripling you call Cú Chulaind? Would his word be
better than that of his companions?' 'I want no bargain
with you,' said Cú Chulaind. 'No doubt you fear death,
wretched fly,' said the churl. At that, Cú Chulaind sprang
towards the churl and dealt him such a blow with the axe
that his head was sent to the rafters of the Cráebrúad, and
the entire house shook. Cú Chulaind then struck the head
with the axe once more, so that he shattered it into fragments. The churl rose nonetheless.

The following day, the Ulaid watched Cú Chulaind to see
if he would avoid the churl the way his companions had
done; they saw that he was waiting for the churl, and they
grew very dejected. It seemed to them proper to begin his
death dirge, for they feared greatly that he would live only
until the churl appeared. Cú Chulaind, ashamed, said to
Conchubur 'By my shield and by my sword, I will not go
until I have fulfilled my pledge to the churl — since I am to
die, I will die with honour.'

Towards the end of the day, they saw the churl approaching them. 'Where is Cú Chulaind?' he asked. 'Indeed, I am
here,' said Cú Chulaind. 'You speak low, tonight, wretch,
for you fear death greatly,' said the churl. 'Yet for all that,
you have not avoided me.' Cú Chulaind rose and stretched
his neck out on the block, but its size was such that his
neck reached only halfway across. 'Stretch out your neck,
you wretch,' said the churl. 'You torment me,' said Cú
Chulaind. 'Kill me quickly. I did not torment you last night.
Indeed, I swear, if you torment me now, I will make myself

as long as a heron above you.' 'I cannot dispatch you, not with the length of the block and the shortness of your neck,' said the churl.

Cú Chulaind stretched himself, then, until a warrior's foot would fit between each rib, and he stretched his neck until it reached the other side of the block. The churl raised his axe so that it reached the rafters of the house. What with the creaking of the old hide that he wore and the swish of his axe as he raised it with the strength of his two arms, the sound he made was like that of a rustling forest on a windy night. The churl brought the axe down, then, upon Cú Chulaind's neck – with the blade turned up. All the chieftains of Ulaid saw this.

'Rise, Cú Chulaind!' the churl then said. 'Of all the warriors in Ulaid and Ériu, whatever their merit, none is your equal for courage and skill and honour. You are the supreme warrior of Ériu, and the champion's portion is yours, without contest; moreover, your wife will henceforth enter the drinking house before all the other women of Ulaid. Whoever might dispute this judgement, I swear by what my people swear by, his life will not be long.' After that, the churl vanished. It was Cú Ruí son of Dáre, who in that guise had come to fulfil the promise he had made to Cú Chulaind.

The Exile of the Sons of Uisliu

Introduction

This, the most stunning tale ever written in Irish, is better known as the story of Derdriu; yet originally it was as much a story of treachery and honour as of romance. 'The Exile of the Sons of Uisliu' answers the question 'Why were Fergus and so many other Ulaid chieftains in exile in Connachta at the time of the cattle raid of Cúailnge?' At this level, Fergus is the key figure: once his word – his guarantee of Noísiu's safety – has been violated, he becomes Conchubur's enemy; any other course would be shameful. 'The Exile of the Sons of Uisliu' moves from personal exile to political exile; it thus marks the decline of the Ulster Cycle.

Underlying literature and history, of course, is myth, the familiar regeneration pattern of old king–goddess–young king: Conchubur–Derdriu–Noísiu. Derdriu passes from Conchubur to Noísiu and back to Conchubur; myth becomes history with Noísiu's death, and yet it is at the threatened resumption of the pattern, with Éogan replacing Noísiu, that Derdriu kills herself. Cú Chulaind is notable by his absence; perhaps he arrived in the Ulster Cycle too late to play a major part (a small one being out of the question), or perhaps he simply never fitted in.

Although much of the tale is presented in verse, the poetry generally repeats and elaborates upon the narrative rather than adding to it. The tone is markedly less severe and more romantic than that of the prose, and the lines do not have the elegant simplicity and chaste beauty of those in 'The Wasting Sickness of Cú Chulaind'. But subsequent versions of the story – and there are many – are less restrained still: Noísiu, Aindle and Arddán, having been captured, are executed with one blow of Éogan's sword so that none will outlive the others; Derdriu seizes a knife and kills herself as soon as Noísiu is dead; the lovers are buried next to each other, and yews growing out of their graves intertwine. These later versions are not without their own appeal; yet it is the earliest (surviving) recension, from the Book of Leinster, that is translated here.

'The Exile of the Sons of Uisliu' is the inspiration (through intermediary translations and retellings) for Yeats's play *Deirdre*, for Synge's play *Deirdre of the Sorrows* and for James Stephens's novel *Deirdre*.

The Exile of the Sons of Uisliu

The Ulaid were drinking at the house of Fedilmid son of Dall, Conchubur's storyteller, and Fedilmid's wife was standing over them and serving, even though she was with child. Drinking horns and portions of food went round, and the house was filled with drunken shouting. When it came time to sleep, Fedilmid's wife rose to go to her bed, but as she crossed the house the child in her womb screamed so that it was heard throughout the court. At that scream the men all rose, and they were standing chin to chin, but

Senchae son of Ailill quieted them, saying 'Do not disturb each other! Let the woman be brought to us that we might learn what caused that noise.' So the woman was brought to them, and her husband asked her:

What is this violent noise that resounds,
that rages in your roaring womb?
The outcry between your two sides – mighty its sound –
crushes the ears of those who hear it.
My heart is terribly wounded:
a great fear has seized it.

Then Fedilmid's wife spoke to Cathub, for he was a wise man:

Listen to Cathub, fair of face,
a handsome prince, great and powerful his crown,
exalted by his druid wisdom.
I myself do not have the white words
through which my husband might obtain
an answer to his question,
for, though it cried out in the cradle of my body,
no woman knows
what her womb bears.

And Cathub replied:

In the cradle of your womb there cried out
a woman with twisted yellow hair
and beautiful grey green eyes.
Foxglove her purple pink cheeks,
the colour of snow her flawless teeth,
brilliant her Parthian-red lips.
A woman over whom there will be great slaughter
among the chariot-warriors of Ulaid.
There screams in your roaring womb
a tall, beautiful, long-haired woman
whom champions will contest,
whom high kings will woo;

and to the west of Conchubur's province
there will be a rich harvest of fighting men.
Parthian-red lips will frame
those flawless teeth;
high queens will envy her
her matchless, faultless form.

Then Cathub placed his hand on the woman's womb, and
the child murmured, and he said 'Indeed, it is a girl, and
her name will be Derdriu, and there will be trouble on her
account.' After the girl had been born, Cathub said:

Though you may have fame and beauty,
Derdriu, you will destroy much;
Ulaid will suffer on your account,
fair daughter of Fedilmid.

And after that there will be still more deaths
because of you, woman like a flame.
In your lifetime – hear this –
the three sons of Uisliu will be exiled.

In your lifetime a violent deed
will be done at Emuin;
repented thereafter will be the treachery
that violated the guarantee of mighty Fergus.

Because of you, woman of fate,
Fergus will be exiled from Ulaid,
and – a deed that will cause much weeping –
Conchubur's son Fiachnae will be slain.

Because of you, woman of fate,
Gerrce son of Illadán will be slain,
and – a crime no less awful –
Éogan son of Durthacht will be destroyed.

You will do a frightful fierce deed
out of anger at Ulaid's high king;
your grave will be everywhere –
yours will be a famous tale, Derdriu.

'Let the child be slain!' said the young warriors. 'No,' said Conchubur, 'I will take her away tomorrow, and I will rear her as I see fit, and she will be my companion.' And none of the Ulaid dared oppose him. Derdriu was reared by Conchubur until she was by far the most beautiful woman in Ériu. She was reared in a court apart, lest any of the Ulaid see her before she was to sleep with Conchubur, and no one was allowed into that court save her foster-father and her foster-mother and a woman named Lebarcham who was a satirist and could not be barred.

One day, in winter, Derdriu's foster-father was outside, in the snow, flaying a weaned calf for her. Derdriu saw a raven drinking the blood on the snow, and she said to Lebarcham 'I could love a man with those three colours: hair like a raven, cheeks like blood and body like snow.' 'Then luck and good fortune are with you,' answered Lebarcham, 'for such a man is not far off, in fact, he is quite near: Noísiu son of Uisliu.' Derdriu replied 'I will be ill, then, until I see him.'

It happened one day that Noísiu was standing alone on the rampart of the stronghold of Emuin, and he was singing. The singing of the sons of Uisliu was very melodious: every cow that heard it gave two thirds more milk, and every man who heard it grew peaceful and sated with music. The sons of Uisliu were also good fighters: when they stood back to back, they could hold off the entire province of Ulaid. Moreover, they were as swift as hunting hounds and could overtake and kill wild animals.

When Noísiu was outside alone, then, Derdriu stole out to him and made as if to go past, and he did not recognize her. 'A fine heifer that that is going by,' he said. 'The heifers are bound to be fine where there are no bulls,' she answered. 'You have the bull of the province: the king of Ulaid,' Noísiu said. 'Between the two of you, I would choose a young bull like yourself,' Derdriu replied. 'No! There is Cathub's prophecy,' said Noísiu. 'Are you rejecting me, then?' she asked. 'I am, indeed,' he answered. At that, Derdriu leapt at him and seized him by the ears, saying 'Two ears of shame and mockery these unless you take me with you!' 'Away from me, woman!' Noísiu said. 'Too late!' answered Derdriu.

With that, Noísiu began to sing. When the Ulaid heard his singing they rose up against each other, but the other sons of Uisliu went out to restrain their brother. 'What are you doing?' they asked. 'The Ulaid will be coming to blows on your account.' Then Noísiu told his brothers what had happened. 'Evil will come of this,' they said. 'Even so, you will not be disgraced while we are alive. We will all take her to another land – there is not in Ériu a king who will turn us away.' That was their advice. They departed that night: three fifties of warriors and three fifties of women and three fifties of hounds and three fifties of servants and Derdriu mingled in with them.

For a long time, the brothers found protection with kings throughout Ériu, though through his snares and treacheries Conchubur often attempted to destroy them, from Ess Rúaid to the south-west and then back north-east to Bend Étair. Finally, the Ulaid drove them out of Ériu and into Albu; there, they settled in the wilderness, and, when the game of the mountains ran out, they helped themselves to cattle. One day, the men of Albu gathered to destroy them, so they went to the king of Albu, and he took them into his entourage; they became mercenaries and erected their dwellings on the green. Because of Derdriu, they built their houses so that no one could see her, for they feared there might be killing on her account.

Early one morning, however, the king's steward went out round the house of Derdriu and Noísiu, and he saw the lovers sleeping. At once, he went and awakened the king, saying 'Until now, we have not found a woman worthy of you. But there is with Noísiu son of Uisliu a woman worthy of the king of the western world. Let Noísiu be slain that the woman might sleep with you.' 'No,' replied the king, 'but go to her each day in secret and woo her for me.'

The steward did that, but everything he said to Derdriu she told Noísiu the same night. Since nothing could be got from her, the sons of Uisliu were sent into battles and hazards and dangerous situations that they might be killed, but they were so hardy that every attempt failed. So the men of Albu gathered to kill them; they told Derdriu, and she told Noísiu, saying 'Depart! Unless you leave tonight, you will be slain tomorrow.' That night, Derdriu and the sons of Uisliu departed and went to an island in the sea.

This news reached the Ulaid, and they said to Conchubur 'A pity that the sons of Uisliu should die in a strange land because of a bad woman. Better that you should be lenient and not slay them – let them return and take them in.' 'Let them come, then,' said Conchubur, 'or let guarantors be sent to them.' That message was taken to Noísiu and his brothers, and they replied 'A welcome message that. We will come; we ask for Fergus as a guarantor, and Dubthach, and Conchubur's son Cormac.'

So these men went to Albu and accompanied Derdriu and the sons of Uisliu back to Ériu. On Conchubur's orders, however, the Ulaid all strove to invite Fergus to feasts and banquets, for the sons of Uisliu had sworn that the first food they touched in Ériu would be Conchubur's. Thus, Fergus and Dubthach remained behind, while Fergus's son Fíachu went on with Derdriu and the sons of Uisliu until they reached the green of Emuin Machae. Meanwhile, Éogan son of Durthacht, the king of Fernmag, had made up with Conchubur – the two had long been at odds – and had been charged to kill the sons of Uisliu, who would be kept from Conchubur by the king of Ulaid's mercenaries.

The sons of Uisliu were waiting in the centre of the green; the women of Emuin were sitting along the ramparts; Éogan was crossing the green with his troops. Fíachu came up to join Noísiu. Éogan, however, greeted Noísiu with the point of his spear and broke his back. At that, Fíachu put his arms round Noísiu and pulled him down and covered him, so that thereafter Noísiu was struck from above through the son of Fergus. The sons of Uisliu were then hunted from one end of the green to the other, and no one escaped save by point of spear and edge of sword. Derdriu was taken to stand beside Conchubur, her hands tied behind her.

This news reached Fergus and Dubthach and Cormac, and at once they went to Emuin and performed great deeds. Dubthach killed Conchubur's son Mane and dispatched Fíachnae, the son of Conchubur's daughter Fedelm, with a single blow; Fergus killed Traigthrén son of Traiglethan and his brother. Conchubur was outraged, and a battle ensued: in one day, three hundred Ulaid fell, and Dubthach slew the young women of the province, and Fergus fired Emuin. Afterwards, Fergus and Dubthach and Cormac and their followers went to Connachta, for they knew that Ailill and Medb would maintain them, though Connachta was no refuge of love for men from Ulaid. Three thousand was the number of the exiles, and, for sixteen years, these people saw that there was weeping and trembling in Ulaid every night.

Derdriu spent the year following Noísiu's death with Conchubur, and, during that time, she neither laughed nor smiled, nor did she ever have her fill of food or sleep. She never lifted her head from her knee, and, whenever musicians were brought to her, she recited this poem:

Fair to you the ardent warriors
who march into Emuin after an expedition;
more nobly did they march to their dwelling,
the three very heroic sons of Uisliu.

Noísiu with fine hazel mead
(I would wash him by the fire),
Arddán with a stag or fine pig,
Tall Aindle with a load on his back.

Sweet to you the fine mead
that battle-glorious Conchubur drinks;
but often I had before me, across the ocean,
food that was sweeter.

When modest Noísiu spread out
the cooking hearth on the wild forest floor,
sweeter than any honeyed food
was what the son of Uisliu prepared.

Melodious always to you
your pipers and trumpeters;
yet today I tell you
I have heard music that was sweeter.

Melodious to Conchubur, your king,
his pipers and trumpeters;
sweeter to me – fame of hosts –
the singing of the sons of Uisliu.

A wave the sound of Noísiu's voice –
his singing was always sweet;
Arddán's baritone was good,
and Aindle's tenor from his hunting lodge.

Noísiu's grave has now been made,
and the accompaniment was mournful.
For him I poured out – hero of heroes –
the deadly drink that killed him.

The Exile of the Sons of Uisliu

Dear his short shining hair,
a handsome man, even very beautiful;
sad that I cannot await him today,
cannot expect the son of Uisliu.

Dear his desire, right and proper,
dear this modest noble warrior;
after his going to the forest's edge,
dear his company in the early morning.

Dear the grey eyes that women loved;
fierce they were to foes.
After a circuit of the forest – a noble union –
dear his tenor through the great dark wood.

I do not sleep now,
nor do I brighten my nails:
there is no joy for me
since the son of Tindell will not come.

I do not sleep
but lie awake half the night;
my thoughts flee from these hosts,
I neither eat nor smile.

I have today no cause for joy
in the assembly of Emuin – throng of chieftains –
no peace, no delight, no comfort,
no great house, no fine adornments.

And whenever Conchubur tried to comfort her, she would
recite this poem to him:

Conchubur, be quiet!
You have brought me grief upon sorrow;
as long as I live, surely,
your love will be of no concern to me.

You have taken from me – a great crime –
the one I thought most beautiful on earth,
the one I loved most.
I will not see him again until I die.

His absence is my despair,
the absence of the son of Uisliu.
A jet black cairn over his white body
once so well known among men.

Brighter than a river meadow his glistening cheeks,
red his lips, beetle-black his brows;
the noble colour of snow
his shining, pearly teeth.

Well known his bright garb
among the warriors of Albu;
fair and brilliant his mantle – a noble union –
with its fringe of red gold.

A true treasure his satin tunic
with its hundred gems – a gentle number –
and for decoration, clear and shining,
fifty ounces of white gold.

A gold-hilted sword in his hand,
two steely spears with javelin points;
a shield with a rim of yellow gold
and a boss of silver.

Fair Fergus betrayed us
after bringing us across the great sea;
he sold his honour for beer,
his great deeds are no more.

Although the Ulaid might gather
about Conchubur upon the plain,
I would forsake them all, openly,
for the company of Noísiu son of Uisliu.

Break no more my heart today –
I will reach my early grave soon enough.
Sorrow is stronger than the sea
if you are wise, Conchubur.

'What do you hate most that you see?' asked Conchubur. 'Yourself, surely, and Éogan son of Durthacht,' she replied. 'Then you will spend a year with Éogan,' Conchubur said. He took her to Éogan. The following day they went to a fair at Emuin Machae, Derdriu standing behind Éogan in his chariot. She had sworn that she would never see her two companions together in the same place. 'Well, Derdriu,' said Conchubur, 'it is the eye of a ewe between two rams you make between myself and Éogan.' There was a great boulder before Derdriu. She let her head be driven against it, and the boulder made fragments of her head, and she died.

Notes

Introduction

1. Myles Dillon and Nora Chadwick, *The Celtic Realms* (New York: New American Library, 1967), pp. 1–2, 214.
2. Leon E. Stover and Bruce Kraig, *Stonehenge: The Indo-European Heritage* (Chicago: Nelson-Hall, 1978), p. 141.
3. Herodotos, 2:33.
4. Strabo, *Geographia*, 4.4.4 (translation by Timothy Gantz).
5. Diodorus Siculus, 5:31.2, 4–5 (translation by Timothy Gantz).
6. Proinsias Mac Cana, *Celtic Mythology* (London: Hamlyn, 1970), p. 127.
7. Julius Caesar, *De bello gallico*, 6.17.
8. Lucian, *Herakles*, 1.1.
9. Lucan, *De bello civili*, 1.444–6.
10. Frank O'Connor, *The Backward Look: A Survey of Irish Literature* (London: Macmillan, 1967), p. 242.
11. A rhetoric is a dense, archaic poetic passage.
12. James Delargy, *The Gaelic Story-teller* (London: G. Cumberlege, 1947), p. 32.
13. K. H. Jackson, *The Oldest Irish Tradition: A Window on the Iron Age* (Cambridge: Cambridge University Press, 1964).

The Wooing of Étaín

1. Frank O'Connor, *The Backward Look*, p. 43.
2. Bóand: 'white cow'; Bóand is also the Old Irish name for the river Boyne. Echu: 'horse'.
3. Macc Óc: 'young son'.

4. Cumal: a female slave, worth three milch cows or six heifers.
5. Síde: the people of the otherworld, often equated with the Túatha Dé Danand (the People of the Goddess Danu). An otherworld mound is called a síd.
6. Feis: originally, a feast during which the tribe's king was married to its tutelary goddess; the meaning later became generalized. The word *feis* is formed from an Irish verb meaning 'to sleep with'; it is not related to the Latin word *festa* or the English *feast*.
7. Fidchell: 'wood sense' – a board game, similar to chess, in which one side's king attempts to escape to the edge of the board while the other side's men attempt to prevent him.
8. Airem: 'ploughman'.
9. Bé Find: 'fair woman'.

The Destruction of Da Derga's Hostel

1. Fían (pl. fíana): a band of roving warriors.
2. Geiss (pl. gessa): a taboo, usually religious in origin.
3. Bretain: the British isle, perhaps the southern part.
4. Deirg: like the name in the title, this means 'red'.
5. Dond: probably the chthonic god Dond.
6. Popa: a term of affection and respect used in addressing an elder.
7. 'Third time': there is no second time.
8. 'Ant of the ancient earth': a wolf.

The Cattle Raid of Fróech

1. Bé Find: in 'The Wooing of Étaín' this name appears as an epithet for Étaín rather than as the name of Bóand's sister.
2. 'Candle of a king's house': a spear.

The Boyhood Deeds of Cú Chulaind

1. Ríastarthae: Cú Chulaind's special battle fury.
2. Féni: the Irish word for the Irish.
3. Del chliss: one of Cú Chulaind's spear-thrusting feats.

The Death of Aife's Only Son

1. Gáe bolga: Cú Chulaind's ultimate spear-thrusting feat; the
name may mean 'lightning spear'.

The Intoxication of the Ulaid

1. Crúadin: Cú Chulaind's sword.

Bricriu's Feast

1. Úaig Búana: Búan's Grave.

Index

271

Index

Index

Index

THE STORY OF PENGUIN CLASSICS

Before 1946 ... 'Classics' are mainly the domain of academics and students, without readable editions for everyone else. This all changes when a little-known classicist, E. V. Rieu, presents Penguin founder Allen Lane with the translation of Homer's *Odyssey* that he has been working on and reading to his wife Nelly in his spare time.

1946 *The Odyssey* becomes the first Penguin Classic published, and promptly sells three million copies. Suddenly, classic books are no longer for the privileged few.

1950s Rieu, now series editor, turns to professional writers for the best modern, readable translations, including Dorothy L. Sayers's *Inferno* and Robert Graves's *The Twelve Caesars*, which revives the salacious original.

1960s The Classics are given the distinctive black jackets that have remained a constant throughout the series's various looks. Rieu retires in 1964, hailing the Penguin Classics list as 'the greatest educative force of the 20th century'.

1970s A new generation of translators arrives to swell the Penguin Classics ranks, and the list grows to encompass more philosophy, religion, science, history and politics.

1980s The Penguin American Library joins the Classics stable, with titles such as *The Last of the Mohicans* safeguarded. Penguin Classics now offers the most comprehensive library of world literature available.

1990s The launch of Penguin Audiobooks brings the classics to a listening audience for the first time, and in 1999 the launch of the Penguin Classics website takes them online to a larger global readership than ever before.

The 21st Century Penguin Classics are rejacketed for the first time in nearly twenty years. This world famous series now consists of more than 1300 titles, making the widest range of the best books ever written available to millions – and constantly redefining the meaning of what makes a 'classic'.

The Odyssey continues ...

The best books ever written

PENGUIN CLASSICS

SINCE 1946

Find out more at www.penguinclassics.com